MW00716712

MIDNIGHT
MATTERS

MIDNIGHT MATTERS

A Novel

Timothy R. Phillips

Twaanévie Publishing House
Blacksburg, Virginia

Copyright © 2017 by Timothy R. Phillips.

All rights reserved. No part of this publication may be reproduced, distributed or transmitted in any form or by any means, including photocopying, recording, or other electronic or mechanical methods, without the prior written permission of the publisher, except in the case of brief quotations embodied in critical reviews and certain other non-commercial uses permitted by copyright law. For permission requests, write to the publisher, addressed "Attention: Permissions Coordinator," at the address below.

Daniel Books, an imprint of Twaanévie Publishing House
845 Deercroft Drive
Blacksburg, Virginia 24060
www.twaaneviepublishinghouse.com

Publisher's Note: This is a work of fiction. Names, characters, places, and incidents are a product of the author's imagination. Locales and public names are sometimes used for atmospheric purposes. Any resemblance to actual people, living or dead, or to businesses, companies, events, institutions, or locales is completely coincidental.

Book Layout ©2013 BookDesignTemplates.com
Cover photo "Equal" © Lassedesignen/Shutterstock. All rights reserved.

Ordering Information:
Additional copies may be ordered at Amazon.com

Queries and/or Quantity Purchase Discounts:
Contact the Publisher at twaaneviepublishinghouse@gmail.com.

Midnight Matters/ Timothy R. Phillips. -- 1st ed.
ISBN 978-0-9660055-4-7
Library of Congress Control Number: 2017907297

Printed in the United States of America

Dedicated

To
Midnight, Catrick, & Tiddy-Beaux
and the mysteries locked within the
Indian Wood

Contents

MIDNIGHT
MATTERS

PROLOGUE: CAT AND MOUSE

Sunday, August 23, 1857
Vieux Saules Plantation ("The Old Willows")

The fourteen-year-old boy hunched in the bushes about twenty yards from the Main House. He was determined to get even with Richard, a boy his age but lucky enough to be part of the richest family in St. Charles Parish, if not the whole state of Louisiana.

Cat, as he was commonly called, knew instinctively to let patience guide him in these matters. From long days of fishing, he had perfected the ability to sit as a statue for as long as it took, if necessary. He could will away the most annoying and persistent of itches or the imminent double sneeze. He had a clever mind, too, like a complicated clock with all its gears in constant motion.

He lived in a black and white world in antebellum Louisiana. The line between the colors was clear to all but a few, which included Cat. Until now he had looked at the world through the eyes of a child. His dearest friends were the fifth-generation sons and daughters of the slaves who kept the vast plantation, *Vieux Saules*, both operational and profitable.

In recent months Cat had begun to notice some of the cruelty and sadness surrounding him. He was approaching an age where the wicked ways were becoming more and more visible. Little by little his parents had lost the ability to shelter him from the harsh realities of the plantation. His eyes were opening up for the first time, and it was a painful thing to watch.

Down the long path to the Main House young Richard had been raised to recognize and even enjoy the white side of the colored line. His education in plantation life began at birth and by the time he reached the golden age of fourteen, he held a full appreciation for being the planter's only son. Unlike Cat, it was not a shock to witness the harshness of slavery, but an affirmation that life was good for him, very good indeed.

To his parents' pride and relish, Richard had accepted without question that his family's slaves were property, not people. He had grown accustomed to this lopsided world and enjoyed without question the privileges it brought him.

For all his privilege, though, young Richard was a lonely, miserable boy and pompous as heck. Cat used other words to describe the boy, but reserved them for moments when his Christian mother was well out of earshot.

Richard both admired and detested Cat, a boy who had a rare charisma that made him an instant leader in any situation. It was a quality much admired by Richard's father and, therefore, richly desired by his impressionable son. It bothered him terribly that God had wasted such a precious gift on a poor white boy.

Perhaps what bothered Richard most, though, was not Cat's lack of social status, but his affinity with the family's slaves over his own kind. In Richard's upbringing, no decent white person would dare associate with African heathens. Yet Cat in many ways lived with them. He would even work the fields alongside his best friend Midnight and the other slaves. And that was the heart of the matter and the driver of the animosity between Richard and Cat.

When it came to the slaves, particularly the boys his age, Richard sharpened the divide. He ordered them about and gave them endless work just because he could. Without even trying, he was developing a mean spirit when it came to Cat's friends. So on this day and time, Cat, the son of a missionary mother, was determined to pay Richard back for the poor way he had treated his best friend the day before.

Cat sat motionless in the humid late afternoon with only his eyes free to survey the land. He watched the comings and goings of the various housemaids and field hands.

Sweat dripped excruciatingly slowly from under his bangs and down his forehead, but he kept his mind focused on the side door into the kitchen. He tensed slightly inside when the sweat crossed his brow and rolled down into his eye. The sting of the salt blurred his vision and broke his concentration momentarily.

The side door finally opened and the two women left the kitchen and headed toward the salt house. '*What grand luck,*' thought Cat. '*Both out at the same time.*' Now was his narrow window to get into the House and up the backstairs to Richard's room on the second floor. But he had to move fast.

Cat grabbed the satchel at his side and ran across the lawn toward the door. It was a mad dash. Before going inside, he looked around. *Good. No one had noticed.* He walked across the kitchen, stopped at the cutting table and, looking around again, snitched a smidgen of cake.

From the window he could see Nancy and Alma leaving the salt house and returning to the kitchen. He had to hurry. He walked quickly to the stairs and began his ascent.

The staircase was long, narrow, and dark. And squeaky. Cat, in bare feet, straddled the steps so that his feet rested on the sides where there was less chance of making noise.

Holding the satchel tight to his chest, he laughed to himself. Inside were a couple of dozen fresh leaves of poison ivy. In his pocket, a pair of gloves. He would rub the leaves all over Richard's sheets and pillows. That would keep the out-of-sorts boy out of his—and Midnight's—way for a few days at least.

The stakes for Cat were high. If he were caught upstairs in the private residence, he would have a lot of explaining to do, and the satchel wouldn't help. The punishment would be severe. Mr. LeBeaux would see to that.

But Cat was confident. He would sneak up the stairs, treat the bed and be back downstairs and outside in just a few minutes. He knew Richard was out riding his treasured horse, Beaumont, and the Mr. & Mrs. were in New Orleans for the day. He had only the House slaves to worry about, but some were unbelievably loyal to the Master.

Cat took another couple of steps. So far, so good. He heard the kitchen door open and then close, followed by the chattering of the two women. They talked so fast, without rest, it was hard to know who was saying what.

The mischievous boy was sheltered in the dark of the stairs. In his mind he replayed the steps he would take once he was in Richard's room. He had been in there once before so he knew the layout. He started to smile just thinking about Richard covered in itchiness from head to toe.

He took another step. Suddenly, the door at the top of the stairs opened revealing a rectangle of bright light. Cat's head snapped up, eyes wide with fright. He fumbled with the sack of leaves and it landed with a soft thump at his feet. His heart froze as he saw a figure fill the doorway.

Sunday

1 CAR SICK

August 23rd, Present Day
Along Interstate 10, St. Charles Parish, Louisiana.

The boy in the middle focused on his *Gameboy* while his head bobbed to the rap coming out of his headset. Nerdy Nate, as some kids in school called him, was on vacation with his newly blended family. And it was going well for no one.

"This will be a wonderful bonding experience," his mother had told him. A road trip through the Old South in their new midnight blue Suburban. 'It will give you a chance to experience history,' she said. To practice French with real Cajuns. To spend quality time with his new stepfather, and the twins, Ryan and Patty. 'Rattie and Bratty,' he called them.

From the first seconds their car pulled out of the driveway, the mood was tense and forced. Nate was still mad he had to sit between them, thanks to Princess Patty's extra luggage that took up the entire back seat. He was also annoyed by Ryan's constant fidgeting.

"Quit it, jerk face!" Nate hissed.

"You're the jerk." Ryan elbowed his ribs. "You're the reason we're on this stupid road trip. We could have gone to Hawaii, but Diana—*Mom*—wanted her little Natey to see his roots. Maybe if you were more normal—"

"—and weren't such a geeky idiot." Patty added, stepping on her new brother's foot.

Nate turned his head and spat out "—and you such a spastic creep."

Mr. O'Shaunessey eyed his rear view mirror nervously. He could see trouble brewing. He quickly pushed the play button on the overhead DVD player. It was his first line of defense.

"Oh, look, kids," said Diana. "It's 'Spy Kids."

Ryan leaned towards Nate's ear. "I believe there's only two kids in that family."

Nate repositioned his headset and tried to ignore the insult. But it was hard. In the new family he was outnumbered two to one, and the two were twins joined at the mouth. One would start the trouble and the other was a ready alibi.

Even his mother was a disappointing ally. She wanted so badly for the two families to merge happily. When push came to shove, it was easier to nudge the one she knew best.

Diana Bouvier O'Shaunessey wore the title of peacemaker. First as a child in a large French Catholic family, then as a young woman married to a French chef wildly detested by her family.

After just a few years and a disastrous restaurant venture, their love account was as overdrawn as their checkbook. Disillusioned, the young Henry Bouvier packed up his pots and pans and left his pretty, but poor wife and young son to brave the world all on their own.

Diana was devastated to say the least. Despite pleas and warnings from her family—or, in spite of them—she had leapt down the aisle and tied the knot. Little did she know it was a slipknot waiting for the first sign of hardship and adversity.

For the next nine years she pretty much raised young Nate on her own. Offers to help came from her family—not his, of course—along with the heavy strings of Toldyaso's and Shouldaknown's. Heartstrings are gentle and require an even hand. Yes, she had been blind; that's what love is, she told herself and any of her friends who would listen.

She looked in her visor mirror at her beautiful son. He was the image of Henry. Round, cherub face. Green eyes and corn silk hair. Blessed with a smile that could talk a hall pass out of the sternest of teachers. That, he had done more than once. Anything to get out of French class with its sappy conversation and mindless repetition. He complained bitterly to his mom that only girls were in the class. But, like her parents, she smiled and said he would look back on it as one of the best experiences of the school term. 'Mom was never a fourteen-year-old boy,' Nate thought hopelessly.

She looked again at his face sandwiched between noise cancelling headphones. In another month he would be starting ninth grade along with Ryan and Patty. She still held hope that all three of them would bond. High school is a bad time to be alone and since she and Nate had moved Uptown, Nate had been spending most of his time glued to his wired gadgets.

For Diana it truly seemed like yesterday that she and her little toddler were moving into their one bedroom duplex. In that first year she took night classes to be a paralegal while Mrs. Grynolachek ("Granolie") watched Nate. It was a constant struggle to stay fed and clothed.

She glanced at her second husband, a partner in the largest law firm in town. He was a confident, successful man. Two qualities lacking in her first husband.

John could sense his wife's attention. He turned from the empty road, caressed her hand, and gave it a gentle kiss.

"Oh, brother," moaned the twins in unison.

Patty yelled 'Personal Jinx" and swung her arm across to punch Ryan, hitting Nate in the process. Forgetting it was Patty and not Ryan, Nate flicked his arm hard against her stomach, knocking the first whine of 'Dad' clear to the back of her throat.

A bit shocked himself, Nate managed to mumble his sorries to the still-winded Patty.

The girlie-girl glared at him. He turned away to look out the window and glanced at Ryan. He had quickly learned to keep a close eye on both. Whenever one was quiet, the other was generally up to something and that something usually meant pain or embarrassment for Nate.

Ryan was looking out the window pretending to be interested in the bayous. Nate knew better.

"Daa-ad. Fox just hit me." Over the years Patty had perfected the tone and incline of her whines to a most refined science. Volume was also not a problem if the situation called for it. And, tears, well, they were always kept in reserve close by.

She also knew how to push her stepbrother's buttons. Two of them, anyway. So what better name to call him than Fox, the ugly American's mispronunciation of faux—the French word for false. Patty knew he hated anything that reminded him of Madame Dupont's fourth period French class and hated even more that he had a false family life as the only Bouvier in the O'Shaunessey house.

When it came to some things, Patty's short-term memory was annoyingly short. "You're not a real brother," she said to him under her breath. You're a fox brother. Get it?"

"I got it the first time, four weeks ago. And the hundred times since."

"Well, I wasn't sure. You seem like a slow fox sometimes. Did you know," she added slyly, "that foxes are afraid of water?" An evil grin lined her face. "Interesting, don't you think?"

Nate gave her a mean look. The twins were never going to let him forget that day. That Day. Just the slightest remembrance of it made him angry inside. "Why don't you just—"

"Kids, please don't fight," pleaded Diana. "We'll be in New Orleans soon. Then we can get out and stretch and see the sights. You are all just going to love the Crescent City." She looked over at her husband with a bit of apprehension.

"I wonder if the hotel will have a pool." Ryan leaned forward and patted Nate on the shoulder. "Ol' Natey just loves to swim— don't you buddy." Now it was Ryan's turn to wear the evil grin.

Nate's mind shot back to *That Day* at the Y, before they had all become a "family." He stood on the edge of the pool watching Ryan struggle as he was seized by a cramp. The boy was shouting for help between gasps of air. Nate, the only one in earshot, was frozen and unable to move limbs or lips.

As Ryan's head went underwater for the last time, the young lifeguard, surrounded by three girls, heard Patty's scream from the high dive. He saw her pointing to the far side of the pool. He sprinted towards Nate and, springing into a long arc, dove cleanly into the water. The rush of air nearly knocked Nate into the water with him, but Nate's eyes remained fixed on Ryan.

Grabbing the side of the pool, Nate felt the goose-bumps of cold and fear begin to cover his skin while, inside, he felt burning shame flow through his veins. *'What is wrong with me?'* he asked himself as he watched two blurry images rising to the surface. *'Why didn't I jump in and save Ryan?'* He knew with a terrible sinking feeling that he would never be able to set things right with Ryan now.

The lifeguard lifted Ryan's head above water and brought him to the side where Nate stood.

"Hey, kid!" The lifeguard looked straight at Nate. "Give me a hand." Nate's eyes were blank. "—Kid, did you hear me?"

Nate's head shook itself back to reality. "Huh?" He almost choked on the word soaked with chlorine.

"He won't help you," a winded but sharp-mouthed Patty shouted as she finished her race from the far end of the pool. "He just as soon see him drown." Before reaching to help pull her brother out of the water, she shot her trademark mean look toward the shivering nerd. "Wouldn't ya?" Then, with seemingly little effort, she raised her leg and pushed Nate into the pool. The resulting splash of water echoed in laughter from the other rising freshmen. Even the water couldn't muffle competely the sound of ridicule directed his way. He had lost any chance of making friends in his class before school had even started. It was going to be a long four years.

Nate later tried to tell Ryan he was sorry but the words never came out right. Besides, the other boy didn't seem to want to listen. He was more of a talker. In fact, by the end of the next day, the whole school knew the story. Everywhere he went, he heard *'Save me! Save me!'* from the other laughing kids. He was either a coward or a heartless SOB. A guy more interested in gadgets than people.

If that was not bad enough, a few weeks later he learned that his mother was going to marry Ryan and Patty's father. The taunting only got stronger as the wedding day approached.

Worse to come, he and Ryan would be sharing a room, and the larger boy made it clear that Nate was not welcome.

Rather than fight it, Nate withdrew. He spent as little time in the house as he could and avoided his stepbrother at all cost. Now he was stuck in a car with him on a long and tortuous road trip.

John glanced again into the rearview mirror. "It'll be fine, Diana," he said in his most reassuring voice. "They're just getting used to each other. It's a lot for them to take in all at once. Some day we'll look back and laugh at it all."

She smiled and squeezed his hand. It felt good to have a strong hand in her life again. She had done well the second time around. With her head against the headrest, she looked once more in the mirror. They all looked bored. With each other. With this trip. With life.

Over her head on an eight-inch screen a brother and sister sped away from bad guys in their parents' getaway submarine. She wished her own family could work so well together.

TIMOTHY PHILLIPS

2 THE TWIN STAIRS

The "happy" family continued their trek into the bayou country and sugar parishes of Louisiana. They couldn't decide what was in greater supply, water or oil wells. The latter seemed to be tucked into every available nook and cranny. The Californians thought it such an odd sight to see stately antebellum homes nestled between water towers and oil derricks.

John O'Shaunessey kept a tight ship when it came to opening the windows. He was a firm believer in climate control whether it was at home, at the office, or in his car. He was a bit spoiled that way. He liked it a cool 68 degrees, all the time.

As they motored over the bayou, they were oblivious to the 98 percent humidity, the noxious fumes from the oil refineries, and the resulting stench of fish who could not survive the condition of the water.

"It sure is pretty country, John."

"A decent lawyer could make a fortune off of all this oil. Downright harmful to everyone and everything—except the lawyers, of course." He smiled.

"But just look at all this history standing side by side with the present. That's a miracle in itself." She looked back at the three sleeping kids. "That's another miracle. Peace and quiet."

John chuckled. "They're a handful, alright. But when school starts, it will get easier. They'll get in a routine, you'll see."

"I hope so. The tension is killing me. I keep hoping Nate will wake up one day and find out how lucky he is. When he was little, he always complained about being an only child. Now he's got a brother and a sister—and they're all the same age. What could be better than that?"

"Well, in his defense, Ryan and Patty can be a tough team to crack."

"Even so, he needs to at least try. Instead he just buries himself in computers and that music." She let her head fall against the seat. "I dread the day he wants an earring—or worse."

"Nate? I don't think so. He's not into shock value. Now Ryan, that's a different story."

"John, look! It's beautiful. Slow down a bit, honey." There was an urgency in her voice, as if she were worried they would pass it by and never see it again. As the tires dug into the gravel, Diana's eyes remained entranced on the plantation house that lay just beyond the oak allée.

John dropped his speed considerably, moving the three bobbing heads in the back forward and then back quickly. The sudden change in momentum brought Nate and Patty's heads together. Both woke up rubbing opposite sides of their heads. Nate mumbled curses under his breath while Patty slapped his arm and complained to the man who caused the trouble.

"Relax, Patty," said John. "Diana wanted to see something. Go back to sleep."

"Oh, John, let's stop. It'll be fun and we've been on the road since lunch." With a quick hand she brought down the vanity mirror in her visor and with the other fumbled through her purse for her lipstick. In the upper part of the mirror she saw the three kids wrapped up in their 'Grumpies,' as she liked to call it.

John looked at his watch. It was nearly four. "We won't make it into New Orleans before dark."

"That's ok. I think we could all use the exercise, and the culture," she replied as she traced the outline of her lips with Evening Shade.

As John slowed to make the turn into the oak lined lane, Diana did her best to bring all three children into an alert, and somewhat cheery, state. No small task.

"Why do we have to stop now? I was just getting comfortable."

Diana ran a comb through her hair and checked for symmetry in the mirror. She adjusted her hair to perfection as she urged the kids to get excited.

"Come on, Ryan, you're going to enjoy this. We'll take a tour of the house and look around the grounds. It will be almost like stepping back in time."

Nate rolled his eyes. He had heard this speech many times; with each trip to the missions in Southern California; the ghost town near Barstow, or the back lots at Universal Studios. When it came to American history, his mom had the perpetual enthusiasm of a docent on emotional steroids.

He turned to Ryan. "Trust me on this one. There's no way out."

For once, Ryan took Nate's advice without comment. He put on his shoes—a pleasant relief to Nate and Patty—and prepared himself mentally for two hours of pure boredom.

"Dad, this had better be worth a hotel with a heated pool."

John laughed. He knew more about Louisiana humidity than he let on. "Whatever you want, son."

The O'Shaunesseys of Whittier, California disembarked and walked toward the inner gate leading into the plantation proper.

The Old Willows plantation rested on a fertile chunk of land surrounded by the Mighty Mississippi on three sides and bisected by a creek. It was well endowed with willows along both river and creek. The main lane off of the River Road into the plantation was an allée of two hundred year old live oak trees.

Diana read the sign aloud, as always.

"Welcome to Vieux Saules, *The Old Willows*. Founded on Mardi Gras in 1762 by Mr. Bertrand LeBeaux, a French-born immigrant. At its height just before the War Between the States, Vieux Saules comprised over 6,500 acres and 818 slaves. The primary crops were sugar, cotton, and indigo. Your tour begins at the Twin Stairs. Plantation and Grounds close at 5pm daily."

"Well, here we go." She took her husband's hand and led the family up the gravel lane to the Main House. It was a two-story mansion with a colonnade of twelve massive white columns and two arch staircases, The Twin Stairs, leading from the second floor portico to the front lawn. As with many plantations in the sugar parishes, the family's residence was on the second floor, while the first contained an extensive wine cellar, food pantries, kitchen, laundry, and maids' quarters.

She turned to John. "Can't you just feel the history pulling us in?"

"I haven't seen you this excited since our second date when I told you we were going ballroom dancing."

She squeezed his hand and gave him a kiss on the cheek, leaving behind a faint print of Evening Shade.

"Oh brother," came a chorus of three from behind.

"Personal jinx!" shouted Ryan and Patty as both slugged poor Nate who was once again caught in the middle.

Nate pulled back and let his new siblings get some distance between him. He slipped the headphones back on and wandered slowly toward The Twin Stairs. As he inched closer, he remained oblivious to all that surrounded him. Instead, he fidgeted with the iPod trying to find the right song.

"Two adults and three children, please." John handed the young boy a fifty-dollar bill.

The boy scrawled '2:3' on a scrap of paper and gave it back to the lawyer along with his change of loose bills and coin.

"We close at five, so y'all'll need ta hurry. Mary Anne's about ta start her next tour. Just ta the right."

Diana grabbed a handful of maps and gave one to each and gently shepherded them toward The Twin Stairs where a young and thin, very thin, docent dressed in a period costume stood watch over her flock of tourists.

"Oh, she's adorable," gushed Diana.

"Looks like Little Bo Peep," chuckled Ryan.

Diana gave her stepson a disapproving look, but Patty clearly thought it was also funny. Diana's face pleaded with the three teens to obey as they joined the ranks of the others.

"Good Evening. My name is Mary Anne. I'll be your guide through Vieux Saules. You will find that many of the furnishings in the home are original and so we do ask you to be most respectful as we walk through. Before we start, are there any questions?"

Diana was first with her hand in the air. "Yes, ma'am?' said the purple-hooped docent with the silver Timex.

"What is the significance of two staircases outside? It seems so unusual? I thought they were usually inside."

"That's a very good question, ma'am. The stairs were built by the original owner. Most antebellum homes have two stairs, one for the husband, and the other for his wife. With the wide dresses"—she pushed hers from side to side for the desired effect—"it was not possible for both to descend at the same time on the same stairs.

"To the people of the day," she continued in a voice designed to suspend, "it seemed very elegant indeed. But why outside? That's a mystery that I will share with you at the end of our tour...along with other mysteries such as why the sugar mill in the distance is painted such a bright blue." She glanced at her watch. "I see we will need to begin. Please follow me up the stairs."

While Nate tied his sneakers, the group moved up the right stairs. They were out of eyesight by the time he had re-tied both and adjusted the volume on his headset. He grabbed the banister to the left and bolted up the stairs. He followed the Southern voice down the hallway.

"The LeBeaux's were among the wealthiest planters in the sugar parishes and some would say in the entire South. They imported only the finest things to furnish their home. The family lived on this floor where they could take advantage of cool breezes coming off the River. Outside galleries allowed them to entertain and enjoy the views both day and evening."

A young girl raised her hand. "How many people were in the family?"

"At the outbreak of the War, the family consisted of Mr. Richard LeBeaux, his wife Evelyn, and their two children, Richard the Third, and Elizabeth. In addition, there was an overseer and a number of white workers, as well as over 800 slaves."

"Where did the slaves live?" asked an older African American from New York or some locale near there.

"They lived on the north side of the Creek that runs through the grounds. Mr. LeBeaux was a shrewd business man and, as a result, ensured that his workers had the best homes, food, and clothing possible."

The gentleman's face told nearly everyone in the room, except the docent and wandering Nate, that her answer was sub-par.

"Did he also provide his workers a 401k plan?" he asked, only half-joking.

The docent looked at a young girl who was thankfully doing something she shouldn't. "Oh, honey, please don't touch that knob. It's a very old door and hasn't worked in years." She corralled the group and continued with her prepared text.

"The first room on the right" she intoned, "was young Richard's. He lived here until 1859 when he turned sixteen. As was the custom, he then moved into the *garçonnière* that Mr. LeBeaux began building for his young son when he was seven.

"That two story, hexagon-shaped building is in a grove of trees to the left of the parterre garden that is outside the back doors of the Main House. Garçonnières provided a playhouse for the young boys and, later, a place to live until they could marry and create plantations of their own or inherit from their fathers."

Young Richard's bedroom was large enough to accommodate nearly the entire tour group. It was furnished simply, though. A large four-poster bed, mahogany dresser, nightstand with chamber pot, and a high boy.

"The furniture in this room, like that of the others, is original to Vieux Saules. You will notice the photograph over the nightstand. That is young Richard and his sister Elizabeth. It was taken in May of 1857 when Richard was fourteen and Elizabeth was twelve."

"Look, kids, he's the same age as you." Diana gushed.

Nate stared into the picture. "Actually, Mom, he's a hundred and fifty eight." He turned to the docent. "When did he die?"

"About five years after that picture was taken. He had gone to Vicksburg when it was seized in 1863. He never returned to Vieux Saules, and the plantation never really recovered." Sensing she had just brought the room down, she switched to her cheeriest voice that suggested The Old Willows will one day rise again as she led them down the hall into the opulence of a planter's daughter in the twilight before the War.

Nate took another long look at the tall, confident boy in the waistcoat and short pants. He had the cockiness that comes with wealth, status, and lineage. How sad for him that he didn't live long to enjoy it. Seeing his face and knowing his future had an effect on Nate. The boy lingered in the room, while the others continued into Elizabeth's.

Nate walked over to the long windows facing the river. The bubbles and waves in the glass told him they were the original thing. If he could imagine, he was standing in the same place where Richard stood so many times himself; he was seeing much the same view, the same sleepy river. The same stables and barn, and acres and acres of cotton. He wondered what the boy was like.

He took one last look at the boy and girl, and left the room to rejoin the group. He had lingered too long, though, and there was neither sight nor sound of the troop.

He came to the door on the left. 'What was it the docent had said about it?' He couldn't remember. He grabbed the brass knob and turned. The door opened. It led to a narrow staircase. 'They must have gone down here,' he thought.

Nate heard a muffled thump and caught a whiff of something that smelled old and musty. He walked down the steps cautiously. The door closed behind him. It was now somewhat dark and the steps were steep.

He waited for his eyes to adjust. With his hand gripping the rail, he moved cautiously down the stairs. About halfway down he heard deep breathing. Was it his own breath echoing to keep time with his hammering heart or was he not alone in the stairwell?

The spooked boy held his breath and listened. Hearing nothing, he took the next step and tightened his ears; he felt sweat now on the back of his neck. Adrenalin led him to the next step down, and the next one. Another step and suddenly his body seemed like cold jiggly jello falling into a warm mold.

His insides felt squishy. The butterflies in his stomach had taken over his voice box, and his legs were now filled with jelly. Waves of warmth followed by cold moved throughout his body, and this collision of opposites gave him quiet hiccups on now near wobbly legs. A strong brain freeze brought his hands up to his temples. He pushed his tongue hard against the roof of his mouth until the icy pain had passed.

'*What was that?*' he thought. It was as if something had passed through him. He looked up the stairs behind him but saw nothing. And there were no footsteps to be heard.

His own foot had stepped on something soft. As he bent down to find a cloth bag, he heard women talking down below. He breathed a sigh. He was always losing track of time and getting lost. He tired of his Mom's lectures on the subject. He quickened his pace down the steps, at one point nearly slipping backwards in his haste.

Near the foot of the steps he stopped in his tracks at the sight of two black women dressed, near as he could tell, like slaves.

"Catfish Hennessee! What in blazes you doin' in the upstairs? You know Master LeBeaux would skin your backside if he caught you."

Nate stood frozen. He knew she was talking to him. His mind was in a foggy mist at the moment, but the name Catfish sounded, strangely enough, actually familiar to him. And, odd as well, he suddenly knew the names of the women in the room."

"Nancy? Alma?" he heard himself say in a breaking voice.

Nancy and Alma looked at each other and then back at Nate.

He turned around a couple of times taking in the details of the busy, but primitive kitchen. *'They really went all out with the dress and actors in this place. Not bad,'* he thought. *'Historic Mr. Anderson in second period would dig this place.'*

"If not you be upstairs, I'd say you been in the sun too long."

"You best get out of this house, Cat," said Alma. "Young Master Richard, he's mighty sore at you."

"Are you talking to me?" Nate turned his head. Was it his imagination, or did his voice suddenly sound like someone else? Like a Cajun Huck Finn.

Nancy lowered her head while fixing her eyes on the bewildered boy. Then she glanced over at her friend Alma. "Is there another white boy in this sorry kitchen, Miss Alma?"

"No, ma'am." She then turned to Nate. "Boy, you ain't got time to stand there and stare. You gotta git."

Nate now felt the cold wood against his feet. He looked down; he was barefoot and dressed in overalls so worn they would fetch a great price in the malls. He instinctively reached for his hip, but his Walkman was gone.

His heart dropped into his stomach as he turned back towards the stairway, remembering the strange sounds and the sensation of cold Jello inside.

"You done so many mean tricks on Master Richard," said the leder woman, "you can't even remember the last. It was a good un, though."

"Cat, he knows, you's the one loosened his saddle. Landed fat slab in horse pilings." said Alma. Both women began laughing hysterically as they re-lived the haughty 'Son of the Massah' in green-stained riding britches. He told them he had slipped on the lawn, but the all-familiar lingering smell gave him away.

"He stormed up those very stairs. Oh, he was mad. Cursin' your name like the blue blazes."

"Yes, suh, Cat, you be smart to lay low in The Cemetery a week or so," advised Nancy.

"Maybe longer, you ask me." chimed Alma. "Oh, mighty sore, boy he is."

Nate looked at his wrist for the time, but his watch was gone with the wind. Nancy and Alma peered at him, their eyes narrowing and gave each other a puzzled look.

"I'z tellin' ya, Cat. I seen Richard here no more 'an ten minutes ago. You best git."

Alma nodded in full agreement. "Quick like."

Nate was finding all of this too much to take. He started to go back up the stairs to rejoin the rest of the tour.

Nancy and Alma rushed over to him and each grabbing an arm led him through the kitchen and out the back door.

"You don't wanna go back up there. Up there's trouble for you. Life? That's out here somewhere." She swatted him on his bottom.

"Now run," commanded Nancy.

"Like a slave." added Alma.

The two women closed the door behind Nate and got back to their cooking. He could hear them laughing on the other side.

The young Californian stepped off the back porch and took a few steps away from the Main House. He looked up at the second story. His family was up there somewhere. The question was how to get back to them.

3 CEMETERY CREEK

Nate turned from the house and looked out over the gardens and fields of the plantation. For a second time his heart dropped along with his jaw as he stared wide-eyed at the scene before him. He stumbled back and caught himself from falling on the brick porch. He sat down slowly on the steps to take it all in.

From every direction sights and sounds bombarded his senses. Wagons of tools and slaves moved down one of the lanes; a pair of white workers on horseback down another. To his left, in the parterre garden, a silver-haired slave worked meticulously pruning roses, while a boy of seven or eight polished the sundial.

Unlike twenty minutes before, the fields nearby were now filled with cotton nearly ready to harvest, and the orchard trees were heavy-laden with fruit. The lawns around him were meticulous, and the horizon was now devoid of water towers and oil wells. The air smelled only of fresh-baked bread, cut grass, and the River.

He looked down at his trembling hands and noticed he was still clutching the map his Mom had given him before the tour began. He opened it carefully and turned it around to match his view.

As he studied the map, a riverboat blew its whistle five times, signaling it was approaching the wharf at Vieux Saules. The barn doors flung open, and a wagon with four slave men bolted into the late afternoon sun.

The men shielded their eyes as they re-entered the daylight. Two of the men nodded and smiled as they passed Nate. He raised his hand. Little Jim and Adam. *'How odd,'* he thought *'that I know their names. What's happening to me?'* He closed his eyes tight, counted to three Mississippi's, and opened them, but the scene before him remained the same.

Nate heard voices from the gallery upstairs and remembered what Nancy and Alma had said about the boy named Richard. Although he wasn't sure why he should avoid Richard, it sounded like a good idea to move on. Maybe he could find this Catfish person and he could help him.

But first he had to answer the call of nature. He looked at the map and with a sinking feeling realized the toilet icons were probably meaningless. Nate stared at the map. He found the barn, stables, icehouse, seed house, kennels, and—there—the closest Necessary, or outhouse, to the Main House. *'How quaint,'* he thought, *'but logical.'*

Using the House as a reference point, he skirted the gardens, passing a slave he suddenly knew to be Silas who was still pruning the orange roses, which were Mrs. LeBeaux's favorites.

'How do I know these things?' he scratched his head.

Nate could see the Necessary just ahead. By now he was more running than walking. Getting home was no longer his immediate priority. He reached the brick and plaster outhouse, grabbed the door, and ran inside. Just in time.

As he stood inside he took in all the scenes painted on the walls. He wasn't altogether sure, but there seemed to be a naked Adam and Eve to his left and a baby Moses to his right. In between and all around were Job, Noah, Jonah, David, and Solomon. Men known to God but to Nate they were just old men in beards and billowy robes.

The shy Nate looked up at a host of angels looking down at him. All eyes seemed on him. He finished quickly.

Nate fiddled with the door latch anxious to leave the spooky place but the door was stuck. He heaved his frame and with a strong push and shove, it sprang open to an unhappy Silas.

"Catfish, you know better dan using dat room. Family only, you know dat. All your life you live here. How many times Ol' Silas haf to tell ya. You otta know better, Catfish. Mistuh Mallock catch you in der, an' he tan my hide, not yours. You git outta here now."

"I'm sorry...Silas, I had to go bad. Too much soda."

"Soda? Soda what!?"

"Uh—I mean, water. I drank too much water."

"Next time you take it somewheres else."

Nate hurried away from the unhappy man and his thorny roses. But the modern boy from Whittier kept looking behind his shoulder.

'Were my ears clogged or did that man call *me* Catfish?' This was getting a bit weird for the young Nate who was on his own now for the first time in his life.

He walked down the path between the barn and the stables and paused between the buildings.

'They said I'd be safe in the cemetery. Maybe I'll find the real Catfish there.' The map showed a cemetery on a bluff above the River just south of the barn.

It was getting late, though. Nate wished he still had his watch, and his iPod. He could only guess the time by the rumblings in his stomach. He wished now he had eaten more off his plate at lunch.

On the map there was an orchard just on the other side of a cotton field. It looked like a large field, though, and Nate worried about getting lost in the dark. Still, he wondered how being in a cemetery would keep him safe. How was he going to find food between the old tombstones?

As he started up an incline in the road, a group of black boys with fishing poles was coming down the road. Even at the distance, Nate tried to concentrate on their faces, waiting for the first spark of a distant memory to rush to the surface and give him a clue. That part was becoming an interesting game for him. Yet as much as he loathed Ryan and Patty, he relished being back in the car with them. He was getting worried inside. None of this made any sense to him, and he had literally no idea what was going on.

The boys were coming closer. One of them hollered to him.

"Ho, Catfish." Nate stared into the boy's face. It was Luke, a boy a year behind him. He was with George and Walter and Noah and Robert. Once again, everyone was calling him Catfish. Something was definitely not right.

Nate nodded.

"We'z caught ourself a mess o' fish." They held up their lines loaded with fish. "We'z eatin' goo' tonight. Where you off to?"

"The Cemetery," replied Nate, with as much confidence as he could push into two words and five syllables.

All the boys laughed. "You mus' haf de fever, Cat," said Luke. "Only cemetery up tha' road is filled with da pale bones o' white folk. No reason to go der."

"Yeah, no reason a-tall," several others chimed in.

Looking around, Nate noticed one boy not laughing. That boy, who he learned was Robert, had a fixed gazed aimed point blank on Nate. Something about Nate was clearly bothering the other boy. Somehow Robert knew what the others didn't. He believed in the unseen. Often, while in the fields under the hot sun, he would talk into the air and ask *Them* to send wind or rain. Which one didn't much matter to him. Rain or shine, he fed his heart on unseen magic.

"What'cha see, Robert?" asked Luke who was only a second behind Nate in noticing the strange intense look Robert was giving their white friend.

"Yeah, what'cha see?" added Noah. The boys moved into a tight circle around Nate, with Robert at the head.

Robert took a small step forward toward Nate who was, by now, nervously shifting his eyes from face to face. Barely an hour ago these boys had all been dead in the history books while he drove seventy miles an hour in an air-conditioned vehicle.

But now he was in their world, their time. Favored or not, they were in their element. They knew the rules of engagement, knew where they could take a chance, and who they could trust.

Although Nate was somehow mentally tied to this as-yet unknown Cat, the California kid had no control over Cat's cranial archive that was now somehow lodged in his brain.

As Nate arched his back to put some space between himself and the seer, Robert took matters into his hands and reached out to touch Nate's face. Suddenly his hands dropped. There was a long silence, at least it seemed long to Nate.

"Don' much know," Robert said finally. "Funny spirits to-night." He shrugged and turned around, but not before rubbing his hand on the top of Nate's head.

Nate was stunned. His hair was a corn-silk blond except for a four-inch ellipse of tow-head white. It had been with him since birth. All his life people were either asking if it was natural or if they could rub it for good luck. He was used to this at home but how did these near-strangers know?

The other four boys quickly followed Robert's lead and rubbed his spot as well.

Luke gave Nate a playful shove. "Come wid us. We'll share the fish."

"Thanks, but Miss Alma said I should go to the cemetery."

The black boys laughed. "You been in the sun too long," said Luke. "Come on with us." They all said in unison.

The boys were lively and playful. It had been a fine Sunday, the best day of the week for them. A day left to themselves. No master or overseer or load of work. A day to fish and play, that was all, provided they could slip away before their Mamas found them and got them dressed for church.

Nate allowed himself to be pulled along into their group. As they walked, he tried to replay the day in his head to understand what had happened to him. Where did he make the wrong turn and fall into another dimension? It was like watching himself caught in *The Twilight Zone*. He wasn't even sure what year it was. Sometime before the Civil War, that was all he knew.

Thomas reached in his pocket and pulled out a ball made of muskrat fur and filled with sand. He threw it to George who was about ten yards ahead. George caught it easily and quickly passed it to Luke, who passed it to Walter and then back to George. Robert, like always, was now back in the middle.

George caught Nate's eye and lobbed it high over Robert toward him. The white boy had to run backwards a ways in order to catch it, which he did to his own surprise.

"Over here, Cat." said Luke.

Nate threw it with ease the thirty yards distance between him and Luke. As the ball approached, Luke crouched and jumped. His timing was perfect.

'That's a first,' thought Nate, remembering his own humiliating tryouts at football last spring.

"Y'all think you're funny. Keepin' the ball from ol' Robert. Keep it." He ran past Luke, giving him a scowl, and cut across an open field.

"Robert!" yelled George. "Come on back!"

"Don't pay him no mind. He always in a bad mood." Luke made a face at Robert's retreating back and pulled his throwing arm back ready to resume the game.

Nate felt a little bad for Robert. He knew what it was like to be the odd man out.

The boys continued passing the ball back and forth on their way to the Cemetery. It made the time pass quickly.

"Well, Mr. Cat, here we be." George swept his hand across the view of rows of cabins and oak-lined lanes and alleys. He seemed to sense this was a new experience for his old friend.

Without thinking, Nate whispered "*Le Cimetière du vivant.*" Cemetery of the Living.

He walked across the wooden bridge, across an invisible line that separated the slaves from the cruel white world around them. Nate would soon discover that here in the Cimetière the boys were somewhat free to think and feel and do what they wanted. They just couldn't be who they wanted.

Some twenty yards away Nate saw a young black boy playing marbles with a pretty girl. They appeared to be about the same age as Nate. When they saw him, they stood up at the same time and waved, almost like they were one person.

The girl ran forward, grinning broadly, and grabbed Nate's hand, pulling him towards their game. As she touched him, Nate felt a rush of affection towards her he couldn't explain. He felt the same surge when the black boy threw his arm over his shoulders, talking excitedly.

"You hear the news, Cat?" he asked. Not waiting for an answer, he blurted out, "Ol' Tiddy-Beaux's gonna git dunked to-night. In the cold crick."

Nate just stared at Midnight for what must, to Midnight anyway, have seemed like a day too long. The excited boy whacked Nate on the arm breaking the spell over him.

"She gonna git baptized, Cat. To-night!" Midnight was clearly overjoyed, as were all the other boys but Pouty Robert, who had since rejoined the group. He more enjoyed the darker side of voodoo. To him it made more sense than holding to a white man's god who also happened, for luck's sake, to be white. Robert reasoned that if there was really a god, and He really loved him like Cat's mom was always saying, He wouldn't let them be treated like animals.

"Your Mama, she jumpin' double-joy right now." Midnight continued. "Ain't seen her so happy, Cat."

As Nate turned toward the girl he felt his face mirror her huge smile.

"The Holy Ghost gonna breathe in me tonight, Catfish. Gonna fill me up!" Her face was all-aglow.

Confused and embarrassed, he tried to look away but couldn't. At home in California no one he knew talked this freely about God, least of all in his family. They were good people, but they just believed religion should be neat and tidy and private. A part of him wanted to hide from the raw emotion and pure joy on Tiddy's face, but the other, unfamiliar part of him wanted to throw his arms out, embrace his friend and shout "Hallelujah!" of all things. He managed to hang onto his comfort zone and stayed rooted to the spot, continuing to grin like a crazy fool.

'Smatter, Cat got your tongue?" Midnight doubled over in a fit of giggles at his own joke, breaking the mood to Nate's great relief.

"Yeah Cat, you'se nevuh quiet," George chimed in. "If we didn't see yo' white skin and white spotted hair, we'd done think you was ol' Pouty Robert." Everyone laughed at this, including Nate who decided the best he could do now was to try to blend in until he found out who or what he had become. He joined in the roughhousing with the boys until, not knowing where else to go, he went home with Midnight for dinner.

Later that night about a hundred slaves from the Cimetière gathered on the bank of the creek. In the distance they could all see the Main House and the outlying buildings.

Midnight jabbed his elbow in Nate's ribs as he pointed at a white couple making their way toward the group.

"Yo' Ma and Mistuh Brett are here," he whispered.

'Ma?' Nate's heart gave a jolt and he strained his neck up to see a familiar face. He should have known by now that he would only meet yet another stranger who knew him as Cat. But the emotions he felt now as the woman approached him and placed her hand on his shoulder were comforting and not at all unfamiliar.

He managed to squeak out "Hi, Mom" accompanied by a weak smile.

Jenna tousled his hair. "So, we've shortened Mama to Mom now, have we?" She kissed his forehead. "I missed you today, Cat."

Nate responded without thinking and reached up to kiss her cheek. For the first time all day he felt like he belonged to someone. He lingered in her natural perfume and made a mental note to remember to call her 'Mama.'

The crowd around them grew silent as Tiddy-Beaux approached the edge of the creek. Monsieur Eduard, the pastor of this flock, waited for her in the water. The old slave gave himself tirelessly to the mission of teaching and preaching to his fellow slaves in the Cimetière. The love and pride he felt toward his new young convert was mirrored in his old eyes as he took her hands and drew her forward.

"Tiddy-Beaux, does you accept Jesus into yo' heart as Lord and Savior?"

"I do," she responded loudly. "I want to be in God's family now."

"Den I baptize you, Sister Tiddy-Beaux, in da name of da Fader, Son, and Holy Ghost."

Tiddy took a deep breath as Monsieur Eduard leaned her back completely under the water and raised her up again. As she looked toward the bank, the crowd broke into cheers which quickly became singing and clapping, one spiritual after another.

Nate turned to his 'mother' and saw she had tears in her eyes.

"Praise God," she whispered, reaching out to give Nate a hug. Seeing Midnight, she drew him to her as well and stood there for a moment before she released them and joined in the singing.

At that moment the man who had come with her to the creek stepped forward.

"Congratulations, Jenna. You work so hard teachin' them the Good News and all. 'Tis a blessin' you get t'see a new lamb come into the fold." His arms around her now, he kissed her soundly and released her grinning. "Enough tears now," he said. "It's time to dance. C'mon, Catrick, I brought ye your fiddle."

'A fiddle,' thought Nate frantically. "Now I'm supposed to know how to play a fiddle?!' He tried desperately to think of an excuse but he had no choice as the man he recognized as Brett dragged him to the center of the group and thrust a fiddle and bow into his hands.

Nate took a deep breath and closed his eyes. He didn't exactly pray, but his entire body cried out '*Help!*' He remembered the times earlier in the day when he had responded to someone without thinking. It had come naturally and seemed right. He tried very hard not to think about it as he raised the fiddle and placed his bow across it. To his great surprise—and relief—his fingers knew what to do and he heard music come from the instrument he held. His relief was so great that he relaxed and surprised even Brett as his fingers flew over the neck of the fiddle

The music and gospel songs even reached the white mansion with the Twin Stairs. Mr. LeBeaux sat with his wife on the gallery with its view of the River to the south and the Cimetière to the northeast.

"The nigras sure like their singing on Sunday night," observed the Mrs. with little emotion in her voice.

"I see smoke in the distance. Someone's been saved it seems."

"Oh, Richard, honestly. Sometimes you forget your own mind. I doubt very much that our God cares one whit about what a nigra does or doesn't do." She continued on with her cross-stitch.

Richard stood up from his rocking chair and walked over to the wrought iron balcony to get a better view. He didn't answer his wife out loud but wondered whether she spoke the truth.

Master LeBeaux differed from the neighboring plantation owners and actually encouraged his slaves to become Christians. He believed Christian slaves were more accepting of their lot, less likely to escape, and most importantly, not at all likely to rebel.

LeBeaux knew his family and the other whites on the plantation were far outnumbered by the slaves. He would do anything to ensure they stayed within his law. He gave the slaves a small chapel, a pastor of sorts in Monsieur Eduard, the missionary Jenna Hennessee, and Sundays to rest and praise the Lord for the bounty of Vieux Saules.

Seeing Silas down below leaving the House, he called out to him.

"Silas, who's in the crick tonight?" he asked.

Removing his hat, he replied "Young Tiddy-Beaux, Massah." He put his hat back on and continued home to the Cemetery to join the festivities, not even noticing his fellow slave Benjamin standing in the shadows.

Richard put the unlit cigar to his mouth—Mrs. LeBeaux would not allow him to smoke in her presence—and smiled. '*So Tiddy-Beaux has found Jesus. Maybe his wife was right about full-nigras, but what about those who were mixed?*' he wondered.

From below, Benjamin could see his Master leaning on the balcony rail. The older slave had wanted to go to the Cimetière with Silas but he would have been out of place there in his bright uniform. The other slaves thought he spit and polished the Master's boots too much. Master LeBeaux thought he didn't do it nearly enough. So the conflicted Benjamin stayed in the shadow of the columns and watched the fire from a far distance.

The celebration in the Cimetière lasted well into the night. In time only a few were left huddled around the fire.

Jenna walked over to Tiddy-Beaux and gave her a mother's embrace. "I am so very proud of you." Jenna's voice was soft and warm. "You have studied the Bible with me for a long time," she continued "and have learned a great deal."

"You a good teacher, Miss Jenna."

Jenna smiled and looked into Tiddy-Beaux's eyes. She wished it were true, but she was bound by her promise to Mr. LeBeaux that she would not teach his slaves to read or write. Like the other planters at that time, Mr. LeBeaux assumed great danger would exist on his plantation should the slaves gain too much knowledge.

"Thank you, Tiddy." She turned to Brett and Nate and said it was time to go home. "We have all had a long but happy day. I am tired."

Nate was relieved. Home sounded good even if it had to be Cat's home. He was anxious to get to a place, a room, where he could sort out all of the things that had happened to him this day. Maybe in Cat's home he would be able to discover some information about this boy who had taken over his body and brought him into so many strange situations. More than anything, though, he wanted to go home with Jenna, the woman he would remember to call Mama, and he wanted to know what made her cry at the creek side.

Monday

August 24, 1857

4 CAT'S EYES

Nate woke up a minute before the sun. That was normal for Cat, but highly unusual for Nate. The teenager lay motionless in the bed except for his eyes which surveyed the room slowly from one corner to the other like a surveillance camera.

As he took in his surroundings, so many thoughts were bouncing against the walls of his head. His thoughts were competing with those of the boy they called Cat. Trouble is, Nate couldn't figure out whether he had somehow fallen into Cat's body, or the other way around. But, either way, he knew he was in Cat's backyard—both the time and place.

He pulled the covers off and walked across the wood floor to the mirror over the dresser. He closed his eyes, counted to five *Mississippi's*, and opened them.

The boy peered into the face in the mirror and examined all the features closely. He tilted his head and saw the ever-familiar blond spot. No doubt about it, he was still in his body.

Nate looked at the rest of his body, and it too looked like his, although he noticed his arms were a bit stronger. And he was a lot tanner. But, still, nothing too out of the ordinary.

So, why, he wondered, did he have this strange feeling that he was also someone else? How could he be two people at once? And, with only two years of French in school, how come these second thoughts were all in French?

The sun was now peering through his window and he could see the pictures on the wall. He felt one staring at him. As he turned around, his face froze. He walked over to the photograph of a boy and his parents.

It was remarkable and mind numbing. He was, somehow, the boy in the picture.

He heard steps in the hall and then a knock at the door.

"Oui," he said. Without thinking he had answered in French.

His pleasant-sounding French mother was on the other side.

"Mon cheri—le petit déjeuner est prêt."

"Je viens, maman—une minute. "

"Hurry up, son. Brett has a lot to do today."

"Oui, maman," he replied.

As the footsteps in the hall faded, Nate stood amazed; he couldn't believe what had happened to him. He had truly somehow morphed into someone else and was now thinking and speaking French.

Nate quickly undressed and put on yesterday's overalls and cotton shirt. He looked around the room and under the bed for shoes but couldn't find any.

'*Am I supposed to walk around barefoot? Like a dumb Huck Finn.*' he thought.

As he stood up he noticed a green bound book on the small table in front of the window. He walked toward it, and saw the glistening white Main House towering over everything in the window frame. Directly outside was a small vegetable garden. Yellow and blue flowers lined the picket fence between the dirt lane and the garden.

The window had been left open all night and now the competing music of the local songbirds, some extinct in Nate's world, filled his small room.

Nate picked up the green book and opened it to the inside cover. It was a boy's journal; a glass bottle of ink rested on the table nearby. He read the inscription, which was written in French.

Cat's Journal
A birthday gift from Mother and Brett
April 4, 1857
Happy Fourteenth!!

Nate's green eyes widened as he and this Cat fellow were born on the same day, and both were now fourteen. He flipped a few pages into the book.

Thursday. April 16, 1857

Worked with Brett painting the stables. Took most of the day. Richard's horse tried to kick me over the fence. Kicked over the can of paint instead. Brett wouldn't stop laughing. I was mad and wanted to paint the horse red. Thought twice about it. Didn't want my own backside red from Master LeBeaux.

Went over to the Cimetière after supper to play with Midnight and Tiddy. Spent most of the time on the porch. All too tuckered to play.

Nate flipped the pages to another day.

Tuesday. May 12, 1857

Warm day. Swam and fished mostly. Caught a couple sunfish. Went into town with Brett. Saw a slave auction starting, but Brett rushed us past. There was a boy there about Midnight's size and age. Made me think.

There were a couple of raps on the door which jolted Nate from the recent past.

"Mon fils! Le petit déjeuner!" Her voice was firmer this time around. Time for breakfast.

"Oui, oui, maman—dans une minute."

Nate had a thought and fanned the pages until he came to the last entry. He hoped it would be about yesterday. Maybe it would give some clues to this whole thing. He stared at the date.

'*Eureka!*' he thought.

Saturday. August 22, 1857.

Couldn't sleep I was so angry at Richard. Someone needs to bring him down a notch or two. Maybe if he rolled in a fancy bed of poison ivy he might not be so uppity. Might even want to crawl out of his own skin! Like the snake he is!!

Nate remembered the cloth bag on the back stairs. It was soft on his bare feet. '*Was it possible,*' he wondered, '*that he had literally run into Cat on his way to Richard's room?*'

"Catrick!" This time it was the deep voice of a hungry man. A hungry Irishman!

Nate closed the journal and put it back by the ink bottle. He took a deep breath, opened the bedroom door, and let himself be drawn toward the wonderful smell of eggs and sausage. He could hear '*his*' mother Jenna singing in the background.

"Bonjour Cat." She walked over to Nate and, holding his face in her hands, gave him a peck on each cheek.

He was mesmerized by her beauty. Last night it had been so dark when he saw her, and he had been distracted by everything that had happened to him, as well as the excitement of Tiddy's baptism.

"Bon jour." he whispered.

"Good marnin' son," said the dark-haired Irishman in his early thirties. He had a sketchpad beside his plate and was busy at work.

Cat had been so taken by his mother that he hadn't even noticed the man in the room. He watched him draw.

"What are you doodling?" he asked timidly.

The painter looked up from his pad. "Doodling? What is doodling?" He glanced over at Jenna.

"Um, your pictures. They're—tres bon." He suddenly became aware that he had the accent of last year's exchange student from Quebec.

"*Doodles?*" his father repeated. "I like that. Sounds Irish." He smiled and continued sketching."

"Come, sit down, Cat. The food is getting cold."

His mother sat down and folded her hands. Nate watched Brett follow and quickly did the same.

"Père Dieu, bénissiez cette nourriture. Dans votre nom, nous prions," she said. Then she repeated in English for Brett's sake. "Heavenly Father, bless this food. In your Name we pray."

The three ate quickly with little conversation. Then Brett stood up, kissed his wife, and was out the kitchen door.

"Où va-t-il?" Cat asked.

Jenna laughed. "Where else? The Paint House. Et vous?" she continued. "What will you do today?"

"Je ne sais pas." he shrugged.

Nate marveled at his newfound French ability. His mom would be gushing worse than she did at her own wedding if she could hear him speaking now.

As far as the day, Nate really didn't know. This was all new territory for him. He was in the middle of a different world without his usual gadgets to give him cover. Nate was in charge at the moment, but he wasn't sure how long that would last. He seemed to becoming more and more aware of Cat's presence within his own mental realm.

What if one moment he no longer thought as Nate? Would he one day forget everything he had known the day before? What if he could never break out of this dream and was forever stuck here? Nate could feel himself starting to panic inside. He got that wonderful trait from his mother.

Jenna noticed Nate's flushed face.

"Êtes-vous malade?" Jenna wiped the sweat from Nate's forehead. "You do not look well."

"Je vais bien, maman," he answered. "I just need some fresh air."

Nate stood up, gave Jenna a kiss, and followed the steps Brett had recently taken.

Unlike Brett, though, Nate didn't have anywhere to go. Unless someone could magically take him back to where he had started. By mid-morning, the young boy was still sitting on the same tree stump he had found shortly after leaving the house.

The boy from California was awe-struck by all that was going on around him. He saw first-hand things barely touched in the history books.

It befuddled him that he was literally in the midst of people who had lived—who were now living—a hundred and forty years before he was even born. He and they were breathing the same air. Old flesh and bones now fresh and very much alive!

What Nate didn't see was also just as exciting. No airplanes overhead. No cars whizzing by the highway. No highway.

He was in his history teacher's paradise.

The sound of the screen door and Jenna's voice broke the spell he was now in.

"Have you done your chores, Cat?"

Nate didn't respond. He still wasn't used to being called a cat. He never liked it when his step sister called him a fox. And now he was a Cat.

"Have you weeded the garden?" she asked, this time with a firmer voice.

"Flowers or greens?" he heard himself moan. Cat's attitude was coming to life.

"Both."

"Ah, maman!" he groaned. "It will soon be too hot to fish."

Cat had suddenly entered Nate's consciousness full on and had decided it would be better to fish than to work. Especially on such a muggy day.

Nate stood up from the stump and turned towards Cat's fishing pole leaning next to the porch. But before his foot touched the path, Jenna stopped him in his tracks.

She could read her son's mind. "Forget the pole and grab the trowel, mon cheri."

"Maman." The fourteen year old was getting impatient, as was his mother. She had watched him from the window all through the morning and had decided he had daydreamed long enough, even for a boy.

"Where is your friend Midnight?" She, of course, knew where he was.

Cat knew as well. "In the fields. With the cotton." he mumbled.

"And how long has he been in those cotton fields?"

Nate lowered his shoulders, grabbed the trowel, and scowled his way to the vegetable garden.

"Peter Hennessee." Jenna rarely used his Christian name. It had the immediate impact on her son she expected.

"Oui, Madame." He had at once found his *I'm-facin'-the-Principal* voice and turned around to face his accuser.

"You have grown up among slaves but sometimes you seem to truly have no idea what they know. Midnight is your best friend, but do you really understand what he endures? Every day. He doesn't have the pleasure to go fishing rather than work the fields.

He cannot tell the overseer that he is too tired to work today. Or that he would rather dream on a tree stump."

As Jenna spoke, Nate looked directly into her eyes. He understood what she was saying. He knew from books he had read, as well as the emerging memories of Cat, that he had certain privileges simply because he was white. It was never said out loud. It was too obvious. It was all given below the surface.

Nate thought now of Midnight working under the hot sun hunched over the cotton, his hands cramped from picking the Master's white gold. He knew from the journal how much Cat thought of Midnight.

"Alright, Maman." The blond boy walked up to his mother and touched her arm. She looked into his moist green eyes.

"I will get out some sweet cider. When you have finished in the garden, you can take some to Midnight."

Nate nodded, grabbed the garden tool and joined the other working souls under the hot Louisiana sun.

After an hour or so of what, to Nate, seemed like back-breaking work, the boy had filled a burlap sack with weeds and carried it over to the compost heap at the corner of the plot Master LeBeaux had allowed them to use for the family garden. As he emptied the contents, LeBeaux's son Richard, the spoiled prince of the plantation, approached him.

Though roughly the same age as Cat and Midnight, Richard was about four inches taller and broader in the shoulders, more so than even Midnight who did hard, physical labor from sunup to sundown six days a week. Here was a boy who was sure of almost every step he took.

"Bon après-midijour, Monsieur Chat." Richard always spoke in French to Cat, and Cat was never sure if it was his awkward way to show his kinship with another Frenchman his age, or if it was to show off his fanciful French that Cat's mother was teaching him in their daily tutoring sessions.

Either way, Cat would have nothing to do with it, and spoke only English to the rich prince. No matter how Cat might have framed the words in his head, by the time they reached Richard, they had lost any trace of their French origin.

"Hello, Richard." There was a mix of boredom and resignation in his voice.

J'ai un bateau sur le bayou. Veux-tu aller pêcher avec moi? *I have a boat on the bayou. Would you like to go fishing with me?*

"I have to finish my chores." Nate replied.

"Partons. Je ferai un esclave fais vos corvées." *Come on. I will get a slave to do your chores.*

"My mother would not look kindly to that. Nor would I."

"Ne soyez pas un imbécile. Avancez. Appréciez la vie. Le fleuve est plein des poissons aujourd'hui." *Don't be foolish. Enjoy life a little. Come on. The river is full of fish today.*

"I need to finish here."

Richard paused. "Pourquoi," he paused again. "Et pourquoi tu ne parles pas en francais avec moi? À un Noir tu parles francais, mais moi, un garçon français, tu parles anglais. Pourquoi est-ce que c'est?" *Why do you not speak French to me? To that dark boy, you speak French. To a French boy, you speak English. Why is that?*

Richard's jealousy of Midnight's friendship with Cat was well known on the plantation, and a great worry to Midnight's mother. She had already lost too much to the whims and emotions of the Master family.

Nate ignored Richard's question and began to walk away but Richard grabbed him by the arm and turned him around.

"Je vous ai posé une question. Reponds-moi!" He paused for effect. "En français." His tone was biting.

Nate, spurred on by Cat, bore his eyes into Richard's. Cat's spirit was digging in its heels.

Richard didn't care for the silence or hard look. He gave Nate a shove.

"Répondez-moi, garçon. Pourquoi faites-vous pour ne pas parler français au fils du roi." *Answer me, boy. Why do you not speak French to the son of the king.*

"Your father is not a king." Nate scoffed.

Nate glared at Richard, and for a moment confused him with Ryan. He was another rich boy who always got his way. Nate could feel his hand clench into a fist. A voice inside kept shouting in his ear *'Do it! Do it!'*

Richard's jaw tightened noticeably. "S'il pas le roi, alors qu'est-il à toi?" *Then what is he to you?*

The planter's son took a deep breath and spoke again to Nate, "Je perds la patience avec cette conversation." *I am losing patience with this conversation.*

Richard continued. "Ingrat! Mon père a pris soin de ta mère quand elle était enceinte. Quatorze ans après et tu tout les deux soyez toujours ici. Pourquoi êtes-vous partis?" *You are ungrateful. My father took your mother on when she was pregnant and on the streets. Fourteen years later and you are both still here. Why not leave?*

Nate looked at Richard, shook his head and turned away.

"Au revoir, bâtard."

At those words, Nate turned around and pounced on Richard. He gripped both hands around Richard's throat and squeezed. Nate's face was flushed and his lips fused as his grip tightened. Nate felt he was back at the schoolyard defending his own honor.

'*Mama's boy*,' they called him. '*Said his dad took one look at him and split.*' It was rubbed in his face often. Literally.

Only, this time, Nate seemed to have the strength and gumption to do something about it. He squeezed his grip tighter and watched Richard's face get whiter.

A frantic Richard put his hands on Cat's and tried to release the hold, but Nate was too determined. In desperation, Richard rocked side to side until he had enough momentum to turn the situation upside down.

He was heavier than Cat by fifteen pounds, and his hands fit around Cat's neck all the better.

"Maintenant, monsieur,"—he breathed heavily as he got his wind back—"répétition après moi en français." He paused for air. 'Votre père est le roi. Je ne suis rien.' Dites-le!" *Now, sir, repeat after me in French. 'Your father is the king. I am nothing.' Say it!*

Now it was Richard's turn to squeeze the life out of the other boy.

The smaller Nate spoke, in a slow, raspy voice. "Votre père est—" The captive boy's eyes shifted to the right as if he were looking for the right word lurking in the bushes. Richard turned his head to follow Cat's eyes. With his left hand, though, Nate reached for a small branch and, still looking to the right to throw off his captor, he started to raise the wood.

But it was no use. Jenna had placed her foot on the stick and began speaking in French to both boys faster than the rush of the Mississippi in a spring flood. At the same time, she seemed to lift Richard effortlessly off her gasping, red-faced son.

"What is going on?" she demanded.

"I came here to ask Cat to go fishing," said Richard as he wiped the grass off his trousers. "But all he does is hurl me insults. He knocked me down. I do not think my father will be happy when he hears this."

"Cat, give Richard an apology."

Nate looked away.

"Peter, son of Andrew, apologize."

Nate stared at Jenna in disbelief at the forcefulness in her voice. *'How could she take the side of this blustering bully in fancy pants? Didn't she hear the way he was asking for a fight?'*

"Apologize before the sun melts. And tomorrow you will go fishing with Richard."

"But mère—"She put her hand to his lips and whispered in his ear.

"Apologize so that life may go on."

Nate stared at Richard until his mother urged the words out of him with a swat on his bottom. As he spoke, he managed to give his dear mother a disapproving face.

"Million de pardons, Richard, fils du roi. Si vous êtes disposé, je voudrais aller pêcher avec toi demain." *A million pardons to you Richard, son of the king. If you are willing, I will go fishing with you tomorrow.*

Richard shook his hand and Jenna's as well. He smiled at the lingering sound of French coming off Cat's tongue to his ears. He had finally succeeded in getting something from the one person on the plantation too independent to care what Richard did or thought.

"Demain alors." *Tomorrow then.* He raised his hand in the air as the picket gate slammed shut with a thud and a cloud of dust.

Jenna returned to the porch and sat down in the chair to watch Cat finish his work in the garden. She marveled at how much he had grown just in the past year. She was sure he had put on at least three inches and maybe ten pounds. Still, he was

the leanest boy on the plantation. All the more to marvel at how
fast he was growing up.

She looked away for a moment and when her eyes again fixed
on her son, he was just a young toddler in diapers running un-
steadily through the yard. She watched him discovering the creatures of the garden. He especially liked the butterflies.
'Butterbyes,' he called them. He chased after them unsuccess-
fully but never gave up the hope of touching one.

Her mind wandered further back in that day her life changed
for the better...

"Good afternoon, Ma'am." The young Irishman, a relative
newcomer to Vieux Saules, had finished painting one of the Ne-
cessaries a frail pink for Mrs. LeBeaux. The lad's face was
touched with the lady's color. It was in his hair as well.

"Well, Mr. Hennessee, that color suits your character most
aptly."

"Between you and me, the Man's a bloody idiot. Whoever
heard of painting an outhouse, even a fancy one at that, pink?
Or, for that matter, any color." Brett sat down on the porch and
put his back against the post. "Ah, now that feels good." He
pushed his back further against the post.

"Be sure not to leave any pink when you go to leave." Jenna
teased the tired man, who would one day be her husband.

He ignored the comment. His mind was deepening in thought.

"What am I doing here?" he asked. "Painting outhouses and
outbuildings and barns. I'm a bloody artist. Pen and ink. Oil.
Watercolors. Serious art, that is." He plucked a few tall blades
of grass brushing against the porch. I have been here a year now
and every day is the same. And I'm no closer to—"

"Her?"

"To anything. At least you have your son." They watched Cat as he stretched up to touch a low tree limb, lose his balance, and fall back on his cloth padding. Jenna and Brett both laughed. Her little boy stood up and walked toward another tree.

"He's not one to give up."

"Nor should you, Mr. Hennessee. I believe God brought you here for a purpose. And some day it will be clear to you. Crystal clear."

"In the meantime?"

"In the meantime, you continue on. You paint. You live. You enjoy."

"And what do you do?"

"I raise my son the best I can, and I be a true witness to the people in the Cimetière and, yes, even those in the Main House."

"The Cold House, you mean. My dear, those people up there are pure heathens."

"I don't believe heathens to be pure. They are sinners like the rest of us and, as sinners, they can be saved like the rest of us."

"I admire your spunk and your pluck. But you are a naive girl."

"Girl? Why thank you, young Mr. Hennessee. And when you are old enough to shave, you must let me know."

"Funny that." He paused. "Do you mind me asking what happened to the late Mr. Argineaux? It's been on my mind awhile to ask."

Jenna looked away for a moment in the direction of the North as if searching for a distant memory.

"He was a river pilot killed trying to break up a fight at a gambling table," Her voice trailed off into the past.

"I'm sorry. Did he, I mean, did he ever get to see his son?"

"No. He died when I was just a few weeks carrying Peter. In fact, before he left, I didn't know myself. It all came as a shock to me, a reminder of the love I had had with him.

"He was a good man," she continued, "though like all of us, he had his shortcomings. He could, for example, never stand up to his father. No matter how much he tried, the courage dropped to his feet within moments of being in the same room as the older Monsieur Argeneaux. It doomed our marriage really, even before his death."

"You are fortunate, I guess, to be here then. At least you're safe. Being a woman on her own, especially with a little one, is not always a good thing."

"I met Mrs. LeBeaux in New Orleans. It was shortly after my husband's funeral. I just couldn't go back to his family; his father really detested me. I think he didn't like the fact I was no longer a Catholic, or that I thought—and dared say aloud—that slavery was abhorrent. He owned a rather large plantation along the River on the Mississippi side."

"Yeah, I cannot imagine that would be a wise thing to say, especially here in the South."

"Anyway, Mrs. LeBeaux and I struck up a conversation. When she found out in the first seconds I was French, she insisted I come out here and teach her the language of her husband's family. That was more than two years ago."

"So as a 'long-timer' who can leave at any time, how's it been? Do you ever want to just get up and leave and go north back to Quebec?"

"It has not been bad. It is pretty country, and I am useful here. I have led quite a number of people to the Lord. I believe that is why the Lord put me here. Cat was born right here in this house. It is a good life for him so far. He even has another boy he likes to play with. They are good mates, as you would say. He's a bright boy; they call him Midnight. Cat's face lights up whenever he is around. Spiritually, they could be twins."

"How will Cat feel when he is old enough to understand what goes on down in the Cemetery? When he finds out his mate is bonded for life? As are his children and his children's children. Life not yet even contemplated. Or will you be gone by then?"

"For a man I thought was shy, you do ask a lot of questions."

"I have a lot of time to think when I'm slopping pigment on the pigs."

"What about you? When will you go north?"

"Unlike you, I have no family North of here. Or East. Just me. Here. But you, why not take your son and go back to your family in Canada?"

"Some day I would like to take him to meet his grandmother Alice. She is anxious to meet her grandson, and I have not seen her in nearly three years. It was heart-breaking to leave, but I felt called to be a missionary in the South among the enslaved. I felt a real calling."

"But then you fell in love with a river pilot?"

"It is, true to life, more complicated than that. I was a tutor on his father's large plantation. Over time we fell in love and were married. His parents, though, never approved so it was an uphill battle."

Jenna lifted her face and watched her little boy watch a caterpillar crawl on his young finger. She smiled and caught a small frog in her throat.

"Did I ever tell you I was adopted?" she said at last.

"Adopted? No, you have not. That is something I would clearly remember." He watched her tug a curl of auburn hair behind her ear. "Would it be impolite of me to ask what happened?"

"As far as I know they are alive and well. It seems I was one more than they needed." Her voice drifted as she finished her thought. "I am not sure why I told you this. It is not something I generally share."

"Perhaps the sight of your young son, shaky as a new-born fawn, brought back a memory."

"Yes," she agreed, "perhaps that is it. But I tell you, as long as God permits me, I shall not leave the side of this one.

The Irishman set his hand gently on hers. "I am sorry, Jenna."

She looked up and smiled shyly. "Jenna. You called me 'Jenna.'"

"Suddenly, you look like a *Jenna* to me."

"Thank you. It's a nice, early present."

"Present?"

"Tomorrow is my birthday."

"Well, then, I better hurry on."

Jenna gave him a quizzical look.

"I can think of a more proper present to give you, but finding just the right green to capture your eyes will not be an easy thing to do." Suddenly, the young artist had a found a project worthy of his talent. He rubbed Cat's blond spot gently before passing through the picket gate and taking one last look at the beautiful and sweet spirit sitting in the shade of the porch.

He walked back to The Paint House with excitement and energy. In truth, she was as lonely as he was and somehow that gave him hope.

As Jenna now watched her fourteen year old finish in the garden, her husband climbed onto the porch.

"Ah, you have put the good lad to work, I see."

"It was either that, or let him crush poor Richard."

Brett gave her a queer look.

"Cat can tell you all about it after lunch while you both repair the roof." She looked into her husband's eyes. "Talk to him for me. He is not at all happy with me right now, but he must learn to get along with Richard."

"I am not sure I am the one to do the talking on that score. I am not exactly a fan of Richard's father, remember?"

"Yes, but you have a better perspective than he. He still sees life through a child's eyes."

"Jenna," Brett cracked a smile. "He is a child."

"Yes, but childhood is much shorter here than in Québec or even your dear Ireland."

Brett put his arm around Jenna and took a deep breath. He knew his wife was right.

5 An Irish Butterbye

Tiddy-Beaux wandered past the edge of the Cimetière as she followed the erratic and whimsical flight of the lone butterfly. She had first set eyes on him from the cabin where he was resting his wings on the rough wood of the windowsill. The bright spots of color stood out against the grey of the old wood. The slow fanning of his wings lifted Tiddy-Beaux's young imagination. Captivated, the pace of her breathing was soon in rhythm with the slow rise and fall of the creature's wings.

Then, as if some word of the wind had spoken, the butterfly lifted off the wood into the open air. Quick as she could, Tiddy-Beaux herself was off. She skipped breakfast as she skipped out the cabin door and down the steps into the shady oak lane that was one of the main 'streets' in the Cimetière.

She followed the flight of the colorful spirit past Toby's cabin and in between Aunt Sarah's and Old Jonah's. It landed on the porch post of Monsieur Eduard who married and buried the Cimetière folk. And who had baptized Tiddy-Beaux the night before.

"Bonjour, Mademoiselle."

The elderly, refined slave sat in his rocker peeling an apple. After seventy years of hard work, his bones were tired from picking cotton and cutting cane. Now, he barely picked more than a child. His value to the Master, though, was not in the amount of cotton he could pick, but in his ability to keep the Cimetière focused on the Lord.

Tiddy-Beaux just stared at a spot right above Monsieur Eduard, as if she were in a trance.

The older man pushed back in his rocker and looked above and saw the scarlet wings.

"Vous avez trouvé un joli papillon rouge." *You have found a scarlet butterfly.*

She laughed. "I didn' fin' her—or him. She foun' me."

"Well, she be a pretty coluh anyway. Une jolie couleur."

Another whispering breeze and the butterfly was off again. He flittered, fluttered, and flattered from post to post, limb to limb, flower to flower. And Tiddy-Beaux followed his every move, further and further out of the Cimetière toward the creek that led to the River and the potential for freedom.

It was as if the butterfly was a messenger from God encouraging her to take the steps out of the plantation world.

Only the quick eyes and stern call from Clara kept her from disappearing toward the Wood, a dangerous place for a girl so young.

Meanwhile, Nate and Brett had spent a good part of the afternoon on the roof of their house replacing broken or missing shingles. From twenty feet up Nate had a good view of his surroundings.

The corners of his eyes were drawn to a bright wave of purple moving quickly from the Main House toward the family's private Necessary, the one Nate had used the first night to Silas' great discomfort. If he were more interested in prissy girls, he would have admitted she was a pretty one, with locks of curly blond hair and a pleasant face. Right now, though, at age fourteen he was more intrigued as to how the young lady was going to fit her melon-shaped dress through the door. He set the hammer down and watched in amusement.

The little princess walked with quite a purpose, sticking the poke of her umbrella into the ground with each urgent stride. When she was nearly to the private door, Nate saw and heard the girl's young servant Sadie come running towards her at full-gallop, screaming her mistress' name as she flew.

"Miss 'Lizabet! Miss 'Lizabet!" There was high-pitch determination in the girl's voice.

'Ah, Elizabeth. Yes, that was her name.' Cat's memories of the little miss flooded Nate's brain in a flash flood. Taunts and put-downs, the shaking finger, and the uppity little nose. He remembered now why he didn't like her.

Brett stopped working shortly after his son took notice of Elizabeth. He had seen that look in Cat's face many times before. *Mischief in the Makin'* he called it. He stood up and re-positioned himself so that he and Nate were sitting side-by-side on the ridge post facing the Necessary.

The door to the Necessary closed, and Brett watched Nate's face.

Suddenly, they both heard the loudest, shrillest scream. The fireworks had begun. First, an unmistakable shriek of horror mixed with panic, immediately followed by the sound of the wood door being thrust out with such a force it knocked poor Miss Sadie off her hinges and smack to the ground. This was followed by a burst of purple running for dear life over Miss Sadie and through the parterre garden.

Sadie was out cold.

Nate, though, was laughing so hard he nearly did a backward somersault down the other side of the roof.

Brett was puzzled. "Cat, what exactly did you do to the poor lass?"

But Nate didn't need to answer. Within seconds, the undeniable smell of skunk had reached the pitch of the roof. Brett pinched his nose, giving his voice a French sound to match Cat's.

"Ah, Catrick, why did ye go and do that so close to home?"

Nate was bright red in a giggle fit. He could barely get out the words "I didn't do anything. Honest. But"—his giggles made it hard for Brett to understand the boy—"she probably scared the stripes off the poor fellow."

Brett looked across the lawn at Sadie still knocked out cold. "Pity that, though." he said. About that time man and boy watched the four-legged hero emerge from the lofty latrine and saunter toward the garden.

"Forget the door, Brett. The smell itself woulda knocked poor Sadie out anyway." He remembered then that he didn't care much for Sadie either. She was always copying her mistress—when Elizabeth wasn't looking that is. So, naturally, she turned her little black nose up at Cat whenever she knew another white person wasn't around.

"Uh-oh." Brett saw imminent trouble in the shape of Master LeBeaux and his son Richard descending the back stairs of the Main House. Brett and Nate immediately put their attention back to the roof.

"You have to admit, Brett. That was funny," Nate said under his breath, as if Mr. LeBeaux could have heard all the way from the garden.

"Just don't let your mother find out. She wouldn't consider it to be Christian charity." He smiled and tussled Cat's blond spot.

"Me? Don't look at me. I've been up here most of the day. One of the favored ones must have left the door open and then— you know—nature calls." Nate laughed at his own joke and held on to the ridge post for safety. "If I'm not careful, I'll be needing the smelly house myself." The last joke was too much for the laughing boy. He lost his grip on the roof and down he slid, taking more than a few splinters with him as he made the steep pitch and landed backside down on a mound of, thankfully, soft bushes.

"Catrick!" Brett inched slowly toward the eaves and the hysterical laughter of his red-faced son holding his hands to his sides.

"Ah, Brett!"

"Are you hurt, lad?" he called out.

"Only where my sides split!" By now, Nate's laughter was as high-pitched as Elizabeth's own voice.

Jenna heard the commotion of something sliding down the roof and came out of the house running. As she bolted down the porch step, instinct told her to look up. A blur near her feet— followed by Nate's fit of giggles—quickly brought her eyes back to Earth.

"What on earth happened?" She looked at Nate, and then quickly up to the broad-smiling Brett. Nate was in no condition to speak, and Brett just shrugged his shoulders.

It was then that Jenna herself smelled the perfumed critter from the other side of the road. She quickly pinched her fingers over her nose.

"Get inside. Both of you. Before it gets in your clothes and inside the house."

Brett bent himself at the knees as if were going to dive into the bushes on top of Nate. Still on his back, Nate spread his arms wide as if to say '*C'mon, I'll catch ya.*' Then he burst out laughing again.

Brett slid down the ladder and helped his son to his feet.

"Let's go have some of that fine bread we smelled comin' out of the chimney." He put his big arm around the boy, and the three of them went inside the house and closed the door tight. Very tight.

Jenna handed Brett and Nate each a thick slab of bread with butter and a pint of cider. The hungry boy wolfed down the bread and drank the pint quickly. Nate wiped the last bit of crumbs from the side of his mouth and dashed toward his room.

"Cat?"

"I want to write this down in my Journal."

She heard the door close and knew he would be lost in his writing for an hour or so.

Nate re-emerged, almost on schedule. "Where's Brett?" he asked.

"He went down to the Paint House. He said you had wanted him to mix you some special colors for something."

"Special colors?"

"That's what he said. Do you want to help me set the table?"

A flicker of Cat's memory switched on. Jenna saw her son's eyes widened.

"What is it, mon cheri?"

"I'll be back," he said as he ran out of the house.

"Where are you going in such a quick rush?" she called out. But the only answer she got was the slam of the screen door. If poor Miss Sadie had been standing on the porch, she would have been knocked into dé jà vu.

Jenna watched her blur of a son tear across the lawn and jump over the picket fence. She saw faint clouds of dust as he ran down the lane toward the carpenter's shop and the Paint House.

Nate was out of breath by the time he reached the Paint House. He spread his legs and bent over to get his wind back before going inside.

The creak of the wood door caused Brett to look up from his colorful work.

"Ah, it's you, Catrick. I wondered when ye'd be joinin' me. What do you think?" he asked as he lifted the wood stick out of the clay pot. "A fine cornflower. Or, maybe periwinkle."

Nate nodded as he entered the room and approached Brett's work. '*So this is the Paint House, where Brett spends so much time.*' The smell of the paints was somehow familiar to Nate. And it was a pleasant one at that.

In the far corner near a window was a small peak of cloth. Brett walked over and lifted the veil.

"You've done a wonderful job on it, Catrick. Looks just like our house. Tiddy is going to be so surprised."

Nate walked up to the little wooden house slowly, as if he wasn't quite sure what it was. Before him sat a small replica of Cat's house. Nate's eyes walked around the perimeter noticing the wood siding, row by row, and the white shutters that were closed over the windows. The eaves were adorned with fancy trim, and the roof was as steep as the one he had fallen off earlier that day. It was a miniature masterpiece.

He turned back to Brett for some sign. But all he got was the happy face of a man watching his son follow in his own footsteps.

"She's a beauty, Cat."

Nate held his breath, it was so perfect.

"A spittin' image of *The Chattery*, isn't it? Look—" he pointed at the shuttered window around the corner. "—there's your room. Oh, you've done well, Catrick. You've got a good eye and a patient hand." He walked over and put his arm around Nate.

For his part, Nate was straining his eyes through the narrow slits in the walls for some clue as to what exactly it was—besides a miniature version of their house. He called out to his other half for a little help with the riddle, but Cat must have been sleeping or off trying to figure out what had happened to himself back at the staircase.

"Where's the door?" he asked at last.

Now it was Brett's turn to chuckle. "Doors? You're lookin' at 'em!"

Nate rubbed his finger along one of the slits and looked up at Brett, disbelieving. "These are the doors? For who? Midgets?"

Brett choked on his own laugh. He looked at Nate wondering if the boy's memory had flitted out of his brain like some daydreamin' Irish butterbye. Brett smiled fondly as he remembered his dear mum back in Ireland. *Irish Butterbye* was one of her favorite expressions when she couldn't remember where she had put something or what the thing was even called, for that matter. "Oh, Brett," she'd say in her lilting tone, "*did ya see an Irish butterbye go by a minute ago? Seems to have taken me shoppin' list.*"

He thought often of his parents. It was always months between letters. If it wasn't for Jenna, though, none would have
ever made their way to Ireland. He wondered if he would ever
see them again. It was so hard to save enough money to go to
New Orleans, let alone across the Atlantic. And Jenna was anxious too to see her mother in Quebec again. *Poor Cat,* he
thought, *already fourteen and he has never met any of his grand-
parents or his fifty-two cousins on his side. It wasn't right.*

"Are you all right, Brett?" Nate nudged his father in the
side.

"What?" He looked down at Nate still holding the butterfly
house in his hand. "I'm fine, Catrick. Very fine." He tussled
the blond spot.

The house was a surprise for Tiddy that Cat had been working on for the past month. He kept it hidden in the Paint House
even though he knew that Tiddy would never have been allowed
on this part of the plantation. He wanted her to be the first to
see it.

All Spring and Summer Tiddy had been fixed on the butterflies. They were so free to go from place to place. She told Cat
she now dreamed at night that she had the wings of a butterfly
and one day she would head north. And the Master would not
even notice.

But as summer started coming to a close, and mornings
brought her no closer to having wings of her own, Tiddy began
worrying that the cold would kill her beautiful butterflies. Lately,
it was all she could think and talk about. It was starting to drive
Cat and Midnight a little crazy.

'*Do somethin', Cat!*' Midnight would plead. '*Anything.*'

One night while he was walking home from the Cimetière,
Cat had an idea. He would build them a house and they could

sleep through the cold, rainy winter. He found some scraps of wood and using Monsieur Devereaux's carpenter's tools and Brett's guidance, he fashioned an elegant looking house for the winged folk.

The Irish Butterbye flew back into Nate's memory, and he could picture butterflies of every color hanging on the eaves and the roof fanning their wings in the sun. He smiled as he looked up at Brett. He could see himself, or rather Cat, building the house from scratch late into the nights. He could see Brett shadowing him, guiding him, along the way.

Now he had moved his work into Brett's Paint House and was ready to create a visual masterpiece even his artist dad would admire.

Cat always enjoyed being in the Paint House. There was every imaginable color painted somewhere on the walls or the workbenches. Beside the oils, he could always smell the scent of his warm Irish step-dad. He loved him as much as he did his Mom.

Brett walked back to his workbench and retrieved the jar of cornflower paint he had mixed. He handed the jar to Nate who grabbed a small brush, and began working on the sides. It was quiet in the Paint House, as the last rays of the sun found their way into the shop. Once in, they too lingered to soak in the merry colors on the wall.

This was a pleasant place for Nate to be. He liked working with his hands, and knowing that he was making something for Tiddy. He kept seeing her glowing face as Monsieur Eduard lifted her out of the creek last night. She had passed on to him the same glow as she hugged him tightly and whispered in his ear. *"I be saved, Cat. I be free as the butterflies."*

Nate knew what it meant to be free. He wasn't so sure about being saved. Didn't really know what that meant. He wanted to ask Jenna, but something told him Cat already knew.

"Brett—?" he dipped the small brush in the paint and scraped it along the lid before sliding it under the eave. Brett could hear the hesitation in Nate's voice. "—Tiddy's saved now, right?" Being 'saved' was all everyone kept saying about Tiddy the moment she came out of the water.

"That she is. Saved for eternity. She's truly in God's hands now. No matter what LeBeaux thinks."

Nate watched a smile come to Brett's face.

Brett looked at his son. "One day she'll bask in God's glory like all of us."

Nate wondered if the *us* included him. *Would he really be with them forever? And where exactly would that be?*

"Am I saved?" Nate asked meekly.

"Brett gave him a surprised look. "Of course, ye be. Why would you be askin' that?"

Nate realized quickly that he had asked a silly question. If Cat had been here instead of him, he wouldn't have had to ask. Nate felt stupid just then, and also a bit left out. Everyone he knew here, everyone he liked had been saved. They would see eternity, whatever that looked like, but not him. He knew for sure, as sure as his hands were turning blue, that he was not saved. He was Nate inside.

As he looked down at his house, he heard the wooden door creak open. He turned around quickly, covering the house with his back.

"You boys look a little suspicious." Jenna smiled as she walked toward the mischievous-looking man and son.

"I'm making something—for Tiddy. Sort of a baptism present." He held his hand out like a traffic cop. "It's a surprise."

"I'm a good one for keepin' secrets, son. Let me take a look."

Nate gave it a hard thought, looked at Brett, who nodded, and slowly the two stepped aside, revealing to his mother an eight inch tall blue house that was a near replica of their own house even down to the shutters and chimney."

There was clear pride in Jenna's eyes that equaled that of Brett. "Why, look at that! It's beautiful, Cat. It's a little Shattery." Brett beamed at his wife; he loved the way she said '*Chattery.*' It was one of those small things in life that reminded him that he was at home.

She walked up to the wet house and viewed it closely from all sides. "Oh, son. It's beautiful. Tres bon."

"It's for the butterflies. Tiddy's afraid they'll freeze their—wings off in the winter."

Brett smiled. He often smiled when Tiddy's name came up in conversation. "She's a sensitive lass," he said. "Always did have a soft spot. And look at you—a soft spot yourself!"

Nate felt himself subconsciously puffing out his chest in a small rush of testosterone. "No way! I mean—I just threw this together—you know that. It's not a big deal. Really." Nate felt his face getting flushed.

Jenna put his hand on Nate's cheek right where it was reddest. "Never be ashamed for making something like this. It is a beautiful gift. I am so proud of you." She put her arm around Nate and squeezed tightly. Brett put his arms around the hugging two.

'*Group hug!*' Nate closed his eyes and for a brief moment imagined it was his long-lost father there in the room with him. The infamous French chef who left when his own kitchen got too hot.

As Brett and Jenna started to let go, Nate turned and hugged tighter.

"You're a grand son, Catrick. The best I could hope to have." Brett looked out the window. "It'll be dark in an hour. We'll see ya back at the house." He took Jenna's hand and left him to his artistry.

"Ok." Nate rolled up his sleeves which had fallen down. "— just want to finish the blue." He dipped the brush into the jar. "I won't be long."

The door creaked shut, and Nate was all alone in the Paint House. Only now he had the lingering memory of his father and mother to keep him company.

As he worked, he wondered if, when he returned back home— if he returned at all,—if the Irish Butterbyes Brett had told him about would take away all the memories of his time at Vieux Saules. All his memories of Brett and Jenna. Midnight and Tiddy.

'*Those blasted Irish Butterbyes!*' He speared his brush into the cornflower soup. From the window he watched his parents strolling down the lane. They were walking almost as one person. Nate stared until they were a distant image and until he was sure they were tucked well in his mind, safe from even the most whimsical Irish Butterbye.

6 MALLOW FIELDS

Midnight watched Miss Tawna as he worked. She was having more and more trouble standing as she hunched over the cotton. It had been a particularly hot day and swampy humid. Bullfrog joked that you could drink the air.

"Miss Tawna, you alright?"

"Jus' a little tired, Midnight. But I be fine. It's in my blood."

Midnight smiled. It was Miss Tawna's subtle reference to her royalty. She was an African princess. Only three years old when she was taken by a rival tribe and sold to the white men on the shore.

Legend says her father was one of the great kings and that he had sent thousands of warriors to find his daughter. Slaves now long since departed told stories of seeing African ships halfway between Africa and the Caribbean in search of the royal girl.

Miss Tawna was the Queen of the Cimetière. The older slaves felt a kinship to her. They, or their parents, had once touched the African soil. The younger ones looked to her as a symbol of their people's greatness. Here, they were lowly people in chains and treated worse than the Master's dogs. But there, at one time, they had countries of their own and ruled as men and women; they were not property.

Even the wicked overseer Mr. Mallock allowed Miss Tawna some latitude. He had been told in no uncertain terms by Master LeBeaux that he was never to touch Miss Tawna. The Master truly feared a mass revolt of murderous proportions should a white man mistreat the plantation's African Queen.

But that law of protection by no means applied to anyone around her. Especially to Midnight, who seemed to bring up a strange reaction from the mean man of Kentucky. The white man rode up on his horse.

"You, boy!"

Midnight stood up straight. "Yes, suh."

"Why ain't chu workin'?"

In even his short fourteen years Midnight had learned what was wise to say aloud and what was not. He knew that anything relating to Miss Tawna would not do well for him. She was off-limits to Mallock, which only made him more angry at everyone else.

"I'm jus' checkin' m' bag, suh." He held up the burlap sack that was beginning to overflow with the picked cotton. "Nearly fol', sah."

Mallock stared at the scared boy for the longest time.

Finally he spoke. "Then git another'n."

Midnight quickly ran over to the wagon where some of the older men were stacking the full bags. It was back-breaking work, but they had done well for the Master that day. It was looking to be a profitable harvest this year.

Mallock watched Midnight from a distance. Until he felt the stare of Miss Tawna. He turned to her, nodded almost imperceptibly, and rode off to another part of the field to stir up yet more fear among the exhausted, captive audience.

Midnight returned to Miss Tawna's side.

"You watch fo' that man, Midnight. Somethin' 'bout him not right. These be things I know. Mus' be careful."

"Yesum." He himself then watched Mallock in the distance. Despite the heat of summer, he felt a cold chill run up his spine.

"Yesum." he repeated.

Midnight stood there shirtless and barefoot watching the man on horseback. The boy was the thinker in the group, the one who watched and figured things out.

He was also the baby in his family, the youngest of six children, though he never knew the oldest brother and sister. They had both been sold a year before he was born, at a time when the crops had failed to provide enough cash for Mrs. LeBeaux's French imports.

Midnight's Mama, Naomi, never stopped blaming herself for the loss. She played it in her mind, sometimes daily, especially when she was left to herself in the lull of the day.

She had sent twelve year old Samuel and his ten-year-old sister Ruth to the common garden to get some green beans. Naomi loved the crisp sound and smell as she snapped the vegetable into the pot. Mixed with potatoes—Mmmm—her mouth watered just thinking about dinner that night. She had noticed an unpicked patch the previous day, and since then found her mind wandering back into the garden. She'd have gone herself if she didn't have the three younger children to watch. She'd have gone herself if she had only known...

"Don't cha come back without the basket full, ya'hear!" she had hollered after them, half smiling. For Samuel and Ruth it was a bit of an adventure and a chance for them to bring food to the table for once.

At about the same time, Master LeBeaux and his new overseer, the odd Elgen Mallock rode across the bridge into the Cimetière.

The poor man had not slept all night as he tried to decide which slaves he would sell. In the end, he determined that he and his overseer, Mr. Elgen Mallock, would ride into the Quarters and each grab a child. Whoever was picked, was picked. Let God decide their providential fate, not their earthly master. And so it was in the early morning that the two men rode into the garden and let God choose the children.

"Only two are needed." LeBeaux's jaw was tightly set. *"We'll each grab one. I do not intend to attempt this a second time so do not fail me."* LeBeaux urged his horse forward toward the slave quarters where groups of younger slaves were milling about outside the cabins waiting for their mamas to call for breakfast. Lost in his own frustrated thoughts, LeBeaux missed the evil glint in Mallock's eyes. He had not known this man long enough to really understand his character. He had no idea how much the odd man from Kentucky was relishing this next task.

Ruth looked up as she heard horses approaching. The basket fell from her hands as she realized too late that the big dark horse was headed straight for her. She screamed and threw herself on the ground, thinking the rider intended to knock her down anyway. She covered her head, bracing her body for the kick of the horse's hooves.

The girl could feel the horse's breath shoot towards her like a hot blast. She looked nervously between her fingers. His nostrils were as big as her surprised eyes. At the last minute, Mr. Mallock, with a deviled grin, veered the horse to the right. As Mallock rode past her, he leaned down and scooped her up like a weightless trophy. He wrapped his arm around her chest tightly, and pressed the horse to speed up.

Leaning far to one side, Mallock dragged the barefoot little girl in a wide circle before finally lifting her up and throwing her hard against the saddle horn. The mad man held the screaming, kicking girl down firmly. The frantic pounding of her fists into the horse's side was in sync with the hooves against the ground. With every gallop, she could feel the hard horn push against her squeamish stomach.

Ruth tried to look up to see where her brother Samuel was, but each time she lifted her head, Mr. Mallock struck her scalp with his riding crop. Warm blood began to drip down the side of her head in a zigzag pattern that matched the shaky movement of the precious little girl's face.

Anyone able to watch the man would have seen the clear pleasure in his face at that moment. He was having a good time, far better than the miserable days he had spent in his native Kentucky. Oh, how he loved Louisiana on this fine morning.

Meanwhile, Master LeBeaux, who had turned away from his overseer at the edge of the Cimetière, set his sights on a young buck who had suddenly stood up in the middle of the green garden like a rabbit sensing danger. Oblivious to the evil behind him, LeBeaux loosened the rope hanging on his saddle horn. By the time he reached Samuel, he had the loop ready and he easily tossed it over the head of the petrified boy.

Samuel woke from his trance just as he felt the rope tighten across his chest, pinning his arms to his side. It was at that

precise moment, the moment he was truly helpless, that he real-
ized his sister was in trouble. The boy screamed out her name
but the time for warning her had passed. As he was pulled back-
ward to the ground, Samuel saw her being lifted off her feet by
Mallock.

The sickened boy felt the rope slacken, and he struggled to his
knees to escape and rescue Ruth. Yet just as he was almost free,
the quickened pace of LeBeaux's horse had stretched the rope
taut. And in the next second he was pulled forward with a quick
jerk. For the first seconds he flew above the ground. Then the
gravity of the situation brought him down. The ground became
sandpaper against his ragged clothes and bare skin.

While Samuel struggled to get to his feet, LeBeaux kept his
eyes focused on the bridge out of the Cimetière. He was disgusted
by this whole affair, and was still noticeably perturbed with his
spoiled wife. It wasn't often that he voiced a complaint about
her, even in his own thoughts, but he hated what she was now
forcing him to do. He hadn't the courage to look behind and look
at the face of the unlucky child. He was anxious to leave the
Cimetière and, for that matter, get this day behind him. He urged
his horse to increase its trot, unaware that the boy had been
knocked to the ground a hundred yards before.

As the horse quickened its pace, the furrows of the field shifted
the boy from side to side. Wind and dust and tears, as well as
being tossed from side to side, made everything a blur to Samuel.
He tried to move his head to see his sister but it was impossible.
All he could do was hold on and hope to God it would end soon.
For both of them.

Master LeBeaux wrapped the rope around the saddle horn,
and pressed the horse again. They were now on the hard dirt
road, and Samuel could feel his skin being made raw everywhere.
He was both numb and in pain in different places. His mouth

was choking on the dirt. It covered his eyes and he could no longer see. Then his head hit one of the planks on the bridge out of the Cimetière and he was out cold.

"Git up, boy!" LeBeaux commanded. He tugged on the rope but there was no response. "You're no use to me dead. Now, git up, I said." He tugged on the rope again, this time with more force.

The sharp pull on the rope jolted Samuel awake. He could hear his Master ordering him up. Still the obedient slave, Samuel forced every part in his body to one task, getting up. But when he stood, wavering on jellied legs and bloodied knees, it was more in defiance. Forgetting his station in life for a moment, the boy lifted his bloody, tear-stained face and stared straight into his Master's eyes.

LeBeaux choked back an oath and his heart lurched painfully when he recognized at last the slave he had chosen to pay for his wife's pretty French curtains. It was Samuel, his most prized and, if possible, most loved slave.

He tore his eyes away from the tortured face before him and began to fumble with the rope tied to his saddle. He was surprised to feel remorse and regret begin to choke him like burning cane in the autumn. His fingers grew almost frantic in their efforts to untie the knot.

At that moment he heard galloping hoof beats and looked behind him to see Mallock approaching with a bundle draped in front of him on the horse. LeBeaux's hands froze on the rope and the burning in his throat traveled to his eyes as he realized he had no choice now. He re-tightened the rope so roughly it brought the shaken Samuel back to his knees, and the boy barely managed to stumble upright before he was forced to follow LeBeaux to the Main House. He looked behind to see his sister's face, but it was still hidden against the dark mane. The iced eyes of Mallock were enough to turn Samuel's head toward LeBeaux.

As LeBeaux and Mallock approached the Main House, the planter saw a blue figure on the portico. The Master uttered some choice profanities under his breath. His wife, Evelyn, small umbrella in hand, was straining her neck to see. She dared not descend the stairs. She knew all too well how angry her husband was over the issue. They had fought well into the night, with Master LeBeaux furious at his wife for putting him in the position of selling children. He was a staunch Catholic and believed that all families, free or slave, were sacred.

Like any man, though, he had at least one weakness and that was for him a five-foot porcelain doll from Vicksburg. He could never say 'no' to this woman, no matter what the circumstance was. In most ways she was not a bad woman, but she had one weakness as well. She liked living the life of a Southern Queen. In fact, LeBeaux often referred to his wife as Queen Sugar, a play on the popular term for his favorite cash crop. Cotton may be King in the rest of the Deep South, but here in Louisiana, sugar was Queen.

The trappings of a queen, of course, cost money. While Vieux Saules was a large and prosperous plantation of sugar, cotton, and indigo, the timing of its vast richness could not always satisfy Mrs. LeBeaux's appetite for fine clothes, perfumes, and furnishings. The problem for Master LeBeaux was that his dear wife had the patience of a two year old. Despite his pleas, she sometimes could not wait for the sugar markets or the cotton merchants. He would then be left to his own devices, however unpleasant, to make it all happen. This was one such time. Mrs. LeBeaux was dead set on having new curtains throughout the upstairs social quarters.

For Master LeBeaux, selling young slaves was unacceptable. To do so for curtains made it all the more ridiculous. In its almost seventy-five years of existence, Vieux Saules had never separated a family. Over the years, when the slave population was greater than his need, Master LeBeaux, like his father and grandfather, would sell some of the slaves. But he would always sell in family units, assuming—naively—that the purchasing master would retain the set.

Mrs. LeBeaux argued that the plantation had over six hundred slaves, with thirty to fifty born each year. No one would ever miss two. Childless herself at that point, she never considered the thoughts of the grieving mothers and how this loss would forever affect their lives. And so, at two in the morning, the Matter was settled in Mrs. LeBeaux's favor.

Master LeBeaux knew all five hundred and twenty-three slaves by name. He should have, for it was his right, one of his pleasures, to grant each newborn the name that would stay with the child throughout its life. He recorded each birth in his Slave Ledger. LeBeaux was meticulous about his record keeping.

Master LeBeaux continued to stare at the bruised and bloodied boy. Samuel was clearly his favorite. He was good with his hands at an early age, and had a natural curiosity for how things worked. He would make a good carpenter or mechanic when he reached manhood. And LeBeaux could always use a good mechanic in the sugar mill during the rolling season when the cut cane was ground to a sweet—and most valuable—juice.

Mr. Mallock brought his horse to a stop, stirring up a cloud of dust in the general area of Master LeBeaux. The overseer threw the crying Ruth onto the ground as if she were a lifeless sack of flour. The stunned girl just lay there at first.

LeBeaux took one look at the little girl and immediately became angry.

"Mr. Mallock, this is the boy's sister. You selected from the same family." The tone of his voice was unmistakable.

"Master LeBeaux, sir, your instructions was to grab the first Negro child I see."

"I assumed, Mr. Mallock, that common sense would suggest they not be siblings."

"Why? It ain't important to them."

Seeing his sister thrown to the ground brought Samuel out of his daze. He let out a loud scream and crawled towards her.

"Ruthie! Ruthie!" he cried.

"What leads you to that conclusion, Mr. Mallock? Intuition or cold observation?"

Mr. Mallock stared momentarily at his horse's mane.

"You like me t' git 'nother, sir?" Deep down, he was hoping to have another chance to terrorize the slave quarters. The rush of power it gave him was his own fountain of youth and had a curious effect on him.

"No Mr. Mallock. This will do." In his heart he cursed God that moment for the double pain He had chosen to inflict on a poor slave mother. "Take them both into town. They can doctor Samuel and Ruth before the auction on Thursday."

With these words the great master of Vieux Saules rode off toward the stables without so much as a look to the two slaves or a nod to his wife.

News traveled quickly through the plantation, both in the Main House and in the fields. As Master LeBeaux neared the stables, he swore he could hear the cries of Naomi at that moment. For many nights afterward the cries followed him to bed and kept him from a good night's sleep.

It would also be a long time before Master LeBeaux would step foot in the slave Village again. And a year before he saw Samuel and Ruth's mama again when he arrived one morning and handed her Midnight, a new-born boy delivered just seven hours before to a slave woman who had died giving birth to twins.

He was clearly trying to make up for the loss of her two children. In his heart of hearts he actually believed that his gesture would make Naomi whole and his conscience clear.

Why he did not also give her the other twin, a beautiful girl, remained a mystery, as did her whereabouts.

No doubt, the baby was precious to Naomi. The still-grieving mother was hoping for a David in answered prayer to defeat the Goliaths around her.

But the Master had spoken: 'Minuit. Finit.' He would be forever named for the exact moment he had entered into a life of slavery. From then on, he was simply called Midnight.

Nate finished his supper quickly and downed the last of his cider. He got up and walked over to the kitchen counter where Jenna had set a small jug of cider for Midnight.

"It is nearly the end of the workday," remarked Jenna. "Minuit will be coming down along the East River Path. You should take it to him." She handed Nate the jug.

With the jug in his left hand, Nate gave his mom a quick kiss on the cheek and was soon out the kitchen door. He ran down the walk and without a thought bolted over the hedge that separated their side garden from the Main Lane leading to the Master's house. Like a true cat, he landed on both feet. He was fired up but not entirely sure which way led to the Cimetière.

He tried re-tracing the steps in his mind, but it had been dark the night before when he followed Brett and Jenna back to *The*

Chattery. Should he go left, toward the Main House, or right toward the Sugar Mill? He reached in his back pocket for the map, but he had left it in his room in the Journal.

'*What would Cat do?*' he wondered. He looked over at the mansion and thought '*Why not?*'

He ran toward the Main House—he could see its grand columns ahead—until he reached the crossway. Another decision point. This one was easier, though. Stables to the left, a winding road through open fields to the right.

The athletic boy cut the corner and headed along the North Fork Path. At the fork, he veered right along the Village Path. It crossed the Creek and stopped at the Cimetière.

Or, the Village, as Master LeBeaux preferred to call it. 'Village' had a more paternalistic feel to him than 'Cemetery.' It helped him sleep better at nights, except on those nights when he was sure one of his dark villagers had focused more on his voodoo than his work.

Master LeBeaux was generally a sensible man, good with his figures and knowledgeable of crops and the business side of running a vast estate. But at times his superstitious streak got the best of him and it would cost him a good night's sleep.

On the mornings after, the knowledge of his lack of sleep reached both the quick and the dead quicker than the dead could return to their places of rest.

The hated overseer, Mr. Mallock, took his cues from the Master's moods. The nastier the better, from Mallock's point of view. He relished every chance he would get to harass the dark folk. In his native Kentucky, he was a poor nobody. Son of the town drunk. But here, at the grandest plantation in the sugar parishes, he was next to king. He held the lives of men in the palm of his hands. And the safety and purity of the women and children as well. What a wonderful life he had been given.

From the footbridge looking down the Main Alley of the Cimetière, Nate could see the strange Mallock on horseback nudging the slaves back to their cabins. He stopped at the entrance to the Cimetière and from atop his horse seemed to be counting the men, women, and children as they passed him by. Not a bright man or a learned man by any means, but he prided himself on his ability to cipher in his head to the magic number of *six hundred and twenty-six.* The exact number of slaves currently in his care.

As the group processed down the Alley, ranks broke off and veered down side streets. Nate didn't wait for Mallock to leave. Following the path he took the night before, Nate walked down the Main Alley, toward the column of slaves, and turned at the first side alley. At the end of this alley was another block of cabins forming a T-intersection.

Nate stopped in his tracks. The cabins all looked the same. He scratched his blond spot and then walked to the corner cabin, resting his back against the wall. He had come this far on his own; Midnight would have to do the rest.

He uncorked the jug and took a swig. The cold cider felt good on his parched throat. His stomach quivered with butterflies tickling his stomach. He was both nervous and anxious to see Midnight. He had never really had a friend before, and there was, according to Jenna, a deep bond between Midnight and Cat.

The Cimetière had been dead until then. Everyone had been off in various parts of the plantation, toiling for the Master's pleasure. In short time, though, the porches of the various cabins began filling with hot, tired souls. They sat, nearly in unison, on rockers, chairs, stoops, and steps, and the heavy weight of a hot Louisiana day seemed to lift the very floorboards of the cabins off their frames.

Nate watched Midnight round the corner from the North. He looked worn out. Nate uncorked the jug and walked over to his friend, handing the jug to Midnight as soon as he was near enough.

Midnight was too tired to even smile. He took the heavy jug, slid his back down one of the porch posts, and landed in a cloud of dust. He immediately took a swig of the cider. And then another, and another.

"Better slow down before you throw it back up," Nate advised his friend.

Midnight lowered the jug and took a deep breath. "It be as hot as the Devil's hell today, Cat." he said.

Nate wiped the sweat from his own brow. He wasn't at all used to the Louisiana humidity. "It still is, mon ami."

Midnight handed the jug to his friend. Nate took a quick swig and gave it back.

Nate could see the lime flickers in the meadow.

"You feel like catchin' some fireflies'?" Nate asked. It was something he had always wanted to do.

"Sure," answered Midnight. "But, later, after I've rested a spell."

"Alright."

"I've gotta git my breath back first, though." Midnight took another gulp of Jenna's cider.

His older brother Jonah joined them on the steps. "Massah's boy drove us hard today, Cat. Right, li'l brothuh?"

Midnight nodded and passed the jug to Jonah. He swallowed. Several times. "Your Mama makes the bes' cidah."

Dogs barked excitedly to the North.

Jonah spoke. "I hears there's an African boy on the run."

Nate's ears perked up. "How'd ya hear that?"

"Ol' Andrew tol' me ths mornin'. His wife be three places down the Rivah. She says a Massah nears by gots mighty mad at a young buck. So he sol's his wife to a man who took her far up the Rivah." Jonah laughs. "The foolish buck took off to find her. He be foolish an' dead by mornin'."

The dogs continued their chorus.

"Sounds like he already be found," said Midnight sadly. "Neve' hadda chance. Foolish to even try."

"What else could he do?" asked Nate. "He had to find his wife."

"Cat, you be black as a white boy can be, bu' you still think like a whitey." said Jonah. "Tell me. Where does a black buck go? Where he gonna hide?"

"I don't know, Jonah, but he's not wrong to try. He ain't dumb to want to find her."

"Tell me, Cat. Where can you hide in the Cimetière and not be foun'? Even the dumbes' an' blindes' slave could pick your white ghost from the shadows. An' you know this place like home. That dumb buck be in a new place. A los' black sheep ready for the dogs."

"Just don't call him dumb, that's all."

"Alright, Cat. I call him '*dead*' instead. That bettuh for ya?" Jonah stood up and went inside.

"My brothuh's right. He'll be dead by mornin'."

"Maybe, but he had to try, didn't he?"

The two boys sat fixed on the steps waiting for the sun to set and the 'Squitos and bats to take flight. All around them the women made ready for dinner. Several of the cabins worked to-gether on the meals as an extended family. An extended family that included a blond cat from the other side of the Creek.

TimothyTIMOTHY PHILLIPS

Tuesday

August 25, 1857

7 For Keeps

Nate woke up to the annoying crow of the rooster after what seemed like only a few minutes that he had been asleep. Poor Nate was still getting used to Cat's schedule and energy. The Louisiana boy was always on the move and was far more athletic than any boy back at Dexter Middle School in California. Certainly more athletic than Nate.

In Cat's body, Nate could now jump over three foot hedges without breaking a sweat. And climb to the top of twenty-five foot trees without getting ill from the height or fear of falling on his head. If only he could get used to swimming. The French Cat loved to swim, but Nate had always been afraid to put even a foot inside a pool. Somehow Diana's nightmare of her toddler floating upside down in a pool had been passed on to her son. Rather than getting him swimming lessons, her solution had been to keep him as far from standing water as possible. Until she realized that her son was the only rising ninth grader who couldn't yet swim.

Nate had tried to tell Ryan on *That Day*, but he couldn't decide which was worse—to admit he couldn't swim or to let everyone think he was a coward. It certainly didn't help his relationship with his new stepbrother, though.

Nate was enjoying being Cat. Back in Whittier, the kids called him Ninny Nate or the Geek Freak or, his personal worst, Whinestein. And, of course, he was always the last one picked to be on a team. After even the girls and all the other boys who were twenty pounds heavier and a half-foot shorter than he was. Now he had the stamina of an athlete and the confidence of a quarterback.

Ryan enjoyed those moments in school the best. He loved seeing his smart step-brother waiting awkwardly on the sidelines 'til the very end. Even after their parents married and he and Nate became part of the same family—even if Nate was stubborn enough to keep the Bouvier name.

The two boys were different in so many ways. For one, Ryan was a twin and even though Patty was an obnoxious pain sometimes, she was loyal to her brother whenever it mattered. And vice versa. They both could always count on at least one person in the circle to pick them first.

Ryan was also a born athlete, a fact that gave his father great pride around the office. There just wasn't a sport invented that Ryan couldn't handle. And handle well.

Ryan, though, was not the brightest crayon in the box, but he picked up quickly that Nate and his mom had little money. The two Bouviers had lived in a tired duplex, and Nate's clothes were an inch and a half short in the legs and frayed in the knees. Haircuts were infrequent, and he never seemed to have enough milk money. Nate even re-cycled his brown lunch bags. What an embarrassment.

The other boy's situation was just the opposite, which he enjoyed pointing out to Nate every chance he could. Ryan's family was among the richest in town. They lived at Dreyer's Patch, one of the fanciest homes near Central Park in Uptown Whittier, and Ryan was given the best of whatever he wanted. His widowed father worried less about spoiling his two children than he did with trying to make up for the twins' growing up without a mother. The spoils, though, went to Ryan's head in a big way.

Nate shook off the memory of his stepbrother—and the rest of the bad dream—and walked over to the dresser. He poured cold water into the basin and splashed his face a couple of times. He stared into the mirror as he did the morning before and again questioned what was happening.

It was his face alright, but also Cat's. He still could not fathom how it was all possible. When he woke up yesterday, he was sure it had all been a dream and double-sure that once he was fully awake, he would once again find himself the butt of Ryan and Patty's jokes. His adventure into the past would be over and he would be back in the unhappy present.

But this was his second morning, and it was as clear as this room he was still a Cat in the Old South. By instinct, he seemed to know what to do. Cat's memory and his shared a room in the same mind. His own green eyes stared back at him. He wondered if maybe Cat was upstairs in the Main House with Ryan and Patty. He pitied the poor soul if he was.

Down the hall in the kitchen he could hear his mother singing in French. Remarkably, Nate understood every word and yesterday found himself speaking more French than English. Except to his Irish step-dad and, of course, to the most obnoxious Richard LeBeaux. Ryan's snobbiness was no match for that Southern blue blood.

He dressed quickly, brushed his spit-licked hand through his hair, and headed toward the kitchen and a hot breakfast. Memories from yesterday's fare brought water to his mouth.

"Bon jour, Maman. Good morning, Brett." He gave his parents a quick kiss on the cheek.

"Good morning, Cat."

"What are you painting today, Brett?"

"Fences along the River Road. Care to help?"

"When will Master LeBeaux ask you to paint real stuff?"

"Doubtful, if ever." Brett shrugged. Jenna gave Brett a sympathetic look.

"But, Brett, it's such a waste. You're an artist." That was evident by all the watercolors hanging throughout the house. Cat's favorite was his father's re-creation of his boyhood home in Galway in the western part of Ireland.

Brett had painted himself in the foreground as a little boy. His five older brothers sat on a stone fence nearby. Even sitting down, they made a noticeable set of stairs leading to a setting sun. The only daughter stood at the doorway knocking. Their mother, he said, was inside the stone house getting ready for Mass, while his father was in the fields out of the picture.

"Talent isn't all," his father answered.

"But why doesn't he let you paint for keeps?"

Brett looked over at Jenna. His son had stumbled into a painful subject for the constrained artist.

"He allows me to earn an honest wage and for us to live here—and for your dear mother to be a missionary to those enslaved. That's enough for now."

Brett was less than convincing—to himself most of all. It was clear in his voice, and Jenna quickly changed the subject.

"So, Cat, you are going fishing with Richard today." she said.

"Oh, Mére, I was having a grand morning 'til now."

Brett smiled whenever his adopted son used an Irish phrase. Over the years the man and boy were becoming more alike than not.

"He is not a bad boy, Cat. Remember, he doesn't have a friend like you."

"No, Maman, he just has all the money and can tell everyone what to do. Which he does, by the way. You should see the way he treats Midnight."

"I can bloody well imagine," said Brett. Jenna shot him a quick look that told him he wasn't helping. "Well, um, Catrick, Midnight is getting older and the harsh reality is becoming just that."

"I know that." He looked at both his parents with the child's eyes. "But it ain't right. And Richard doesn't have to go out of his way to prove he is on top."

"No," said Jenna. "There is much in this world that isn't right. It is man's sinful nature—ever since his Fall. Our God gave us free will, and this is how we respond."

She placed the warm bread on the table next to the fresh-made jam.

The sun should have passed over the horizon a full half-hour ago but the sky was still a dark color. Just then, the three could hear thunder rolling in the background.

"It is fortunate you both repaired the roof yesterday," said Jenna.

Brett smiled. "I shant be painting fences today, love."

"I won't be fishin' with Little Rich Boy—and Midnight won't be picking cotton!" Nate got up quickly, grabbed some bread and headed toward the backdoor.

"Take your coat, mon cheri."

"Maman, it'll be too hot."

"Then take an umbrella so you don't get all wet."

"Argh. Umbrellas are for girls."

"Take it or don't go." She held it under her son's nose, and he took it—reluctantly.

"What will the other boys say?"

"Go!" She gave him her best *Mother-knows-best* look and shooed him out the door.

Nate stood on the back porch and surveyed the surrounding country. This was all still pretty new for the modern Californian. He noticed there were a few lights on downstairs in the Main House, but the second floor, where the Family lived, was still sleepy-dark. In weather like this, they would all probably stay in bed 'til noon. If Nate were lucky, Richard would not be in the mood to fish on such a stormy day.

The boy took a deep breath and stepped out of the porch and into the rain. He walked the now muddy path to the lane and rounded the hedge on his way to the Cimetière. He looked back at his house, thought a moment, and then closed the umbrella and stashed it in the bushes. He was a typical boy after all.

Soon, he was a completely wet boy. He ran all the way to the Cimetière, stopping only once beneath a thick pine that gave him a dry place to catch his breath and eat some of his Mama's fine French bread. Unfortunately, without the umbrella, the bread was now more soggy than flaky. Which was a sure shame considering his Mama's renowned baking skills.

In the distance Nate could see the smoke rising from several of the cabins in the Cimetière. He hoped that Midnight's was one of them. His clothes were soaked, and he was starting to shiver in the cold. He wished he had hidden the umbrella a lot closer to the Cimetière. He took a deep *I-can-do-it* breath and ran from under the cover of the pine. In a dash he was across the footbridge, in the Cimetière, and almost at Midnight's cabin.

"Why, Catfish Hennessee," said Midnight's mother Naomi who was, in many ways, Cat's second mom. "You be as drenched as a cat who done fell in the well. Where's ya coat and hat? I know ya mama not let you outta the house like that. No suh."

Nate looked around for a clever response but found none. Naomi grabbed him by the shoulders and ushered him to the fireplace to get dry.

"Bon jour, mon ami." Midnight walked over and put his arm around the teeth-chattering Cat. "This morning, you got the speed of a cat, but the brains of a dog."

Nate took off his shirt and hung it near the fire. His arms were covered with goose-bumps, and his skin had a bluish tinge.

"Dang, Cat, you be whiter and bumpier than a fresh-picked chicken."

"Yeah, and I'm shaking like one too."

Naomi handed Cat a cup of weak coffee. He took a sip but mainly held it in his hands for heat.

The spirits in the cabin, all nine of them, were high. In this foul weather even mean Mallock would not want to venture out and risk losing a slave to sickness, drowning, or Freedom Fever. No, better to keep all the sheep in the pen where they can be watched. That, of course, meant a bonus holiday for the slaves. Nate could almost hear the collective music playing beneath the shingled roofs of the hundred and thirty-two cabins.

Or, crypts, as Cat called them. If he had been born a slave, Cat often told himself, he would have run away the first chance he got—or kill himself right off. Midnight told Cat he was too ignorant on the subject to make such a claim. *'You don' know wha' chu don' know'* was Midnight's favorite line.

Midnight walked to the side of the fireplace and knelt down on the floor. With his fingers he counted a certain number of bricks up and across. Then he pushed on one of the bricks, and out it popped. Midnight called this his hiding place, though everyone in the family knew all about it.

Midnight reached in the hole and pulled out two small bags tightened with drawstrings. The sight of the bags brought a flash of memory of the two of them playing marbles in the dirt alley. He smiled at once.

Nate took the second bag from his friend, opened the drawstring, and poured the cool glass marbles into his hand.

"Come on, let's go." He pulled Cat's arm toward the door, but his dear Mama put herself between them and freedom.

"Where you boys thinks you're goin'?

"Just outside, under one of the oaks. It'll be dry."

Naomi knew these play days were rare for them. She walked over to the window and looked beneath the trees. Despite the persistent rainfall, the ground beneath them was still dry.

"But you stay under the trees, y'hear?"

"Yessum," both boys replied at once. She opened the door and out they flew. As Nate passed by, she threw him one of Jonah's shirts. "You catch cold, and your Mama will have some words for Ol' Naomi."

Under the oak, Midnight drew a wide circle in the dirt and then a smaller circle inside of the first. The boys then emptied their glass marbles from their pouches. As they settled into play, Tiddy-Beaux joined them.

"Hey, Tiddy."

"Hey, Cat." She watched the game start. "You playin' for keeps?"

"Nah, not today." he answered.

"Want to play?" asked Midnight. He and Nate each took some of their marbles and handed them to Tiddy-Beaux.

"Sure."

Each of them threw a half dozen of their marbles into the inner ring. Nate handed Tiddy one of his shooters, or Taws.

"That be your lucky Taw, Cat. Don't give me your lucky Taw."

"That's ok, Tiddy. The luck is in the hand, not the glass."

"You say that now, Cat. But not for long." Midnight placed his Taw just outside the outer ring and shot at one of Cat's prized blues. He missed by at least an inch.

"Hah! Missed by a good mile." Nate took his ruby Taw and rolled it between his fingers. There was a magic in the red glass and he could see Cat as a younger boy playing the game in this very spot. He knew what he had to do, and aimed his Taw straight at Midnight's favorite emerald.

"Just try, Cat. Go ahead, but beware. It's got magic inside. One touch to your Taw, and you be jinxed the whole game."

Nate lay down and squinted as he aimed. "Sounds like you are spending too much time with Pouty Robert." He released his thumb on the Taw and it sailed straight for the emerald glass. A soft clink later, and Nate was holding it in the palm of his hands. He kissed it for good measure.

"I warned you, brother. You might as well put the Taw back in your pocket."

Nate aimed again and shot but missed his target.

Midnight howled. "See? You all done now, Cat."

It was Tiddy's turn next. The rain started coming down in buckets.

"I hear they never caught that runaway. The dogs lost him somewheres." Midnight was looking in the direction of the Wood.

"Well, this rain will cover his tracks for sure. If he's smart, he will move while the Masters are all asleep in their warm beds."

"What if he can't?" asked Tiddy.

"What do you mean 'can't'" asked Cat.

"Maybe he got hurt runnin' from the dogs. Maybe he be sick and hungry." she said.

Cat always had a soft spot for a hurt soul. "Do you think that's possible, Midnight?"

"He could be. Who knows?"

"We should find out."

Both Midnight and Tiddy gave Cat the same *I-don't-think-so* look. But they knew him well enough to know he was serious, and he knew them well enough to know they would follow his lead. Inside, Nate had some doubts.

"Come on. Let's find out."

"Cat, Mama will kill us all if we go out there. The Wood is scary for black folk."

"It be cursed, say Pouty Robert."

"Oh, Tiddy, what does he know? He places his faith in voo-doo-mumbo. He's the one who's cursed right now." Nate stood up and turned away from the game. "Tiddy, you should stay and cover for us."

"If he's goin', I'm goin' too."

"Come on, Tiddy," said Midnight. "The Wood has danger. You gotta stay."

"You make me stay, I just follow once you're gone. Danger come to Tiddy, you both be in trouble."

Nate and Midnight looked at each other and both nodded.

"Ok, Tiddy, but stay close. You hear dogs, and you lay low. Then come back home. Understand?" Nate was serious.

Tiddy-Beaux nodded.

"Alright," Nate continued. He looked around at the cabins and saw several coats and hats on the porches. He had a plan. "Come on, let's go. This way."

Soon, the three now warmer dressed kids were at the edge of the Cimetière and headed for the Indian Wood. As they ran across the last open field in the rain, Nate remembered what Midnight said about the magic in the emerald. One touch, and a cursed game. As he led his band into the green Wood, he wondered whether there was any truth behind the curse.

8 In the Indian Wood

The three souls walked into the dark Wood shortly before noon. Despite the steady rain all morning, the ground ahead and on all sides was dry. And, in spite of the noon hour, the air was dark. The storm and the canopy of the trees blocked the light at the top of the Wood.

The Indian Wood, as it was known on the plantation, was a mature seventy-plus acre forest of water oak, live oak, river birch, sugarberry, tulip tree, beech, sweetgum, pawpaw, and others. In between the massive trunks of these giants were possum haw, Southern Arrowwood, swamp rose, and Devil's Walking Stick. Many of the trees had been planted nearly two hundred years ago by the Indians well before the first white and black people ever slipped their feet into the nearby Mississippi.

The natives had planted the Wood to house the animal spirits. It was considered both a magical and a sacred place, and few members of the tribe other than priests were allowed to enter.

Local legend, according to the LeBeaux family, said that the original LeBeaux—Bertrand Olivant LeBeaux—had entered the Wood shortly after arriving to establish the plantation. He saw the magnificent trees in the distance and determined that they would be more than suitable to build the Main House.

They say the first tree fell in an unexpected direction and killed a slave by the name of Rubideaux. He was the Master's favorite. The remaining men were pressed onward, and several days later another slave was bitten by a Diamondback Rattle-snake. He died that night.

By then, even though Bertrand and his slaves had come from New Orleans to the South, all had heard of the history of the Indian Wood and now believed it to be cursed. The strength of voodoo in the original band of slaves fueled the legend more.

Bertrand, half-blessed with the LeBeaux gene for superstition, battled nightly with his more pragmatic, ambitious side. *Leave the Wood alone; it is sacred. You'll be doomed…Are you mad? It will make the finest house in all the French land, both strong and beautiful… You'll be doomed, a cursed man… Don't be a fool! The wise man harvests what the Lord provides… Do not come any closer! You are standing on sacred ground!*

He slept in starts and fits night after night until his ribs became so bruised from the sleep-deprived Mrs. that he was no longer able to sleep peacefully anyway. On most nights he paced beneath a canopy of stars, the weight of the Wood threatening to crush his very soul.

In the end, the practical side won out and the now-determined Bertrand pushed his men, slaves and freemen, like a mad man to make up for lost time. He kept one eye on their work and one over his shoulder. He was convinced the storms would come before they had finished. His more pragmatic side may have won the debate, but the spooked side was just below the surface and whispered in his ear whenever possible.

At last, after much nail biting, a rough frame of the first floor was completed, and Bertrand could feel himself relax a bit. It was going well, and the wood was far superior than that which graced the king's Palace of Fontainebleau, which Bertrand had once visited as a young man. This wood had a magical quality to it as well. The men were drawn to it, touching it and smelling it whenever they could. At night they would curl up beside the cut pieces much like a young boy in his father's lap. It was invigorating even, lifting their spirits in some mysterious way.

Seeing this effect on mere mortals, Bertrand was more sure than ever before that the finished mansion would bring great blessings and fortune to his family, and the generations that would call Vieux Saules home.

One night, when the new home was more a skeleton than a shell, a horrendous wave of storms arrived north and west of the new Vieux Saules plantation. Within hours the River had flooded its banks and with little notice in the middle of the night engulfed and consumed not only the sacred Wood but also the makeshift camp nearby and the shallow grave of the unfortunate Rubideaux.

Bertrand's wife Sarah and youngest daughter vanished also in the muddy, raging currents and were never seen again. The Frenchman cursed his fate, his inability to hold on to the two sweetest parts of his life.

He was devastated. Any man other than Bertrand LeBeaux would have packed it all in and taken his things and remaining slaves back to the Crescent City. But, instead, he became more determined than ever to turn his untoiled land into the greatest,

richest estate in all of the Louisiana Territory. The new plantation would become a living memorial to his wife and their baby
girl, he told himself day and night.

His loss, though, saved the Wood from further intrusion. For
the rest of his life, Bertrand would allow no one, not even himself,
to enter the Wood. He went so far as to specify in his will that
no one could ever enter or destroy the Wood. To do so, he was
convinced, would be to curse the Family and the estate forever.

This prohibition was passed down from one generation to the
next so that, even though every other square inch of fertile land
was devoted to crops, milling, living, or otherwise contributing to
the family's wealth, the 77.7-acre crescent Indian Wood remained
undisturbed in the north part of the estate near the edge of the
River.

To further protect his family from the curse, he altered the
design of the House so that the grand staircase was no longer the
jewel of the main foyer, but became the welcoming arms leading
up to the front doors. While no one understood LeBeaux's logic,
the Twin Staircase became synonymous with Vieux Saules.

What wood was not carried away by the flood, he had ordered
burned. He then, at great cost, brought in lumber from the distant, more rural territory in the north. To this, he added fine
brick, Italian marble, millwork, silver, gold leaf, and brass.
French artisans applied plaster to the lathe, and reliefs to the
rounded ceilings. And the deepest, richest colors possible. When
finished, all who saw the House compared it favorably to any
found on one of King Louis XV's country estates.

What Bertrand never knew, however, was that his oldest son,
Philip, low on lumber and in fear of missing his father's deadline,
had hidden some of the Wood before the burning, and he even-
tually used it to build one of the stairwells. It was a youthful
indiscretion that could never be undone; and to his dying day,

Philip refused to take the back stairs into the kitchen. He was sure that if he did the Lord would strike him dead for what he had done.

Now, the lure of finding and helping a runaway led the three young kids into the sacred Indian Wood. If Master LeBeaux discovered them all three would be whipped furiously and disavowed from the Plantation as quickly as the auctioneer could say "Sold!" and Brett & Jenna could pack their bags. It would be the only way to appease the Wood and undo an impending curse on the whole lot.

It was that threat that gave the three the cover to go into the Wood in the first place. No one else, other than an ignorant runaway, would dare go into it themselves. They would just have to be careful coming out.

"What we doin' in here, Cat? You know this is haunted groun'."

"Hogswill! It ain't but a grove of old trees. Come on!" He led Midnight and Tiddy further into the Wood. The two did not look as sure as their friend Cat. They had heard the whispered stories of the forest haunts.

"D'ya think he's still here, Cat?" Tiddy asked.

"Could be. If he'd been caught, we'd have heard about it."

"Could be up river, now," added Midnight.

"Might be. So all we can do is look around and see what we find."

"This a mighty large Wood, Cat. How we gonna look it all over?"

"Can't, Tiddy," shot Midnight.

"Yeah, all we can do is scout around a bit; see what we find. Maybe we'll get lucky."

"Ain't luck, Cat. If we find him, it's because God wants it," said Tiddy.

"Let's stop talkin', and keep our eyes open. So we can git outta here soon." Midnight was getting a bit nervous. "Too dark for my likes," he added.

"At least you two can blend in," joked Nate. "I stick out like a pale thumb." He pushed his hat down over his ears a little more.

"So what we looking' for, Cat?" asked Midnight.

"Well, I don't know exactly. 'Cept no one comes in here so I 'spect we should look for bent branches or trampled brush. You know, footprints in the forest."

"We might hear somethin' too."

"Yeah, if we can all stop talkin'." Nate was starting to get edgy. They could hear the eerie sound of rainwater hitting the canopy above them. Slowly, the water meandered its way down to the forest floor, with some dripping on their heads and shoulders. Some of the rain ran along their hat brims and down the raised hairs on their necks.

Poor Nate was still pretty soaked from his morning run to the Cemetery. The wet pants chafed his legs and made him grumpy. He too was beginning to wish he was back in Midnight's cabin in front of their fire.

"Cat!" Midnight whispered loudly. "Look, up there."

Nate and Tiddy looked ahead where Midnight was pointing. A large shadowy figure was running away from them.

"Is it a runaway?" Nate asked.

"Can't tell. Most likely, though. C'mon."

Midnight led Nate and Tiddy quickly to where they remember the shadow being. When they got there, they could see footprints in the soft dirt and yellow wood sorrels.

Nate's eyes followed the footprints to a thicket of swamp rose with its bounty of pink flowers and prickles.

"Ow." was all Nate could manage to say at first.

"That gotta hurt," said Midnight as he pointed at the prickly Swamp Rose."

Midnight took off his coat and wrapped it around his arm. He walked over to the thicket and parted it. Nate and Tiddy followed him.

"Maybe we should call out; tell him we be friends," suggested Tiddy.

"Friends?" uttered Nate. "Tiddy, he doesn't know us, and we don't know him. Could be anyone, maybe even a murderer or a thief. Could be a hundred reasons why he'd run away. And ninety-nine of them could spell trouble for us."

"Cat's right, Tiddy. We gotta follow his tracks, get a good look and then—maybe—show ourself."

The three continued to follow the blazed trail of parted Swamp Rose and squashed yellow Bear's Foot. As they went, they crouched like Indians themselves stalking the animal spirits. Only they weren't sure what they would find.

They could hear the rain stomping harder on the canopy of trees. The tops of trees were swaying more than before.

"The storm's gettin' stronger," said Nate.

"Maybe we should go," added Tiddy.

"Maybe. We could look in here for days and not see 'nother livin' soul. All I see is green and colored flowers. But I know others are seein' me. I feel it, and I don't like it, Cat. Maybe Tiddy's right. Maybe we should go."

"Y'all are a superstitious lot." Nate's impatience and fear were coming through.

Midnight took a step closer to Nate and whispered. "You don't feel anyone starin' at you now?"

Nate thought for a second. "No." he said flatly. "I don't. Now c'mon." He led the two further along the crushed trail until it stopped suddenly.

"Where'd he go?" said a surprised Tiddy. "He done vanished."

"Can't be," shot Midnight. He looked around intently at the vegetation but nothing seemed disturbed. It was as if the person they were following just vaporized.

"What d'ya think, Cat?" he asked.

Nate rubbed his chin in thought. "I don't know." Then something caught his attention. A patch of blue. He walked over to a Jack-in-the-Pulpit, reached down, and picked up a rectangular object.

"It's a book," said Nate.

"What kind of book?" asked Tiddy.

Nate opened it to the middle. "Some kind of poetry, I think." He flipped to the front inside cover and stared at the name written in pen. His eyes traced the curves and caves of the lettering like an old schoolteacher. He threw the name into the far corner of his mind for something, anything. 'Rubideaux,' he whispered. At the sound of the name, something clicked, and a sliver of Cat's memory—whispered stories of Rubideaux the slave—pierced its way through into Nate's realm. Nate froze, and his face had the look of a new ghost.

Tiddy and Midnight looked at Nate and then each other, and then at Nate again.

"What is it?" they both asked.

"The book—it, it belongs to—" He stopped.

"Who? Who, Cat? Who does that belong to?"

Nate turned the book around and put it at their eye level. Thanks to Cat, who, unlike his mother, had not promised LeBeaux he would not teach the slaves to read and write, both Midnight and Tiddy did quite well—in both English and French.

As they read silently, Nate echoed the word in the Indian Wood.

"Rubideaux."

The three-syllable name flew through every open branch in their periphery, and the mystery of the Wood overtook Nate, affecting him in an odd way. Cat, who had been all but asleep the past two days, was suddenly racing to the surface. He wanted to see the name for himself. He had long heard the stories in the Cimetière about the ghost of Rubideaux.

Nate's hand began shaking as Cat's thoughts flew at light speed through his mind. He held the book up and said the word again. "Rubideaux." Then louder, "Rub-i-deaux!" He let the word echo through the Wood. "Rub-i-deaux!" he shouted this time as if trying to call the man back before he slipped into the grave again.

Both Tiddy and Midnight were spooked at the sound of the name. They had also grown up hearing the legends of the first black man to die at Vieux Saules, and the first to die from a curse. Pouty Robert talked a lot about that part.

Midnight looked at Tiddy's scared face; he knew they should leave quickly. He touched Nate's arm. "We gotta leave, Cat." There was noticeable sweat on Midnight's face. "Voodoo or no, it ain't safe here, brother. C'mon." He tugged on Nate's arm.

"C'mon Cat." Tiddy was tugging at him nervously, almost panicky, as if she needed to find a Necessary. She was feeling as uneasy as Midnight and knew if they didn't leave soon, she could get out of control like Cat. She also knew Aunt Tilly would be shouting a blue streak if she knew she had gone into the Wood. And she would skin both Midnight and Cat for taking her.

That very thought had crossed Midnight's mind more than once.

Midnight tugged on Nate's arm again, but Nate was strong and wouldn't budge. Midnight started to drag him back out but Nate kept shouting 'Rubideaux!' at the top of his lungs. Midnight put his hand over Nate's mouth to muffle him but Nate fought to be heard. Poor Midnight was sure as the Wood was green that Cat would bite him.

He whispered in Nate's ear. "Cat, relax brother. Relax. And let's go." Tiddy watched nervously as Nate's large green eyes darted from side to side and overhead. He was paler than normal for a white boy, and he seemed determined to be free. But Midnight, a bit stronger than Nate, tightened his grip and led his white friend and Tiddy safely out of the Wood.

Along the way, in their haste to leave the Wood, Nate dropped the blue book. It was not until Nate was safely out of the woods and they ran into Brett halfway back to the Cimetière did they realize it had been lost. Their proof of Rubideaux had disappeared, as had the man.

9 Whiskey Jack

The two boys eyed the warm beignets cooling on the windowsill. It was late afternoon, and their appetites were growing. They had not eaten since coming back from the Wood.

The spooks of Rubideaux were still with them as they knelt down to be hidden by the bushes. They could smell the sweet pastry with the melting sugar.

"I'll go."

Midnight started to move into sight, but Nate pulled him back.

"No, I'll go."

"Why you? I'm the faster runner."

"But who's the cat?"

"Catfish. You're the catfish. And, they ain't the fastest swimmers, ya'know."

"So what, I'm gonna get it."

"I'll be there and back before you can spell your name. C-A-T!"

Midnight began to bolt but was not quick enough for Nate's hands, which wrapped around his ankles and knocked him down before he could really start.

"Not so fast, Midnight. I'll get it."

Nate looked left and right and when it was clear, dashed over to the window, grabbed a handful of the beignets and then ran back to the bushes.

"Come on, let's go," he said, a bit out of breath.

Midnight just sat there sulking.

"Midnight, come on."

The boy stood up and walked away from Nate.

"Where you going?" he whispered, more than a little self-conscious that he was holding stolen goods.

"I'll get my own."

"Midnight, come on, don't be sore."

"You always be tha whiskey jack. Every time. It ain't fair."

"The what?"

Midnight looked at Nate and shook his head in disbelief. He looked into Nate's eyes. "Ol' Rubideaux done took your mind when he gave ya the shakes back there."

When Cat was a little boy, his mother had told him and Midnight the story of the whiskey jack birds in Canada who would boldly steal their food. Since then, it had become a game for the two to take turns snitching food from Miss Alma, the finest baker on the plantation.

The boys, though, were getting older and the risk, for Midnight, greater. Cat was a smart lad. He knew that a white boy caught taking a pie or two would get a stern scolding; a slave boy would be given a whipping. Over the last six months Cat had been the Whiskey Jack more often than not, a fact not unnoticed by Midnight.

Nate ran up to his friend who was, by now, walking toward the Cimetière. He handed Midnight one of the sweet pastries.

"Next time your turn, all right?"

Midnight looked annoyed at his friend but grabbed the beignet anyway. He took a bite of the warm fried dough.

"Mmm. Miss Alma is a fine baker," he said finally, after having swallowed the last of his pride with a bit of beignet.

Nate took a bite as well. "Sure is. Very fine."

The two boys enjoyed Miss Alma's fine pastry the whole way back into the Cimetière.

Up ahead the boys could see the outline of another boy a little older standing at the footbridge leading into the Cimetière. It was Richard LeBeaux. He was waiting for Cat.

"Bon jour." The young planter's son was obsessed with the French language. Partly because it was refined, like his parents, and partly, Nate figured, because he had a crush on his French teacher, Jenna. Which Nate found most disgusting.

"Hello, Richard." said Nate in English.

Richard turned to Midnight, who quickly looked to the ground. "Goo' mo' nin', Massah Richard."

"Minuit." he said, noticing the sugar and flour around both boys' mouths. "Helping yourself to the kitchen, boy?"

"No, suh."

"It came from my hands." Nate shot in.

"I see." He paused. "So, Catfish, how about going down to the River? My father has given me a genuine Indian canoe."

"What 'bout Midnight?"

"I am sure the Overseer has work for him to do. Isn't that right, Minuit?"

"Yes, suh."

"Come along, Peter." Richard put his arms around Nate and led him back toward the Main House. Nate turned his head back and watched Midnight give a simple wave, turn around, and walk toward the cabins.

"Why did you do that, Richard?"

"Do what?"

"Cut in like that and push him away."

"He's a slave boy, Peter. And one day he will be a slave man. Working fourteen hours for my father six days a week. Doing whatever my father or the overseer tell him to do. And maybe some day my father will let him get married and have slave babies of his own. Little Minuits." Richard laughed. "And those babies will grow up to work the fields doing whatever they're told. And one day, Peter, I will own that boy. So you should, my friend, care what I think."

Nate bristled at the words '*my friend.*' He put his hands in his overalls and followed the rich planter's son into the parterre garden. The green hedges were meticulously cut and shaped. The garden was the domain of Mrs. LeBeaux. Richard liked to cut through the garden so he could pass the nude statues Mrs. LeBeaux had added a year earlier. They were fine marble from Italy.

"What do you think?" Richard giggled.

Nate stared at the unclothed woman. "I think she must get cold at night." Nate felt his own curious eyes lingering on the stony curves until, that is, Richard punched him on the arm.

"You're funny, Peter. Come on, this way." He led the poor white boy beyond the garden and down the path to the stables. There, one of the stable boys had a horse waiting for them.

The planter's son climbed on first, and then helped Nate get on behind him. After a quick prod with his knee, Richard had the horse galloping away from the stables and down the South

Path past the cotton fields and sugar cane and then East to the River.

Richard rode the horse hard. He left the Path and bolted over a natural hedge, sending Nate's rump into the air. He held on tighter to Richard. Otherwise he would surely have fallen off.

"How do you like the horse?" Richard had to yell to be heard over the sound of the horses' hooves pounding the ground.

"What's the hurry? The River ain't goin' anywhere."

"Why go slow, when you can run. He-yah." Richard leaned forward as if whispering in his horse's ear. He prodded her with his feet and they were again in the air. Four hooves and four feet sailing over a ditch. By now, Nate was getting a little green in the stomach.

"I like my feet flat on the ground, Richard--if you don't mind."

"Don't be a sissy," he sneered. But Richard slowed the horse down anyway. They were now on a small bluff overlooking the grand Mississippi. Vieux Saules had perhaps the best views of the River of any other plantation in the region. From the galleries on the South and East sides of the Main House, they could see the beautiful Mississippi with all its traffic. The sun and moon danced across its back and in the early mornings it was shrouded in mystic fog like dry ice.

As soon as Richard had slowed his horse to a trot, Nate slid down to firm ground. He stomped on the ground to be sure, causing Richard to let out a good laugh.

"You're a funny cat."

"Yeah, well, I think I'll walk back."

Richard dismounted. "Come here, let me show you the boat." He tied his horse to a low branch and led Nate down a narrow trail to the riverbank. On the dryer ground sat a brand-new canoe made by the local Indians for Master LeBeaux, who liked to spoil his son with gifts.

Richard pushed the front of the canoe into the water. "Get in. There's two oars. Grab one."

Nate felt his feet sinking deeply into the mud—and liked it that way. He had never been comfortable around water. On the refrigerator at home, Diana still kept the newspaper clipping announcing his miraculous revival after drowning in a neighbor's pool. To Diana it was a miracle that masked the pain of her husband's sudden departure; for Nate it marked a life-long fear of being overwhelmed and swallowed up.

"That's all right, Richard. I'll watch from here."

"I will have to start calling you Elizabeth. Now get in!"

"No, I don't think so." Nate started inching his way back up the bank but Richard walked over and grabbed his arm.

"Get in!"

"I don't know how to swim!" he blurted out.

Richard laughed loudly. "Do not know how to swim. Right!" He punched Nate on the arm again. "Now, stop bragging, Peter. You know you are the best swimmer around here."

Nate started to protest, but Richard grabbed him around the shoulder and pulled him toward the water.

"Come on. We don't have all day."

Nate pulled away. "What's the hurry?" Nate asked, his voice breaking. Inside, he was scared to death, but he knew there was no way to convince Richard that he couldn't swim. Cat's reputation as a river rat was near legendary, especially to those on the plantation.

Reluctantly, he moved towards the canoe. Trying to avoid looking at the water on either side, Nate climbed nervously into the rocking canoe. He crouched down and maneuvered slowly to the front.

"Well, hurry up, Elizabeth! Honestly, Peter, you are worse than my sister!"

Nate was tempted to knock Richard into the River with the oar, but didn't want to chance tipping over the canoe with himself aboard.

He knelt down in the front and as soon as Richard was aboard, put the oar gingerly into the water. The canoe was well crafted and moved nicely in the River. Nate was grateful for that, though it didn't take away the chattering of his teeth or the shakiness of his hands on the oar. *This sure wasn't like* Rivers of America *at Disneyland,* he thought.

Nate stared straight ahead like a blind man. He dared not look down at the fast current just feet away.

"Let us go further out from the bank," said Richard. He was excited to be the captain of a ship in the mighty Mississipp' and just as pleased to have Cat out there with him. Most of the boys his age on the nearby plantations were more obnoxious than himself and he tired of them quickly.

Cat, though, was different. He was a boy who had fun with whatever he did; down-to-earth, self-assured, and full of adventure. In short, he had charisma, and Richard was both awestruck and jealous. Here, on the open river he had him all to himself. There was no slave boy around to steal Cat's attention.

Today was different, though. Even Richard noticed that Cat was lacking his usual carefree adventurism. Right now he seemed to be a bigger sissy than his own sister. And that was saying something.

Little did Richard know that at that moment the River had already stolen Nate's attention and most of his courage the moment the canoe had left the safety of the tree-embraced bank.

Nate was now facing his own Mallock in the water, and any thought of relaxing was not in him.

Richard urged the canoe farther and farther out into the shipping lanes. He was on a mission, a mission he kept from Cat. Farther out, the current became stronger and the turbulence greater.

"Richard, we should turn around." Nate tried to check the panic in his voice.

"Just a little further, Peter. We are almost there."

"Almost where? I don't see anything but riverboats and barges." At this point the wind picked up, and Nate had to shout to be heard, and he had to turn his head in order to hear Richard.

"Here she comes!" Richard roared. "Quick! Paddle! Faster! Come on, Peter!" Richard dug his oar deep into the Mississipp'.

"Poussée!" *Heave!*

Pause.

"Poussée!" *Heave!*

Pause.

"Plus Profond, Peter! Plus Profond! Un plus rapidement!"

"What are you doing!" Nate yelled back.

By now they were aimed to hit the riverboat Queen of Vicksburg broadside.

"Are you crazy?!" Nate stopped paddling. The displacement of the riverboat made the water choppy for the little canoe and two boys.

The passengers on the riverboat congregated at the side watching the little craft edge closer and closer. Some of the women on board let out shrieks in horror.

"You boys," yelled one of the crew, "come to a full-stop, y'hear? Now! Stay back!"

"Should I tell the Captain to stop?" asked one of the stewards.

"No. They've stopped. Foolish kids."

They had come within ten yards of the majestic ship. As soon as the paddlewheel passed by, Richard was again paddling furiously ahead.

"Hurry, Peter!" Richard was heading for the wake of the ship. At once they were sucked into the turbulent churning of the water, which tossed the canoe around like a spinning top. Both the boys dropped the oars and held on to both sides of the canoe to ride it out.

Richard was laughing wildly the entire time. He was having the time of his life. Ever since he had asked his father for the canoe, he had planned for this moment. A wild ride on the sea.

After a few minutes the River around them was again a swift current, choppy but without serious waves.

"Richard, are you tryin' to get us both killed? Or just me!"

"Come on, Peter. You must say it was fun."

"Let's turn around and go back home."

"I thought you were the brave boy of Vieux Saules."

"I ain't chicken if that's what you're thinkin'." Nate thought about *That Day* at the pool and then grabbed his oar to turn the canoe toward the west. "But I ain't stupid, either. So, Captain, how do we get home?"

Richard looked at the distant shore. He had neglected to take into account the swift current. "Where is Vieux Saules?" His voice was sounding remarkably like Nate's when he had first set foot in the little craft.

"We're several miles south. If we don't get to shore soon, we'll end up in New Orleans. And that'll be a long walk back with a canoe on our heads."

Richard picked up his oar and helped Nate try to steer the canoe westward. By this time, though, the current had actually taken them further into the shipping lane and, to a now-nervous Richard, further away from the security of Vieux Saules, his father's kingdom.

It had been a morning of storms and a cloudy day, and the sky at this hour was getting dark, making their feeble navigation all the more difficult. Both boys were on edge. For Richard, the thrill had ended, taking what little confidence he had with it. For Nate, whether in Wood or water, this was not his day. Any lingering courage he once had had been left back at the River's edge.

"Richard, we're not getting any closer."

"What do we do?" The Captain was now looking to his first mate to make the decisions. It was a mutiny from the top.

"We can't make it to the bank ourselves. My arms are too sore." Nate answered.

"Mine too. So what do we do?" His voice was gaining in pitch.

"We'll have to catch a ride...on something slower than the *Vicksburg*." Nate looked around full-circle, but there was nothing in close proximity, and it was getting darker and colder."

"Where do you think we are now?" asked Richard.

"Probably half-way between the plantation and New Orleans."

"Look! There is a light!" The boy was a bit giddy, which only annoyed Nate further. He was already cursing Richard in his head for bringing him to the brink of a watery death. He was too young and too far from his home for his life to end now.

Nate turned and saw it too. "Come on, Richard! This is our chance!"

The boys paddled furiously toward the moving light. It was another paddle wheeler but at this point they no longer cared. They just wanted to be on something larger than a log.

As before, the closer they got to the riverboat, the choppier the water. The boys were tired and scared and unnerved by the rough water. This time, though, no one on the large vessel noticed the boys, and the Captain was sailing full-speed to reach New Orleans on schedule.

"We ain't gonna make it, Richard! Stop paddling! Richard! Stop!"

But Richard kept paddling as fast as he could. He was on a new mission. Survival.

Nate crawled, carefully, toward the back of the canoe. He didn't want to upset the delicate balance, which was more fragile in the current situation. He grabbed Richard's paddle at mid-stroke.

"Richard! Stop! *Arrêt!*"

Richard tried to yank the oar away from Nate, which nearly toppled the canoe. In the struggle, though, Nate lost his balance and fell into the cold water. It was a shock to his system and his bare feet could feel the air bubbles created by the wooden paddlewheel. The suction pulled him completely under.

Nate was back in his worst nightmare, his worst fear. The current from the massive paddlewheel was turning him in aquatic somersaults. He was so dizzy from spinning around that if the bottom of the canoe were the backend of a donkey, his hand would never find it. Never mind that the water was muddy as well.

He struggled to figure out where the surface was, where the air was. He could hear someone screaming for him. The voice was high-pitched like his mother's. Nate wondered if he would pass out and wake up in Heaven.

"Peter! Peter!" Richard cupped his hands to be heard. He looked from side to side for his first mate. He was now within a few yards of the *Southern Princess* and the wrath of her wheel. He himself was beginning to panic.

"God help him! Peter!" Richard was now screaming at the top of his lungs. In this state he couldn't even think what to do, other than to yell for God to help.

Nate broke the surface with a large gasp for air. His hands reached frantically for the side of the canoe and safety. He grabbed onto the side of the canoe and pulled himself into the cold air. He clung to the side while he sucked in as much air as possible. His water-soaked clothes weighed him down, and his body was convulsing from the cold water.

Richard was still staring into the water on the other side. He wanted to jump in and save Cat but knew it would be useless. The River was too vast. Most likely, he thought, Cat was already well down river.

Then he felt the canoe lean back, nearly knocking him off balance. He turned and saw what was then the happiest moment in his short life. The boy he secretly worshipped was alive after all.

"Merde! Tu me fait peur!" *Damn you! You frightened me.*

Richard scrambled quickly to the other side. "I was sure you were dead." He reached down and hoisted Nate back into the canoe.

"You ain't the only one. I told ya I couldn't swim." Nate fell backwards in exhaustion. He looked up at the clouds and wondered if there wasn't someone up there like Jenna said. Maybe someone was looking after him.

A minute later they crossed the early wake of the ship and the waves lifted the canoe up out of the water. It came down with a crash, and the second wave slammed into the side, capsizing the canoe, and knocking both boys smack in the water. For Nate, it was dé jà vu.

The shock of being thrown into the water, as well as the cold water itself, seemed to knock the wind out of Richard. In that nano-second of wondering whether he would ever breathe again, the side of the canoe slammed against his head, knocking him out cold.

Nate saw him go under, and without thinking, dove down like Cat, waving his arms frantically until he touched something. It was Richard's arm. Nate slid his hand along Richard's arm until he reached his wrist. He grabbed it tightly and, with all the strength left in him, he pulled them both toward the surface.

The canoe, though capsized, was fortunately only a few yards away. Reaching his arm round Richard's chest, Nate turned his other arm into an oar, and with his feet, swam the best he could toward the canoe. He worried that it would float down river faster than he could swim but he was lucky and reached it before he had lost the rest of his strength.

Nate tried to turn the canoe over with one hand, while he held onto Richard with the other, but it was no use. He was too tired and too cold, and the canoe too long and bulky.

The poor boy was also frozen in fear. He looked around. They were surrounded by choppy, deep and muddy water beneath a darkened sky. He could hear his mother Diana fretting in his ear. It was not an encouraging voice at all. Even through this time warp she could convince her son he was in a hopeless situation.

Nate worried that he would lose hold of the canoe. It was his and Richard's only lifeline. He knew he couldn't swim to the shore on his own, let alone carrying Richard. Worst of all, he wasn't sure Richard was even breathing. Nate had his arm around Richard's chest holding him above water but there didn't seem to be any movement at all from the boy.

There was no time to think or worry. Nate worked his way around the narrow end so that the he and Richard were now separated by the hull. Holding tightly to the base of Richard's arm, he moved them both closer to the wider center. It was frantic work for the fourteen-year-old Nate but finally the boat was wedged tightly between them.

Pressing his chest against the side of the canoe, he put his other hand under Richard's other arm and, pulling back heaved the unconscious boy onto the keel. Nate hoisted himself onto the boat as well, and sat up with one foot on each side of the center. He then grabbed Richard by the seat of the pants and swung his one leg to the other side so that he was now straddling the upside down canoe.

Richard was breathing, but it was shallow. Nate looked over toward the western shore. It seemed awfully far away on an upside down canoe with no oar.

Nate was cold and scared. They were on the big river, the Mighty River who swallowed children for snacks and riverboats for meals.

He edged toward Richard, careful not to rock the boat, and touched his forehead. There was a large goose egg near the temple, and he could see a dark bruise forming. 'This isn't good,' he thought. But at least he was now breathing, even if it was shallow.

Up ahead there was a sharp bend in the River similar to the one at Vieux Saules. Nate could make out small moving lights along the horizon. He put his chest against the canoe and paddled hard with his hands. He knew it was his and Richard's only chance.

As the canoe got closer to the bend, he could see that the darting lights were lanterns. When they were even closer, he could hear the muffled voices on the shore. He knew he was now within earshot.

"Hello! Hello!" Nate screamed.

The lights stopped in their tracks.

"Hello!" came a chorus in return. A man with a deep voice spoke out "Are you Richard? Richard LeBeaux?"

Nate sat up. "I'm with Richard. He's been hurt."

"Boy," said Mr. Clarington, the deep voiced man, to one of his slaves. "You get Mr. Elks and tell him to send a rider north to find Mr. LeBeaux. Tell him his son is injured."

"Yes, suh." The young, barefoot man ran all the way to the stables, through briar and brush, without stopping.

Nate continued to paddle to the shore and when he was only thirty yards out, he jumped into the water and pushed the canoe along with his kicking feet. Another ten yards and he could almost touch the river bottom.

Half a dozen men jumped into the cold water and met the boys. One burly man lifted Richard off the canoe and another swept Nate up and out. Within minutes Richard was on the ground and Nate huddled on a log.

The men stood in a circle around Richard while an older gentleman, the local doctor, examined the still unconscious boy.

Nate tried to see Richard but he was a blur between the legs of the men.

"He ain't breathin', boys."

The legs shifted at the worrisome words, and a couple of the men leaned down for a closer look.

Nate immediately threw off the blanket and forced his way into the circle. He pushed the doctor aside, and began using CPR to revive the planter boy. His afternoons at the Red Cross with Diana were finally paying off.

The men watched in shocked disbelief as Nate alternated between pushing on Richard's chest and kissing him! They looked at each other, not knowing what to say, or think. The nearby doctor watched Nate closely, trying to figure out what he was doing. From his vantage point, the boy was forcing his own breathe into the young LeBeaux. Oddly curious.

While they watched in silence, Richard responded and began alternately throwing up and choking on the water he had swallowed. Nate turned him on his side so the river water could drain out of his lungs.

The men were even more in shock. They had seen a miracle, a young Lazarus waking from the dead.

As Richard's breathing strengthened and he became more alert, an exhausted Nate fell back on his bottom. He could feel the dozen or so men staring only at him. He would have done anything at that moment to be anywhere else, but at last he could feel the shame of *That Day* melting away inside.

The sound of approaching horses broke the silence.

"I think Mr. LeBeaux is here," said Mr. Clarington, owner of *Felicity*, a large plantation a few miles north of New Orleans. "Simon, show Mr. LeBeaux the way."

"Yes, suh." He disappeared as quickly, as obediently, as the boy in the briars.

Dr. DeMain, the plantation's physician, was examining Richard as Mr. LeBeaux arrived while the rest of the men continued to watch Nate closely.

The elder Richard jumped off his horse even before it had stopped and ran over to his shaken boy.

"What happened?"

Richard was in shock, so LeBeaux turned to Nate. "What happened, boy?"

Nate was silent. He wasn't sure how much to tell Master LeBeaux. Should he tell him that Richard wanted to chase after riverboats and ride their wakes? Should he tell him he thought his son was a bit crazy? Should he—

"Peter Hennessee! What happened?"

"Richard wanted to try his canoe on the River. The current was stronger than we thought. It swept us toward the middle and we capsized when one of the riverboats passed. Richard hit his head." *'There, that was pretty safe,'* he thought.

"My God!" He looked at his son's growing bruise. "I'll have that Captain's head. Which ship was she?"

"I don't know, sir," Nate lied. "It happened so fast."

"LeBeaux, you are lucky they even survived."

"What about my son?"

"He'll be fine," said the doctor. "He'll have a whale of a headache, though. But you can thank the boy," he said, pointing to Nate. "Not sure exactly how he did it, but he somehow brought him back to life."

"Ow." Richard had touched his forehead. He focused his eyes on his father kneeling beside him. "Papa?" He turned and saw a bundled Nate to his side. "Where are we?"

"*Felicity*, son."

Mr. LeBeaux squeezed his son's hand and looked at the shivering Nate. "I owe you for my son's life."

"No, sir. I'm just glad he's alright."

News traveled quickly up the River Road to Vieux Saules and beyond about the wild adventure of the planter's boy and the wild Cat.

Jenna and Brett were waiting for Nate at the entrance to the oak allée. As the carriage turned into the drive, it slowed so they could climb aboard. Jenna too cradled her only son and smothered him with praises to God for keeping her son in the palm of His hand.

Death tried boldly to take two sons of the earth today, but it was not to be. Not today.

Wednesday

August 26, 1857

10 THE COLLYWOBBLES

The night owls and the bats alone were awake. As they flew over the crude wooden cabins and the trees that embraced them, they could see only darkness below.

Bullfrog and his wife Carolina were dead to the world. In deep sleep they somehow managed to be in the same dream. One had crossed over to the other. They had been married so long they could often read each other's mind. But even in sleep, the baritone snores of Bullfrog could be heard through shutter and rafter. A blind man could orient himself through the Cimetière by snoring sounds alone.

Across the way and three houses down, Tiddy-Beaux walked knee-deep in the Mississippi with her father. Or, at least a vision of a man to be her father. She, like other children in the Cimetière, didn't know her parents. Like Midnight, her mother had died giving birth. Her father was never known.

She loved her Aunt Tilliman immensely, and it was comfort whenever others in the Cimetière commented how much Aunt

Tilliman looked, sounded, and even acted like her mother. It helped her feel as close to her natural mother as was possible.

'*But what about my father?*' she wondered. Nearly every day since her eighth birthday. She was sure that Aunt Tilliman knew, but could never get the kindly woman to tell her anything. As an inquisitive fourteen year old, the silence about her father was more than frustrating for Miss Tiddy-Beaux. So she was reduced to having to create her own image of a father in her nightly dreams.

Across the plantation, Nate slept in the deepest of sleep where dreams delve into the heart of matters. The film production running in his mind kept switching from *The Indian Wood* to *Tipped in the Mississipp'* to *Techno Nate Tanks*. And back again.

By morning, he was one tired boy. He lay under the covers waiting for his kind Mama to tell him it was time to eat. As he lay staring at the ceiling, he considered going back to sleep to get rest.

In the distance he heard Brett open the front door and talk to what sounded like one of the slaves. Moments later, Jenna knocked on Cat's bedroom door.

"Bon jour, mon cher." Her voice was soothing in the morning. "You have an important letter." She handed him the sealed envelope with its fancy manuscript.

"Who's it from?"

"I believe from Master LeBeaux himself."

Nate immediately sat up. "From Master LeBeaux?" He was surprised by the attention. "Why would he write to me?"

"Hmm, I wonder. Could it be because you saved his only son last night?" She smiled. "Your father and I are very proud of you, Cat. You kept a cool head, and were very brave." She kissed his forehead, still smiling.

"Open it," she urged.

Nate slid his finger under the flap and pulled it open. He opened the letter and read out loud:

To Master Peter Hennessee

My Dear Peter,
It is with extreme gratitude that I write this letter to
you. It is clear that without your brave efforts, our
beloved son would have drowned in the River. For this,
the LeBeaux Family of Vieux Saules will be eternally
indebted.

Please join me in my Study this morning at 10 o.clock
so that I may show my appreciation in a more
tangible way.

In Gratitude,
Richard Bertrand Olivant LeBeaux III

Nate let the letter fall on his lap. He was stunned. The High King of Vieux Saules had actually written to him and used words like '*extreme gratitude*' and '*brave efforts*.'

"Oh, Cat," exclaimed Jenna. "That is some letter, especially for Master LeBeaux. You do not know him as well as I. That is a letter you will not see again for quite some time, if ever. You should show it to Brett." She thought for a moment. "Oh, what are we thinking, you must get up and get ready. It will be 10 before you know it, and you cannot be late. Not for Master LeBeaux. He is very strict about being prompt."

She pulled the covers back and pulled her son up and out of the bed.

"Ow!" Poor Nate was sore in every muscle of his body.

Jenna immediately let go. "I'm sorry, mon cher. I'll go draw a bath."

"A bath!" Nate shrieked in disbelief. "I don't need a bath. I took one in the River last night."

"In that muddy River! No, mon cher, that will not do."

"Mama, not a bath. It's only Wednesday."

"That's your reward for being a hero." she smiled and left him to grouse in his bed alone.

"Argh!" He grabbed his pillow and threw it across the room. Unlike everyone else at Vieux Saules, Nate hardly felt like a hero. *'If I had had any courage, I would never have stepped into the canoe in the first place,'* he told himself. Repeatedly.

An hour later, Nate stood on the front porch of his house waiting to make the journey to the Main House. Jenna had insisted that he wear his fine Easter clothes, including a high starched collar. To Nate, it felt like having cardboard pressing into his lower jaw.

His hair was heavily oiled down, the knickers were itchy wool, and both the stockings and shoes were tight. He felt as stiff and awkward as a puppet dragging his strings in a crowded stadium. To top it off, his mouth was dry as fresh-picked cotton.

As he left the front steps, Brett walked over and tried to give his nervous son encouragement.

"I remember my own first meeting with the man, Catrick. Though the circumstances were different—and far less favorable than it is for you today—the feelings you are having and the way you look are probably the same. You're bloody well nervous, I can tell."

Nate looked in his father's eyes. "Are you trying to help, Brett?"

"Uh, well, yes. I—I'm tryin' to tell ya that it will be fine. You did a grand thing for the great High King. So thar's nothin' to be frettin' about. Maybe he'll even give ya the keys to his bloody kingdom."

'Keys to the kingdom.' Nate filed away the thought. Just like back home, his mind was always working.

Nate walked around the House to the front where the grand Twin Stairs stood. The southpaw put his hand on the banister of the left stair and remembered now so clearly the past Sunday when his own family was climbing the stairs as they began the tour. He took the first step up. Again.

As he walked up what appeared like marble steps, he was in the shadows and grandeur of a dozen massive columns. He was walking into the bastion of wealth and it made him dizzy with fear.

This was a scary, mind-numbing time for Nate as he stood on the front steps, knocked on the massive wood doors, and waited for his entry.

He could feel the sweat beneath his arms and the back of his neck. His underclothing was moist and clammy on his skin. Spasms surfaced in his legs and hands, and his mouth was as dry as the warm Santa Ana winds back home. Most annoying, he felt the Collywobbles of dizzy butterflies.

The nervous Nate could taste the beginnings of his stomach coming to light. *Wouldn't that be grand?*, he thought. *Puke right there on the beautiful brick design. Or better yet, on the ancient houseboy Nathaniel who must have been alive when Jefferson was declaring all men equal. Or, worse, on Master LeBeaux himself. That would probably be worth ten lashings and a splash in the gator pool.*

While he waited and thought of how he would act and what he would say, Nate watched his hand mechanically reach for the knocker again. He froze when the door opened. It was the Master himself.

"Peter, come in!" He grabbed Nate's hand and yanked him inside.

Before Nate could wipe the sweat off his upper lip, he was standing in the main parlor. He had never seen such richness in his life.

"Come, Peter, let us go down to my study." Mr. LeBeaux talked as he walked. He was a man constantly on the move. He ran a vast estate that included not only Vieux Saules but also lesser known plantations in Vicksburg and Natchez, as well as commercial properties in New Orleans and Memphis. He was a multi-millionaire at a time when a man earned only fifty cents a day.

From Mr. LeBeaux's demeanor and those around him, it was clear that the world revolved around him. He was the center of the universe. Servants in starched clothing, much like Nate's, waited on the balls of their feet to spring into action to meet the largest and smallest of the Master's requests.

LeBeaux, however, seemed oblivious to their waiting, or even their existence. He only knew that when his fingers snapped, his requests were met instantly.

They walked out of the main parlor and down the hall. As they passed young Richard's room, Nate stopped and peered inside. Richard was still asleep in his bed.

"The excitement of last night took the sails right out of him," said the elder Richard. "Quite some adventure you both had, I would say." He patted Nate on the back and led him further down the hall.

When they came to a nondescript door on the right, Richard stopped and opened it, revealing an oak staircase, glistening from polish and careful use.

"This way, my boy. You are about to enter the inner sanctum. Mrs. LeBeaux likes to call it the Throne Room." He let out a hearty laugh. "She's enamored by the royalty in ol' England. Likens herself to their nobility, I guess."

Nate took a step onto the top landing and immediately sensed the competing smell of oak and—he cocked his head, trying to figure out the other—

"—cedar. You smell cedar," said the Master.

Nate took a deep breath, thought a moment, and nodded. LeBeaux had read his mind and filled it in. "Yeah, cedar." Nate answered.

He looked at LeBeaux the way Pouty Robert had studied *him* the other day on the road when they had first met. Nate wondered if it was true what they said, that the Master could read people's minds. He seemed to know everything that went on at Vieux Saules.

Nate walked down the stairs, expecting to end up in another hallway but instead found himself directly in the Study. From all accounts, there were no doors out of the Study. The only way in seemed to be this staircase.

LeBeaux let Nate take in all the sights before he finally spoke. He watched the boy's eyes move slowly from wall to wall of bookshelves.

"Kinda like a rabbit hole," said Nate at last, though he knew any good burrow had at least two ways out.

"That is a good one, Peter. I'll have to remember to tell Mrs. LeBeaux that at supper tonight." He continued. "I pride myself on my reading," LeBeaux said at last. "I can read in French and German, you know."

"I didn't know that, sir," Nate replied simply. His stomach let out a loud gurgling sound, which made LeBeaux chuckle.

"Where are my manners?" he said. He walked over to a table and rang a silver bell. Within seconds, a servant entered from a hidden side door.

"Benjamin, bring Master Hennessee some cold lemonade and a plate of Alma's almond cookies." He smiled at Nate. "They are simply the best in the South, if you ask me. Just wait and see."

Nate smiled to himself as a memory from Cat came to mind. Unbeknownst to the Master, Cat had been eating Miss Alma's almond cookies since he was three years old. The boy well knew and appreciated their incredible taste.

"Yes, sir," he managed to say.

Mr. LeBeaux led Nate over to his prized roll-top desk. "This," he said, "is where the real action originates, Peter. It is not in the fields or even in the cotton market in New Orleans. It is right here."

LeBeaux pulled out one of the ledgers and opened it up for Nate to see.

"Every step I plan to take is noted here; every result as well. These are the battle plans. Every move I make or want to take is recorded in ink. For my knowledge and for the future kings of Vieux Saules."

Nate knew from his parents, as well as from young Richard, how Mr. and Mrs. LeBeaux saw Vieux Saules as their little kingdom. And, why not, they had absolute power over the lives of real people. Life and death—and misery in between—was firmly in their grasp, and supported by the State.

"Peter, I have watched you grow up here at Vieux Saules. You are an exceptional boy and, no doubt, have the potential to do great things. In this country, with talent, hard work, and God's blessing, anything is possible."

The hidden door opened again and Benjamin came in and deposited the refreshments. In seconds he was gone and the door closed silently. Nate tried to pay attention when it closed to remember where exactly it was.

LeBeaux seemed to guess what Nate was trying to do. Laughing, he said "Do not waste your time, Peter. That door can only open inward. There's no way out but up." He pointed to the fine oak staircase.

'*Funny. That's what Jenna had told him yesterday.*' he remembered. She had stayed in his room last night until he had fallen asleep. He liked that. Nate was quiet as he lay in bed, listening to her talk. Over and over she kept thanking God for saving his life.

Nate told her how when he was underwater, he kept hoping he would make it to the surface. And Jenna, in her soft, mesmerizing voice, said simply, '*When you are in danger, mon cheri, there is no way out but up.*'

'*Interesting,* thought Nate, *that LeBeaux would use the same words.*'

"Now, as I was saying—please have some cookies and ade—I see great promise in you. Who knows, some day you may be a planter yourself."

"Me?" Nate asked incredibly.

"Of course! Why not? You are bright, and you think quickly on your feet. You have spunk—I have seen it first-hand."

Nate looked unconvinced. "I don't know, sir, I never—I mean, I don't think I could—"

"Of course you can. And, as I wrote in my letter, I am eternally indebted to you for saving my son's life. He is the heir to my fortune. What good is a kingdom without a Crown Prince?" he asked. "When you are of age, and ready to start an estate, well, I will be here to help."

"That's, um, that's generous of you, sir. I just don't think I—" he wanted to say that he could never see himself owning another person, but LeBeaux, in his enthusiasm, cut him off.

"—nonsense. You can. This is for you. Take it." He handed Nate a parchment with a wax seal. It looked very royal.

"What is it, sir?"

"Your start to prosperity." He let Nate open the letter and read for himself.

"You're giving him to me?"

"I know how close the two of you are. Minuit is a good, healthy boy and will make a fine and profitable slave when he grows up. Naturally, you're not old enough to own a slave.

"This transfer will become legal on August 25, 1867. The tenth anniversary of your saving my beloved Richard. You'll be 24 years old by then. Until then, he will be in my most benevolent care."

"I don't know what to say, Master LeBeaux." Nate did the math and knew that by then the South and its plantation system would be gone. He wondered where Midnight would be in 1867. Maybe up North.

He wondered too where he would be. It was an hourly question. *If he could just walk into the past, would one day he just fall back into the present? Would it just happen without notice? What if he was here for ten years? Would he be caught up in the Civil War? Would he get stuck being a Rebel? Would he one day die in the past? Would he ever see his real mom again?*

Nate had the most quizzical face, and LeBeaux could see Nate's mind working overtime.

"My boy, you are far too easy-going to get your drawers tied up in the details. For now, relax and enjoy the adventures of boyhood."

He held up a glass and waited for Nate to follow. Nate reached nervously for his own glass, at the same time remembering his great spill last month at *The Cat & the Custard Cup* at his step-dad's birthday bash. Crimson punch on French white linen. The color matched his face then.

Nate grabbed the glass of ade so tightly not even a wet frog could have slipped through. He crinkled his eyes closed as their glasses clinked.

"To bravery and chivalry, and our way of life. To you, Peter." He lifted his glass higher and then brought it to his mouth. "Ah, nothing beats a strong julep."

Nate sipped his lemonade quietly. His wool pants were beginning to itch in the heat of the room, and he was anxious to go up the rabbit hole and leave his Collywobbles behind.

"Ah, one more thing, Peter."

Nate cringed. '*What now?*' he thought.

"Ten years is a long time to wait for a reward. I want you to have something you can enjoy here and now." He opened up a small drawer in his desk and pulled out a twenty dollar gold coin.

"It is the latest Liberty Double Eagle. Just minted last week in New Orleans. Spend it wisely and well. You earned it."

Nate held the shiny coin in his open palm. He stared at the date '*1857.*' Nate finally had something tangible in his hand that said he was in the past. He continued to stare, which caught

LeBeaux's attention. He was clearly impressed by the impact his gift had had on the young boy.

"A man these days could work a long time and never see that in his hand. Remember this day, Peter. Remember it well."

Master LeBeaux rang a bell, and Thomas returned to escort Nate out of the rabbit hole and back to the Twin Stairs. As the heavy front door closed behind him, Nate opened his hand and stared at the Liberty coin in the bright light of day. The sun bounced off the gold and blinded him. He moved his palm back and forth and up and down, playing with the sunlight.

With his other hand, he patted his coat. Inside was the most precious gift of all. Then he frowned. *'What good is ten years? The War will be fought and won by then.'* He alone knew that LeBeaux's gesture was meaningless; it was an empty gift.

Nate put the coin in his pocket and walked down the grand curved staircase. Halfway down, he looked back. It was a beautiful house, he had to admit. It was sad to know that in a few short years the height of its beauty would be gone forever.

As he left the shadows of the Main House and walked the lane back to his own house, he realized that he was no longer nervous. The big test was over, and the Collywobbles had been left back in the Rabbit Hole.

He started to smile, and the smile got bigger the closer he got to home. He was busting inside to share with his parents his half-hour of fame and glory.

He wasn't sure, though, what he would tell Midnight.

11   Fiddlers & Fiddlesticks

The French and the Irish were in a good mood that afternoon at *The Chattery*.

"Catrick, m'boy, get your Irish fiddle. I feel songs bunched up in me elbow that are dyin' to get out into the summer air." Brett put his own *Ginny Dee* up to his chin and stretched his arm sending the bow on a seismic sketch across the strings.

He had had his fiddle, Ginny Dee, since he was sixteen and still in Ireland. He named her after the first girl he had a crush on. Later, long after Ginny had moved to the next county, he joked that his fiddle was his best and finest way to meet Irish lasses on the streets of Galway.

The fiddle had an even more fetching power on the lasses in Savannah, Pensacola, Mobile, and the wild and adventurous New Orleans. He liked to remind Jenna of that from time to time. She would smile and continue folding the laundry. She knew how lucky she was to have such a gifted and caring man for a husband, and was smart enough not to let it go to his head. Funny, though, Brett always managed to catch the smile on the side. He knew well his place in her heart.

With all the windows open the music soared into the outer landscape like ruddy Irish spirits leaving one wake and heading for another. Brett was bringing the house down with his music.

Inside *The Chattery*, Nate had joined his dad with a second fiddle. While in his room he had discarded the warm itchy woolen shorts and long sleeve shirt in place of his favorite overalls and bare feet. He was back in familiar territory. And happy that the Collywobbles of the morning were now behind him.

Nate played his fiddle as he rounded the corner into the front room where Brett was already in the middle of one of their favorite tunes, *Galway in the Morning*. Its lively rhythm made even the French Jenna kick up her heals and kick the house dust around.

LeBeaux, enjoying a good cigar and drink on the gallery heard the strings down the lane. Soon he heard a second fiddle just as lively and knew that Peter had joined in. He smiled knowing that it was his generosity that was bringing out the mirth in the poor whites down the lane. His private lane.

'*Life is good*,' thought the planter. '*Very good*.' He sat down on a rocker, closed his eyes, and enjoyed the sweet music of the Irish.

Father and son played for nearly an hour, until Nate's arm and fingers needed a break. While they rested and drank cool cider, Nate replayed the entire meeting he had had with Master LeBeaux, describing in as much detail as he could the rich furnishings and the uniqueness of the Rabbit Hole.

Jenna and Brett both had to slow Nate down from time to time. He was speaking so fast he blurred the sounds together and left some words out altogether. His mom and Brett glanced at each other from time to time, smiling at their son's wild enthusiasm.

It was great to see him excited about something. He had been so preoccupied with Midnight not being free, and they knew the coming years would be even harder as Midnight became a man and felt the full burden of slavery.

Nate saved the best bit of news for last. "This is the best part." He pulled the *Transfer of Ownership* document out of his pocket and let them read it slowly, as Master LeBeaux had done for him. He waited for their blank faces to pull themselves upward in grand smiles and excitement.

The wait seemed endless. 'How long does it take to read the words '...*assigned to Peter Hennessee in perpetuity...?*' he asked himself. His fingers rubbed the four strings of his fiddle while he waited.

"I don't understand, Cat?" Brett said finally. He seemed in shock.

"Do you mean that Master LeBeaux gave you Midnight? That he is now free?" asked Jenna in disbelief.

"No, not exactly. Not—not yet anyway." He pointed further down the sheet. "Not until 1867. In ten years." Even though Nate knew slavery would be gone by then, he was still excited. The document gave him the chance to give Midnight immediate hope in his future. By the time 1867 came around, Midnight would already have been enjoying his freedom for a couple of years. But he knew that, right now, what Midnight needed most was to know that he would not be a slave all his life.

Nate knew that that was all he could do. If he told him the real truth, even Midnight would think he was daft and out of his mind.

Jenna's face was lost in a broad smile, and her eyes were beginning to drip like they did at the creek side when Tiddy was baptized.

"Oh, Mom." Nate gave his mom a warm embrace. "I mean, Mama." He knew how much she cherished Midnight. She had helped Naomi care for him when he was first given to her and had even nursed him because Naomi couldn't. It was an unheard of act of kindness and humility for a white woman to do in the South in the 1850s. She had been with him when he first walked and first talked. She had watched him grow from diapers to now the brink of manhood.

"Oh, Cat, this is truly an answer to a decade of prayers. I give thanks to God for His grace and mercy." She kissed her son and held on to the hug.

Nate turned to Brett, who had been silent all this time. "What about you, Brett? You are so quiet."

Brett was lost in his own world. Nate nudged him on the shoulder. "Brett, are you alright?"

"Yes, I am fine, Cat."

"You do not seem happy for Midnight."

"Oh. It is grand news, me boy. Truly. I am very pleased, and like your dear Mama, I am thankful to God that He chose to rescue one of his sons." Brett put his large hand over Nate's and squeezed. "It's truly grand. You should go and tell him. Thar be music in the Cimetière tonight."

The usually spirited Irishman sat somewhat stunned in his chair, with *Ginny Dee* still resting on his lap.

"Cat, you should go and tell him." Jenna seemed to be shooing him out of the house. "But be back by supper."

"Yes, ma'am." Nate kissed Jenna on her cheek and ran out of the house.

Jenna walked over to the window and watched Nate sail over the hedge and fly down the lane. When he was well on his way, she turned back to Brett.

"Brett, darling, what is wrong? Cat is right; you do not seem happy at all for Midnight."

Brett was quiet for a minute. Then he spoke.

"I am happy for Midnight, but I keep wondering, why him?"

"What do you mean, '*why him*'?" she asked.

"Master LeBeaux does nothing without a reason. It is another game of Cat and Mouse, and I'm still the bloody mouse." His voice picked up anger as it grew.

"How is this about you? Master LeBeaux knows that Midnight is like a brother to Cat. He knows that Cat will free him the second he is his. He was being extremely grateful to Cat for saving his son's life? That is all." She seemed annoyed that Brett was turning something so wonderful into something about him.

"Gratitude. That's all?" he inquired.

"Yes." she replied simply. "I don't understand why you are getting so upset."

"Of course not. Why should you? You do not have a child in slavery!" His voice boomed clear to the new shingles on the roof.

A look of instant recognition was on Jenna's face. She held her hands up to her mouth. "Oh, Lord. Tiddy." Tears came instantly. "Oh, Brett." She ran to him and put her arms around him.

"Why Midnight in ten years? Why not Tiddy now! A generous man would have released both friend and daughter," he said, his voice shaking. "What kind of man plays with the deep emotions of others like they were nothing but fiddlesticks?" He picked up his precious bow and threw it across the room.

The breaking of glass as the bow broke the window and landed near the hedge woke up the resting Mr. LeBeaux who had fallen asleep on his gallery listening to the Galway tunes.

A slight, but definite smile appeared on the sleepy planter. *'The good news has reached the poor house now,'* he knew. *'How great to be the Master; to be the first to know and the last to give up.'* He closed his eyes and settled back to a satisfying nap, replaying the fiddles in his mind.

12 MIDNIGHT

"Bonjour, Monsieur! Bonjour Madame!" Nate tapped his corn silk hair as if he were wearing a cap. "It's a beautiful day, a fishing day, n'est ne pas?"

"Bonjour Monsieur Cat." Sylvie handed him a piece of stew meat as he passed.

"Très bon. Merci." he replied as sauce dripped down his chin. He wiped it with the back of his hand, and continued on through the Cimetière.

"Où est Minuit? L'avez-vous vu aujourd'hui?" *Where is Midnight? Have you seen him today?*

"He be ten hours from here," remarked Noah.

It seemed that Cat was always looking for Midnight, and the slaves made a joke of his perpetual question by telling him how many hours it would be until the stroke of midnight. Of course, on the plantation, it had a double meaning, or a hidden wish— that they could all be so many hours away from Vieux Saules. Preferably north, although there was always a debate among them as to whether it would be quicker and much safer to go the short distance into the delta and out to sea. But that had its own set of dangers as well.

"You are funny today, Monsieur Noah." Nate smiled even though he understood the hidden message. Many times Cat had wished he and Midnight could leave the plantation and live the rough life away from everyone. And now, thanks to Master LeBeaux—or, rather, his crazy adventure on the River with Richard—it could now come true.

Nate remembered then that last year, when he was thirteen, Cat had hired himself out to Master LeBeaux as a stable boy so he could earn enough money to buy Midnight's freedom. A month later he did the math and realized he would be 83 before he had enough money. Midnight's market value increased day by day the closer he got to manhood. Poor Cat knew he could never work fast enough to free his friend.

As Nate walked past one of the many willows on the Old Willows plantation, he reached up and snapped off a small branch. He bent it back and forth as he walked and with a quick jab into a bush he was a buccaneer pirate off the Barbary Coast.

A small boy approached. Nate pointed the end of the willow sword at his bare stomach.

"Bonjour mon Ami. Where be your treasure?"

The little boy pointed to a spot directly behind Nate. When Nate turned around to look, the child was gone from sight. Nate smiled and looked around, but the boy was nowhere. Just like Midnight.

While Nate was a playful pirate, a frightened Midnight stood at a dangerous crossroad. He was growing toward manhood and could no longer hide behind his mama's skirt or blend in with scores of the other black kids. As the boys in particular grew taller, Mallock was ever more determined to bring them down a notch or two.

On this day Mallock was in a frightening foul mood, and was bothered more than usual by Midnight's friendship with the white Cat. He had told Midnight to clean up the supply shack that stood at the edge of the Cimetière. He had determined before even stepping back inside that the boy had done not a lick of work. He entered the shack an angry man.

"Mais, Monsieur Mallock, j' ai balayé le plancher." The young black boy spoke in a soft voice.

Mr. Mallock struck his hand across Midnight's face. Hard.

"Don't play no fancy French with me, boy. This ain't Paris, and you sure as trash ain't white."

Midnight had crossed the line, and he knew it. Problem was, there was no way to take a step back. And he knew that too. He had heard that Mr. Mallock was in the worst of spirits today and that fact was covered all over the overseer's face.

"You've been in here all morning. And you ain't swept a lick." He pressed the broomstick against Midnight's throat. "Why is that, boy? You tryin' to cheat your Master?"

Midnight swallowed hard, his Adam's apple held back by the broomstick. His nostrils flared and he took a deep breath, taking in also the foul breath of the overseer.

Midnight's mind raced while he tried to find a way out. Hot sweat melted from his armpits and he started to wet his pants but held back tightly. He wondered where Cat was. Cat could get anyone out of trouble. He was quick on his feet like his namesake, and his tongue was even more clever. His eyes shifted towards the window.

The overseer pressed the broomstick harder against Midnight's throat. "Whatcha lookin' for, boy? A knife to split old Mr. Mallock's head? Is that whatcha want right now, boy, is it?"

"No, sah." His forehead was a slope of sweat pebbles. Warm water now ran down his pant leg.

Mr. Mallock noticed the puddle forming around Midnight's bare feet. He smiled. He had the poor boy right where he wanted him. In that shack, Mr. Mallock was at the height of power and it affected him in peculiar ways.

In one of the side alleys Nate continued looking for Midnight, peeking up into the trees that lined these dirt lanes in the Cimetière, and peeking under the raised cabins. No sign at all of his friend. *'Where could that rascal be?'* he wondered.

"Catfish, your twin be in the supply shack," said the kindly, elderly Miss Geraldine.

"Merci, Madamoiselle. Merci."

The shack was about fifty yards ahead just at the edge of the Cimetière. It was a rough log cabin with an elevated porch in front. It had a door that squeaked terribly, which suited the overseer well. He trained a dog or two to bark at the sound. More than one hungry soul over the years tried to sneak some extra food in the middle of the night. They paid a heavy price with the whip.

Nate was in a playful mood and full of excitement about his good news. The whole way over he had tried to imagine Midnight's face and reaction when he found out he would one day be free.

But first Nate thought he would play a trick on his *bon ami.* He climbed up the wooden steps slowly like the cat he was. He walked over to the small, dusty window and peered in. His friend was on the far side.

He watched Midnight drop his loose trousers and assume the position.

"What's he doin'?" said a disgusted Nate under his breath. "'Doesn't he know that Master LeBeaux has given him to me? Can't no one whip Midnight now." declared the naïve boy.

Further thought of play vanished quickly. Without thinking, Nate put his hand on the door. As he turned the latch, a large hand covered his own.

"Leave it be, boy. Won't do no good." It was the familiar but now muffled baritone voice of Bullfrog.

"Bullfrog, you don't understand. It's different now." Nate whispered.

"What is different is you and Minuit. You the blue sky, Cat. You'se go where you go. Minuit, be the dark cloud. He go where storms go. Pushed from there to there where no one care."

Nate looked at Bullfrog. He was a bear of a man, dark and grizzly. The other slaves called him Bullfrog because of the boom in his voice, which seemed to grow in intensity the closer he was to the water. He often said God lived in the water.

Nate pushed the double-sized hand away and looked back in the window. He focused on Midnight's crumpled face. He knew now why Midnight hated the man so much more than the other slaves. The whipping continued.

"How can a man do that to a boy for no reason at all?"

"Git away, Cat. Don't let the man see ya. That'd do no good. Not for you or Minuit."

"I gotta help him." He reached again for the door but Bullfrog's long left arm swooped around and picked him up like he weighed no more than a sack of cotton.

"You get him killed. That whatcha want?" With Nate kicking and squirming, Bullfrog carried him down the wooden steps toward the sanctuary of the Cimetière. He had to put his hand over the boy's mouth to keep him quiet. He could feel Nate's hot, moist breath against his palm.

"He soon be done." He dropped Nate on the grass next to Timothy's cabin. It gave him the best view of the storehouse.

Crouched with his hands on his knees, an angry Nate stared at the far-off door. His body quivered with each sound of the whip on the young boy's flesh. Nate could feel the Collywobbles returning. This was set to be Midnight's best day ever, and now hate was changing it all.

Nate grew more impatient. "Why doesn't the man stop?"

"Why does he start? Cuz he can. An' there's no stoppin' once hate gits in."

Hearing that, Nate got up and started toward the shack. Again, Bullfrog's long reach of an arm pulled him back like a bishop's hook.

"You know, I could kill Mallock with my own hands. That Monsieur Poubelle, he's garbage."

"No, Cat, you gotta let it be. It be in the Lord's own hands."

"It ain't right. Never is, but especially now that he's gonna be—" Nate stopped himself from giving away the secret. He wanted Midnight to hear it first.

Bullfrog let out a hearty laugh. "Too bad you ain't the Master's son. Be a whole lot different in ten years, I 'spect."

Nate gave Bullfrog a serious look. "You can count on that, Bullfrog. Things will be different."

The two heard the creak of the door, and the hard sound of boots descending the steps. The satisfied overseer adjusted his hat as he went. On the path ahead he saw three black men idly talking in whispered voices. He quickened his pace toward the bigger men without a fear in the world. For the ravaged boy behind him, he gave no passing thought.

Nate immediately got up to run to his friend but, again, Bullfrog stopped him.

"Don't go just yet. Give the boy his place. And don't go tellin' him whatcha know. Leave him have his pride."

Midnight emerged from the shack into the bright light of the Louisiana day. It seemed all the sweat from his brow had found its way into his eyes. They were awash in stinging salt. As he walked back toward the cabins, his chest seemed to heave in constrained crying.

He saw Cat resting in the shade. *'Where was he just a half hour ago? Where was he when I was crying out inside? Cat always knew to come. Why not today?'*

Midnight stared at the ground while he sought some answers. He couldn't look at Nate's face right now. He stopped twenty yards out and counted his toes while the black birds sang.

Nate started to get up, but he could almost hear Bullfrog telling him to stay. Like a lazy Southern dog.

"Minuit, viens-ici! Reste sous l'arbre avec moi." he called to his friend. "You must be tired from all your work."

There was no response from Midnight.

"Viens-ici. S'il te plaît." Nate stood up and walked toward his best friend.

Midnight looked up. Tears began to stream down his thin face. When Nate came eye to eye with Midnight, he wiped his friend's tears and gave him a long and tight embrace. This was a new experience for Nate but it had come naturally to him without a thought. Back home he never would have embraced a friend, even one in such pain. But slowly over the past several days, he was becoming more and more like Cat.

"Some day, you and I will leave this place alive," he whispered to Midnight. "Some day, I promise you."

Midnight shook his head slowly, still in shock.

"Il est un homme stupide. "He can't even speak French."

Midnight started to laugh and cry at the same time. Pain was mixing a strange humor.

"Ah, oui. A very stupid man."

Nate put his arm around Midnight and walked him back to the cabin while telling him about his visit with Master LeBeaux. He thought his friend could use a good lift, and the ending to his story would do just that. As he described the Rabbit Hole, Nate could hardly keep his secret in the bag.

As Nate got to the rich part, there was a loud commotion in the main alley of the Cimetière. Dogs were yelping excitedly, and there were horses in the street. It was clear that Mallock and his men were involved somehow.

Pouty Robert appeared at the corner of one of the cabins and was motioning to them excitedly. "Come quick, you two. C'mon." He was waving his arms like he was fighting off a horde of mosquitoes.

"Let's go see." Midnight started to go, but Nate pulled him back.

"I ain't finished with my story."

"It can wait, Cat; c'mon." The noise was getting louder, and they could hear Mallock shouting, obviously at a slave. Midnight was anxious, but also nervous inside, to see who was in trouble. "C'mon, Cat."

"I would think you'd have had your fill of Mallock today."

"I don't wanta think about it. You wants to stay, stay, but I'm goin'." He started to leave without Nate.

"All right, I'll come. But when you hear the rest of my story, you gonna regret leavin' now."

The two boys walked down the side alley and rounded the corner to the main alley. There, about twenty yards in front of them, was Mallock and three of his men on horseback. Each of the men held a rope that was tied to either a hand or an ankle of a poor slave. The young man was bloodied everywhere; from the marks on his body, it was obvious to the boys that he had been dragged by the horses for some distance.

"Mallock's been busy today." He glanced over at Midnight. "I ain't seen him before."

"D'ya think he's the runaway they was lookin' for the other day."

"Most likely." Nate figured. "Wonder where they found him."

"He must not have been in the Wood after all," said Midnight.

"Poor boy. He looks mighty tired and terribly beat."

"An' mos' likely they ain't done yet. The stupid man has to show his stupid slaves who the boss is."

Nate knew Midnight was right.

"C'mon, Midnight, let's go. Won't do us to watch him suffer. And I have a story I wanna finish. You're gonna like the ending. I promise."

Nate tugged at Midnight's sleeve and pulled him away from the dogs and whips and the suffering that would surely follow. Midnight now knew first-hand the brutal end of the whip and pitied the runaway and his fate. He wished he could go into the thick of it and help, but knew it was all useless.

He was depressed as he walked away with Nate, and he had a hard time focusing on his story about LeBeaux and a rabbit hole.

Nate led Midnight far away from the Cimetière and close to the Indian Wood.

"You takin' me back to that haunted place, Cat? You know, they's right, it's cursed, and I can show you my backside to prove it."

"I don't see it that way at all."

"An' why's that Cat? We went in there yesterday, and look at me today."

"Yeah, we went in yesterday, and last night I was saved from drowning in the River and saved Richard."

"You shoulda let him drown."

"No—"

"—No?! Cat, he's just gonna grow up and be another Massah."

"Maybe, but he won't be your Massah."

"How you know that, Cat? You been talkin' to Pouty Robert and his tea leaves?"

"That's what I've been trying to tell ya, Minuit. Massah LeBeaux done give you to me." He paused. "Not now, but in ten years."

Midnight cocked his head sideways in disbelief. "Wha'chu tellin' me, Catfish? I'll be a free man?"

"Oui! Ten years from yesterday, and I have the papers to prove it."

Midnight started to sit down in the lush grass, but halfway down found it too painful. He stood tall and gazed at the cloudy sky.

"I don't believe it. I'll be a free man." He looked over at Nate with skepticism. "You sure about that? You read it through?"

"Yup. So did my Mama and Brett. The paper has Master LeBeaux's wax seal."

"Why would Massah set me free?"

"I saved his son's life."

"He be happy now. Maybe tomorrow he change his mind, go back to his ol' self."

"He can't, Midnight. He signed the paper—it's legal. He can't go and change his mind. Just can't."

"He's the Massah here. He can do anydthng he wants." Midnight started to turn away.

"No." Nate put his hands on Midnight's shoulders and turned him back and looked him square in the eye. "He wouldn't do that, Midnight. His whole life here is based on the law. That's what it all rests on. He's bound to it. Trust me on this."

Midnight gazed in his friend's face, and a small smile appeared. "Course, gotta git through the next ten years. Won't be easy knowin' what I know."

"We can go out west together."

Midnight smiled even more at the thought of riding a horse on the open range and going anywhere he wanted to go. He and Cat had always taken turns reading stories about the open west. It was their dream to see it together.

"You know what I think, Cat? I'm gonna wake up in the morning, and find none of this be true. I'll die a slave."

"Trust me. This is true. I'll pinch you to prove it." He moved his lobster hands toward Midnight.

"Get away Cat." He waved Nate off with his hand.

The boys sat looking at the sky for the longest time in quiet— Nate proud as can be of his brave deed and what it brought for Midnight, and Midnight wondering how he could leave his family behind. *How could he enjoy his freedom knowing that they were still slaves? He was sure Cat hadn't thought of that.*

"Cat, you think there'll be slaves in a hundred years?"

"Not likely," Nate responded. Nate wondered what—or how much—he should tell Midnight. Wasn't his news now enough to give him hope for his future?

"What about fifty years?"

"Naw. Maybe twenty," Nate lied.

Midnight did the math. His mama would be an old woman by then. Too old to know what to do; too old to see what's in the free world.

Nate was smart enough and a good enough friend to know why Midnight was asking these questions.

"Cat, I knos I gotta trust God. He will make all things right. For me, and my Mama, and Tiddy, and Jonah, and all of us.

"Like your Mama says, Cat, Jesus has already bought my freedom. Done shed His blood for me. When I be in Heaven, I will be free. Tht's fo' sure. I may be a black boy, but I be free and in the presence o' the Lord."

"And where, where Minuit, is the curse of the Indian Wood? Gone, I'd say, all the way down the Delta and into the Gulf. Probably clear to Africa and Rubideaux's village."

Nate picked up a rock and threw it in the direction of the Wood. "Yup. Gone forever, I'd say."

"If I was Pouty Robert, I'd say you done jinxed it all now, Cat. Shouldn't mock a curse. Ain't lucky."

"There was no curse. Ever. Just hokey-pokey superstition."

"Well what about Rubideaux's book we found there?"

"I bet Richard put it there as a joke."

"How would he know we'd go in there?" Midnight challenged.

"Heck, I don't know, but it sure ain't a dead man's book.

Midnight began shifting his feet. All this talk of curses and Rubideaux made him nervous. He was also anxious to run and shout and tell the world he was on the road to freedom. If his bottom wasn't so sore, he might have done it, too. But, in the end, his reality set in, and brought his mind back to earth and back to the present.

"Let's go, Cat," he said quietly. It'd be supper soon." As they walked back toward the Cimetière, he put an arm around his best friend.

"Cat, I didn't thank ya fo' my freedom. I know it was because you saved Richard an' risked your life. Thanks." He held his hand out to Nate, and they shook and then embraced.

"But, Cat, let's not tell the others 'bout this."

"Why not? Your Mama will be so happy for you."

"No, it'd be better 'tween us. Ten years is a long time. I don't want no one treatin' me diff'rent 'til then. Or think I'm uppity. Jus' be easier fo' me—an' everyone—that way."

"OK. It'll be our secret."

One more among tight friends was not too much to ask. And so they walked back to the Cimetière only to find the horses and dogs had gone. The runaway slave had been taken into Monsieur Eduard's cabin and was being tended to by Jenna and Nancy. Unlike Midnight, the prognosis for this young man was not good.

Back in his room that night Nate sat at his desk and un-capped the ink well. He thought for a moment, touched the dry tip of the pen to his lips, and then dipped it into the black ink.

August 26, 1857

Saw today what I never thought I'd see. My best friend being whipped like a dog. Wasn't right at all. Wish I had had the courage to pass Bullfrog and rush in and free

Midnight. Some day Mallock will get his and he'll know what it's like. Some day he'll know hell, that's for sure.

Nate re-read his words. He knew Jenna would not approve. She would want to try to save Mallock, make him a believer in God and the blood of Jesus. At least he thought that's what she would do. He wasn't entirely sure about the blood of Jesus part but that sounded like what she would say. Monsieur Eduard would say it too, he reckoned.

He was also mad at himself for not doing anything to help Midnight. He could see on Midnight's face how desperate he was; his friend needed him back there and yet Nate had done nothing. He could have run around Bullfrog, or at least screamed out loud so Mallock could hear. That might have stopped it all. But, instead, he did nothing.

Nate stared out the open window into the night air. There was barely a breeze to wipe the sweat from his skin. He ran his hand through his hair, very near his lucky spot. Out there in the pitch dark lay the Cimetière all quiet and sleeping. And in a cabin there lay his best friend, most likely also thinking about what had happened. Nate wondered what Midnight thought of him. Did he wonder why he hadn't done anything at all to help him?

He dipped the pen again.

I'm writing in a borrowed book; living a borrowed life. Not sure at all what I am doing here, or what I should do next. There's no one at all to tell me what to do and I feel totally lost.

Would someone, anyone, please tell me what I am to do. Am I a Cat or a Fox? Is Midnight a Slave or Free?

Frustrated, Nate put the pen down and stood up and stretched. He left the book open so the ink could dry in the night air. Then he blew out the lamp beside the desk and got undressed in the dark. He was tired from all that had happened but wasn't entirely sure he would be able to sleep. Shadows from the curtains wavered on the far wall.

Once in his nightshirt he lay in bed staring up into the ceiling. He tried to answer the big questions of Life but the quiet mumbles of Jenna and Brett talking in the next room kept breaking his concentration. Every now and then, in frustration, he beat his pillow to a puff, and settled back to deep pondering.

Some time past midnight his mind drifted out of the room, along with the questions he had raised, and he found himself floating a knee's whisker above the trees. He could see the brown ribbon of the Mississippi streaked with the moon's quicksilver. He knew around the bend and miles beyond stretched the Crescent City that was his mom's favorite haunt. He knew the thrills it would give her to see it in its 1857 heyday. To see anything in 1857. She was the real history buff, not him. Why wasn't she the one to be led downstairs into the live history drama? It would be heaven on earth for her. Not for him. He just wanted to float out of here and head to the West Coast back to his old miserable self. For a long moment he wondered if he could make it before morning, but then he looked down and saw the cabins of the Cimetière and slowly, effortlessly, he felt his body sink back into bed.

Thursday

August 27, 1857

13 INK & WATER

Richard rode up to The Chattery in his best riding outfit. A bandage was still wrapped around his head. It gave him a gallant look, he thought. He wore the bandage with honor and pride.

His mother had made him stay in bed one day to recuperate, but now he was somewhat free to ride about and get some fresh air. His first thought was to ride over to *The Chattery* to thank Cat properly for saving his life. It was the chivalrous thing to do.

Jenna, in a broad-brimmed garden hat, was out watering her marigolds in the front yard when the boy arrived on horseback.

"Bonjour, Ma'am. Est-il Peter à la maison?

"Oui, il est à l'intérieur. I will get him for you. By the way, how is your head? We are all thankful it was not more serious."

Richard touched the lily-white bandage both for effect and now out of habit.

"I still have a bad headache, but it is much better, thank you."

"Bon. Je vais trouver Peter."

"Mon père said he looked well yesterday."

"Il est énergique en tant que jamais," she said good-naturedly. *Active as ever.*

Richard sat on his large chestnut named Beaumont while Jenna went into the house to retrieve Cat.

"What does he want, Maman?" Nate asked.

"I don't know. He is on his horse. He probably wants to know you are ok. You did save his life. He is grateful, I am sure."

"How does he look?"

"Well, he has a large bandage across his forehead and a blackish eye. Other than that, the same."

Nate put down the pen and walked toward the front door, grabbing his hat as he went by. The squeak of the screen door startled Beaumont, who had been grazing a little too close to Jenna's marigolds.

Richard straightened up when he saw Nate appear on the porch.

"Bonjour," he said.

"Bonjour, Richard. Votre front blesse-t-il?" Cat touched his own forehead as he asked.

"Meilleur." Richard dismounted and tied the reins to the post. "J'ai voulu vous remercier—I wanted to thank you for saving me on the River. I know it was a stupid thing for me to do. I am sorry I put you through it. You could have been hurt as well."

He held his hand out to Nate.

Nate shifted his weight from foot to foot. Richard was getting too mushy for his taste. "That's Ok," he said. "Just glad you're ok." He shook Richard's hand but glanced in the direction of the Overseer's house to avoid looking at Richard directly.

"Say," said Richard now in English. "I'd like to make it all up to you. How about a ride around Vieux Saules? Nice and slow-like. You can pick your own horse. No pranks, I promise."

"Ah, um, that's not necessary, Richard. Your father has already been quite generous." Nate turned to face Richard direct. "You know, he gave me Midnight."

"I know." He looked directly at Nate. "It was my idea."

"Your idea?"

"Yes."

Nate tried to quickly process this new information. Why would a rich, snotty kid who seemed to enjoy taunting him give up the one carrot-and-stick in his arsenal? It didn't make sense.

"Why?" asked Nate. "You told me your father was giving Midnight to you when you were old enough to have your own plantation."

"He was, but I changed his mind. C'mon, ride with me and I'll explain why I did it."

That was just the tease Nate needed to go along with Richard, and the planter's son knew it. He was starting to learn from his father.

Richard put his foot back in the stirrup and swung his other leg over the saddle. He reached his arm out for Nate to get on the saddle behind him.

"We can ride over to the stables and get you your horse."

Nate stayed put for a second then gave Richard his hand. In the next instant, the two white boys, a rich and a poor, were headed toward the Main House and the dozen or so outbuildings that surrounded the estate's crown jewel.

The stable was a long rectangular building with an elevated foundation of stone and packed earth behind. The elevation protected the valuable horses from floods that occurred from time to time. Like the other buildings at Vieux Saules, the stable was well built and well maintained.

Inside, the forty stalls were kept clean by a dozen slaves charged with keeping, feeding, and grooming the thoroughbreds and draft horses.

Not much of a rider—and Nate not entirely comfortable on large beasts—he picked a horse that looked tame enough to ride on but not so feeble that he'd be stuck walking ten miles back to the stables with the saddle slung over his shoulder. His name was Whisper.

Richard seemed to know where he wanted to go so Nate followed about a quarter furlong behind. Seeing the plantation atop a large horse was an insight for Nate. Things looked 'different;' the slaves seemed smaller.

After a run down the Northern Loop past the Cimetière and the haunted Indian Wood, Richard stopped Beaumont on a small bluff overlooking the River and a huge cotton field. It was a large field of white cotton and black slaves. The field seemed to be itself moving as the eighty or so slaves inside it worked diligently in the morning sun to pick the plants clean of cotton.

Men on horseback with whips and guns ensured that the diligence continued. One of the men, Mallock's lieutenant, noted the planter's son on the distant bluff and nodded. He then rode off to the other white men. Within a short time, the movement in the field subtly, but noticeably, picked up the pace. That was the kind of power and influence resident in the Master and his family.

"Peter, tell me, what do you see down there?"

"Well, it's too far away to pick out faces. I know Midnight's down there somewhere."

"So what do you see?" he pressed.

"People working."

"No, not people. *Things.* Legally, they are things, Peter. Pieces of property. From here, they are just dots of ink on a green field. They are just ink dots on my father's ledger. You saw his ledgers, right?"

Nate nodded.

"Page after page of property and profit. But at the end, Peter, that's all they are. Property. Here to make Vieux Saules the greatest plantation there is."

Nate was starting to get angry inside. He remembered Midnight's cruel whipping. "Is that why you brought me here? To tell me they are worth nothing to you or your father?"

"I didn't say that. They are worth a great deal. You know, my father gave up something substantial to give you Midnight."

"That's it? Black ink in your ledgers? Nothing more?" Nate looked back at the field of busy, and undoubtedly tired, workers.

Nate continued. "Whatever gave you even the inkling of thought that they—" he pointed to the field—"are not people? Does a 'thing' cry or sing? Can a 'thing' play a fiddle or dance? Can a 'thing' have babies? Can a 'thing' care what happens to someone else?" He looked straight into Richard's eyes. "Can a 'thing' believe in God?"

Richard put his hands halfway up. "Calm down, Peter. I didn't mean to get you so stirred up." The planter's son tried to laugh it all off. "You listen to your parents too much. Your mother is a kind woman, kindly to all, but she thinks too much like a Northerner."

"She's from Quebec."

"Not that far north."

Nate remembered what the docent said in Richard's room, that the rich boy would die in Vicksburg in 1863. In just five years. He remembered from history class that Vicksburg fell to the Union in 1863. Most likely, Richard would get caught up in that.

It was hard to look at the youthful aristocrat and not feel sad for him. Not only did he not realize how far off he was morally, but he had no idea that he would be dead at twenty, and that his beloved Vieux Saules, in which he put so much of his faith, would be past its heyday in just a few short years.

"Richard," he thought carefully what to say next, "what if slavery gets abolished in the next couple of years?"

Richard let out a hearty laugh. "Now I know you listen to your Mama too much. Slavery is our life. It is not going any-where. The North would have to come down here and burn every plantation there is, and then fight us on our home ground. That will never happen."

"I think you listen too much to your father."

"Why should I not? He is a great man, and a leader in Lou-isiana. He knows what he is talking about."

"Maybe in most things, but not this one."

"We should get back." Richard started to turn his horse around."

"Richard—"

"What?" He seemed annoyed now to be around Cat.

"Maybe I shouldn't say this, but if there is ever a war or something between the North and South, stay at Vieux Saules."

Richard gave him a puzzled look.

"I mean, don't go to Vicksburg, ok?"

"What are you talking about? Why would I go to Vicks-burg?"

"I don't know, but, um, Pouty Robert told me yesterday that you, um, should stay away from Vicksburg at all cost."

"Now, you are listening to Pouty Robert? Do not tell your mother; I don't think she would approve of you and the voodoo boy being together."

"Laugh, but when things get rough around here and someone tells you to go to Vicksburg, remember this day, and don't go."

Richard continued to smirk.

"Don't go, OK?" Nate implored.

"I think maybe you hit your own head out there on the River; you are crazier than Pouty Robert. At least he has the Louisiana sun to blame. H-yah." Richard kneed his horse and off he went. "See ya back at the stables, Omniscient Peter!" He pushed the horse at fullspeed.

Nate could feel himself getting angry inside. He wasn't sure, though, if he was mad at Richard or himself. '*You try to do someone a favor,*' he could hear Cat say, but Nate answered, '*Not just a favor but his life! And the way he talked about Midnight and the other slaves.*' Now Cat and Nate were both fuming inside, and ready to get even with the bloody rich boy.

Nate leaned into Whisper's ear. "Come on, ol' boy, let's show him what you can do." He prodded the grey horse and they were soon in hot pursuit.

Occasionally, Richard looked back at Nate, but they were so far behind, he knew he needn't worry. But Nate kept pushing Whisper, and it was only the growing sound of his hooves that prompted Richard to look back and see Nate within a half furlong. The surprised boy quickly turned back to the road, leaned forward, and urged Beaumont onward.

It was a neck-and-neck race, and both boys and horses were giving it their all. Nate had long since lost his hat, and Richard was in danger of losing his bandage, which was now no longer lily-white.

Several slaves along the path leading to the stable stopped to watch the race between rich and poor. Naturally, inside, they rooted for their friend, Cat, but they knew it best to stand and watch with little emotion.

As they approached the Duck Pond behind the stable, Richard blew a whistle with his fingers, and Whisper immediately stopped and bucked Nate from his saddle. The ejection sent Nate flying about ten feet in front of the grey horse. Fortunately, Richard had timed it to send him straight into the pond.

When he surfaced, Richard was busting his stitches. He trotted Beaumont back to the edge of the Pond. "You should have seen your face as you flew. I will be remembering that one for a long time." He was laughing hysterically. "The look as you knew you were going into the water was, um, cat-like." Richard dismounted Beaumont and handed the reins to a waiting hand.

"I better visit the Necessary before I soak my pants." Poor Richard's face was bright red. Nate and the slaves could hear his laughing as he headed down the road on foot.

"You all right, Cat?" Toby and Micah came to his defense and offered their hands. But Nate was too stubborn and mad at himself.

"I'm fine, Toby." He spit algae out of his mouth. His jaw and eyes were set tight. "You try and help someone, and he just pushes you down. Well, I ain't tryin' anymore. That sorry boy's on his own now."

His pride deflated, the soaked Nate walked back to *The Chattery* and a fresh set of clothes.

As he walked into the front room, the screen door smacked him on his wet bottom. A nice cap to his day so far. He walked to his room.

"Is that you, Brett?"

"No, Mama, it's me."

She met him in the hallway. "How was your—oh, Cat—what happened?"

"Richard. That's what happened. He fooled me into picking a tame horse, but he had it all rigged." He looked at his mom. "It's not funny."

Jenna hid her smile behind her hand. "Of course not. It is a hot day, though."

"When I go swimmin', I like to know that first." He went into his room and slammed the door.

After changing, he climbed out his window and headed to the Cimetière to see Midnight and commiserate. At least, he knew Midnight would be on his side.

But when he got to the Cimetière, he realized Midnight was not yet back from the field. So he wandered over to Monsieur Eduard to see if the runaway slave was better.

"Bon jour Monsieur. How is the runaway?"

"He has a name, Cat."

"What is it?"

"Come in. I'll let him tell you." Eduard had an interesting look on his face.

Monsieur Eduard led Nate into the sparse room. On the far side on a mat lay a young man, perhaps twenty, on his stomach. His back was covered with herbs and medicines. It was obvious that the whipping had been severe.

"Is he awake?"

"Oui." There was clearly pain in his voice.

Nate walked over and knelt beside the man.

"Je m'appelle Peter. My friends call me Cat."

The educated man leaned to his side so that he might shake Nate's hand, but he was in too much pain. He fell back on his chest.

"Je m'appelle —aah." The pain seemed present even when he breathed. "—Rubideaux. Je m'appelle Rubideaux."

Nate's hair seemed to stand up like the days when Nate would spike his hair for school.

"What did you say?"

"Rubideaux," the man repeated. His voice seemed hoarse.

"D'où êtes-vous? Nate asked in earnest.

"Une plantation près de la Nouvelle-Orléans."

Nate leaned close to Rubideaux and whispered "Were you in the Wood to the North by the River?"

Rubideaux nodded his head slightly. "Je vous ai vu là." he said. "You were with two black children. A boy and a girl."

"We looked for you, but never saw you."

Rubideaux laughed, but it hurt too much. "I was in a tree above you. I hid well."

"How did they find you? It is forbidden to go there."

"When I was running from you, I dropped my book. I went looking for it into the meadow outside the Wood. I thought I was careful, but a white man saw me."

"You risked your life for a book? I don't understand."

"Not for the book, but the drawings inside it. My wife drew them for me before she was sold and taken away. It is all I have left of her. My only memory."

Nate had never seen a grown man cry before. He wondered how pictures could be worth the risk to body and life. Nate knew his own father would never have devoted himself to his mother; he instead left them when life together became too hard. As far as Nate knew, in all the years, his father had never asked to see Nate or to even wonder how he was getting along.

He could imagine Jenna and Brett doing such a thing for each other, and for him. He loved his mom back home because she was his mom, but he loved Jenna because of how she carried herself and cared for him and others, especially those in bondage. It was easy to support minority rights in the twenty-first century; few did so in 1857, when the stakes were real and high. Jenna, though, was one person who did. And he admired her tremendously for that.

Nate didn't tell Rubideaux that he had found his book and that he was the one who carried it out of the Wood and lost it. Guilt flowed through his mind as he realized that had he left the book at the base of the tree, Rubideaux would still be free and well in the forest green. One careless step and he had changed another person's fate.

Nate walked home very much depressed. The distance between the Cimetière and *The Chattery* had never seemed so great. He was anxious to get home and crawl into bed even though the sun was still high in the sky. He felt like a walking fool and hated it.

14   PIGMENTUM INDICUM

The Paint House. Yesterday.

"Master LeBeaux, sir. Observe. When I add pigmentum indicum to the base," Brett poured in some pigment "and stir…" *He pulled out the wooden paddle and let the deep violet paint ooze and drip. "Is it not still paint, though a lovelier shade perhaps?*

"And does it not cover the wood all the same." He flipped the paddle toward the side of the whitewashed paint house. He then looked at LeBeaux directly. "And if the paint gets in the eyes, does it not blind the same?"

LeBeaux stared at the blue-speckled wall and walked away without a word.

This morning, Brett received his instructions, and by 8:30 was dangling in a wooden chair thirty feet above ground painting the eaves of the sugar mill a bright indigo glow. Quite a payback for a man not quite comfortable with heights.

Brett looked down from the high-flying trapeze. His view of the earth kept moving side to side, making him all the more dizzy and queasy. With his free hand he tried to grab the frieze of the eave to stop the swing from rocking side to side. He nervously edged further out of the swing to get a better hold.

Close but not quite. Just an inch or so more. He could hear his arm stretch and pull from the socket.

"I got it! Whoa, oh, oh-no, whoa!" His hand had held the wood for a short second, but when it separated it sent the swing quickly to the other end of the pendulum like a carnival ride. He was now going side to side and in circles, braiding the ropes together like a little girl's pigtails.

"How's it going up there?" came a lovely voice from below. It was Jenna.

"Fine. No problems." Brett was a true man. He wasn't going to admit he was having a spot of trouble.

"I can see that." She paused. "It's an interesting color. Your choice?"

"Sort of. I tried to make a point yesterday with Master LeBeaux. I think he's trying to teach me something back."

"So what have you learned?"

"I do better with my feet on the ground. This stuff here's for the bloody birds."

Jenna laughed. "Yes, your Irish is coming out; you're looking a little green."

"With a mix of violet here and there." From his vantage point Brett could see that neither LeBeaux nor Mallock were anywhere nearby so he lowered the swing down to Jenna.

"I could use a break." He looked up at his work. "Bloody, look at that. The man's daft. You'll be able to spot the mill all the way from New Orleans."

"I brought you some cold water."

"Why thank you, Mrs. Hennessee."

"You are most welcome, Mr. Hennessee." Sometimes, to Cat, his parents acted like downright newlyweds even though they were in their eighth year of marriage.

Jenna laughed. "You've given yourself a mustache."

Brett grabbed a rag from his back pocket and wiped the blue beard away.

"I'm a bloody mess, in more ways than I could count."

"What do you mean?" she asked.

"It's useless. How can we beat him?"

"Who? Master LeBeaux?"

"Exactly. How? We're stuck here, and I can't figure out what to do. We're as much slaves here as the others.

"No matter how badly I want to leave, I—we—can't. Not as long as Tiddy is left behind. My God, Jenna, it kills me daily to see my daughter a slave. Can you know how that feels?"

"No...and yes. I have become very close to Tiddy from the time of her birth all ze way up to her re-birth last Sunday. To all of them, really. I don't want any to be slaves here—or anywhere. Each one pains me, and it takes a bit of the life out of me. With Tiddy, we are faced with something that seems truly beyond reach. But is she?"

"Of course she is. For fourteen hellish years I have lived with the thought that my daughter would be in bondage forever, and my grandkids as well. It is like a knife slowly draining the bloody life out of me.

"I was a seventeen-year-old kid off the boat," he continued. "What did I know of life in America? What did I know of slavery? I fell in love, or maybe it was just youthful lust, I don't know."

"It was love; you know it was. You loved Martha; she was a beautiful and wonderful woman. She would have been so proud of Tiddy, especially her baptism. And she would have been proud of the way you have stayed near her to watch over her the best you can."

"You are such an optimist, you know. You see the lovely light in all things, the good and the evil."

"Why shouldn't I? God is good. All the time. When Martha died giving birth, God found a place for her in the Cimetière. He found a home for you so you could watch over her; He brought me a wonderful husband, and Cat an honorable father."

Jenna put her arms around Brett and gave him a long kiss. He returned the embrace, leaving fresh imprints of his arms on the back of her dress.

She opened her eyes and saw her son at the corner of the mill. "Cat!"

Brett immediately turned around. He wanted to ask Cat how much he had heard, but it was obvious from his face that it was more than Brett would have chosen.

Still holding hands, Brett and Jenna walked toward their son who seemed frozen in his tracks.

"You left a note that you were here," he said at last.

"I wish I hadn't." she replied.

"Why? So you could keep this from me?"

"Cat, this is a difficult subject for your mother and me."

"Not much of a joy for Tiddy either," Nate said sharply. "Does Tiddy even know?"

"No." Brett answered softly.

"Why not? She lost her mother. Shouldn't she know her father lives a stone's throw away?"

"It's not that easy. How could she live a life as a slave knowing she is half-white? She wouldn't understand why her white father couldn't just pick his little girl up and carry her home."

Nate's images of his own father abandoning him surfaced quickly and exploded with force.

"Maybe I don't understand that either. Why *didn't* you just pick her up and carry her home?"

"It's not that easy, and you bloody well know that. You have lived on this plantation all your life. Does anyone just walk in and carry one of LeBeaux's slaves away?

"Tiddy's not just a slave; she's your daughter. Maybe you can sit by and paint things purple til you're blue in the face, but not me."

"Cat, you must calm down. You are very upset right now, and when you get this way, you are too impulsive. Your father is right to be careful. Master LeBeaux and Mr. Mallock are powerful men. You saw what they did to Monsieur Rubideaux."

"Does Master LeBeaux know Tiddy is your daughter?"

"Yes," they both answered.

Nate's eyes welled with tears. "I saved his son's life. Why—why, didn't he give me her in return? If he knows she is your daughter, why keep her a slave? What kind of man is he?" Nate was getting to the heart of the matter.

"Is that why we stay here?" he asked. "Why we never went back to Quebec? To your real home?"

"Cat, God has plans for each of us. I pray daily for guidance to know what I should do each day. Your father does the same. When you are older, you will see that zings are not always just black and white. Life is very complicated at times."

"Or maybe we're just taking the easy way and pinning it on God."

"Do you think this has been easy on me?" his father asked him. "Do you? Your best friend is a slave and that has bound you in knots since you were old enough to understand. Well, magnify that by a thousand and you might come halfway to how I feel. Half-way!" Brett mimed with his fingers.

"Well, God's plan or not, I'll not sit around and do nothing. If Tiddy is family, then, with God's help or without, I'm taking her to freedom."

Jenna grabbed Cat's arm firmly. "No. You will do nothing. And you will say nothing. This is a matter for your father and me to handle."

"Then handle it!"

Jenna slapped Cat soundly on his cheek. "I won't allow you to talk to your father and me this way. And you most certainly will not talk about God that way. You act like God is unaware or uncaring about this. You know God, that is, you recognize who He is, but you—we—cannot hope to know everything about Him or about His plans. Patience is truly a virtue."

The sting of Jenna's hands and words hit Nate hard. The stable world Nate thought he had fallen into was more confusing than his old one. He felt just as helpless now as he did back in Whittier.

"I have to go." Nate turned away.

"Cat, please, just go home." Jenna pleaded. "We'll be there shortly. Promise me, all right?"

The confused boy nodded.

She leaned over and kissed his reddened cheek. "I love you son," she whispered.

As he walked back home, his mind was packed with memories and emotions of two worlds in two centuries. He had naively mistaken the rural life this week for a calmer, more logical world, at least for Cat. He, of course, knew that slavery was a harsh and cruel thing, and that it was always just under the surface waiting to explode, but it never occurred to him that it would blow up in the middle of his own family. After all, the three of them felt the same way about it all.

But Nate realized that he, and Cat, had been living in the world only half-aware of reality. There were most likely clues all along the years that Cat never saw, or somehow chose not to see, that would have told him that Brett was Tiddy's father. It wouldn't be possible for a father like Brett to be able to hide them from him all these years. Nate gave himself a brain freeze trying to reach way back into Cat's memory for the answer to that question, but he was already passing the Paint House without uncovering a single shred of light on the matter.

He noticed that the door to the Paint House was open, which was odd. Brett treated his shop, and the paints inside, as if it were a colorful version of Fort Knox. Nate decided to walk over and check it out.

As he approached, he called out. "Ho! Anyone in there? It's me, Cat."

But as he peeked around the open door, he saw that it was empty. Perhaps, in a rare lapse of protocol, Brett had forgotten to shut it tight. He was, after all, under a huge amount of pressure. Events from the Rabbit Hole had ripped open a fissure, pushing years of angst over Tiddy's situation straight to the surface.

'*Events from the Rabbit Hole...*' Nate marveled somewhat at how the whole chain of events was playing out. He had absent-mindedly opened a door in the Main House that he shouldn't have, which led him literally back into the past...which led him to the Indian Wood to find a book, which led a runaway slave out of his sanctuary to most likely early death...and on the very same day allowed him to save a boy's life. He knew it was unlikely that the real Cat would have been able to do that without knowing CPR...which led to his winning Midnight's freedom, which unlocked a secret about Cat's father and Tiddy Beaux...which brought him now to the place where he was just as conflicted as he was back in his own home. All the security and contentment and sense of true belonging he had found these past few days in Cat's circle of family and friends were quickly disappearing. A strong hand, perhaps God's, was shaking the snow globe that had brought the Cat and the Fox together.

"Why put me here just to tear me up!" Nate grabbed a brush from the workbench and started to throw it hard against the wall. It was then he noticed the spackle of violet across the once pure white wall. He caught himself.

'Now, that's odd,' he thought. 'Why would someone do that? Back home, it wouldn't have surprised him. Kids—hooligans, his 'with it' mom called them—tagged anything, even trees. But here at Vieux Saules, not even a scrap of litter was left on the ground.' Something about it was not right, but Nate couldn't put his finger on why.

On the far end of the room he saw his little version of The Chattery. He had finished the butterfly house for Tiddy and was waiting for the last paint to dry.

A wave of emotion overcame Nate. All at once he felt like an idiot. He had taken such pride in building the house for her, as if it alone would bring Tiddy complete happiness. He had walked home with such a puffed chest after he had finished it. Even the artistic Brett would marvel at Nate's fine detail, he was sure.

Nate picked up the house and observed it, much as Tiddy would do with a fine butterfly that had landed on her hand while she was in the Meadow. The boy moved his hand and strained his neck so that he could inspect all four sides, and under the eaves, and through the windows.

It was beautiful. The more beautiful he realized it was, the angrier he became. "I'm a bloody fool!" he yelled to no one but himself. He stared at the house, and then the indigo-splattered wall, and again at the house. He could feel his arm getting hot and in a pitch of fury, he threw the magnificent house at full force against the colorful wall. The house broke apart instantly, sending bits of pieces in every direction.

"Hey, what's all the commotion in here?" Brett's head appeared from around the door. He saw the shreds of the destroyed house.

"Catrick, what—what happened? —Why did you—"

"It was stupid, don't you think?"

"Yes, for sure it was. You spent a lot of time building it."

"No, not throwing it! Building it. It was stupid. Tiddy doesn't need a home for her butterflies. She needs a home for herself!"

"She has a home, and an aunt who loves her. Aunt Tilliman has been very good to her."

"But she should be in your house. She deserves to be with us." He pounded his fist on the bench.

Brett noticed then Nate's tight grip on a bit of shattered roofline. His fist was whiter than normal. Brett walked toward Nate, putting his own hand over Nate's.

"Let it go, son."

Nate stared into Brett's eyes.

"It's not fair. Why couldn't I—Tiddy—have you as a father?"

Brett coaxed the wood from Nate's hand, and opened his palm.

"Ah, Catrick, look now. You've cut yourself." He pulled the deep splinters from Nate's hand and pressed his own against Nate's to stop the bleeding. "It'll work out. You'll see. God does have a plan."

Brett put his hand under Nate's chin and lifted the boy's eyes to his own. "Don't be angry with God. If you have anger, put it to me. I am Tiddy's father, and I have chosen—or followed—this path. God lets us make choices; you know that. And we can look back and wish we had taken another route, but we cannot—we should not—ever blame God for the things we choose."

"I wish I could—" Nate's voice trailed off.

"Could what?"

"Doesn't matter." Nate looked at the small amount of blood on his hand. "It's fine now. I'll go wash for supper." He started to leave the room.

"Cat?"

Nate turned around.

"The path that gave me Tiddy also gave me you. I met with Master LeBeaux the day Tiddy was born, and I offered to buy her. If he had given her to me, I would never have met your mother, and never known you as a son, my only son."

He held his arms out, and Nate ran right into them. "Ah, Catrick, all things work together for good, for those who love the Lord. You must remember that. Always."

Nate buried himself in the grand chest of the man. It was a wonderful feeling to be loved by a father. It was a feeling he never wanted to end, even if it meant never leaving Vieux Saules.

15   RUBIDEAUX'S REQUEST

Nate walked alone along the Sugar Mill Lane feeling sick inside. He felt guilty about not helping Midnight get away from Mallock, and he was sure it was his fault that Rubideaux had left the Wood and been captured. If only he had stayed with the rest of the tour group and not gone down those stairs. Maybe Rubideaux would have made it North after all, and Cat—the self-assured Cat—would surely have raced into the shack and saved his friend.

In the humidity Nate's shirt was plastered annoyingly to his back. It was just after supper, and he knew the mosquitoes would be out in force before long. He was already starting to scratch just thinking about it. He was in a glum mood, and he knew it, and he also knew that everything in the next few hours was going to bug the heck out of him.

In his mind he kept replaying the scenes back at the sugar mill and the Paint House. The side of his face still stung, but what stung more was the big secret his Mama and Brett had kept from Cat all these years.

Cat had a sister in Tiddy, and he didn't even know it. As bad as slavery was—as evil as the Devil—the idea of having a relative as a slave somehow made it all the more terrible. Yet, that didn't make sense to him; Tiddy-Beaux was still the same person today as yesterday. So how could her enslavement today be worse than it was yesterday? Or last year, or the year before?

Nate felt terribly guilty for thinking that way. He knew his feelings were probably natural, but he felt like the biggest hypocrite in the Deep South just then.

Halfway to the Cimetière, he decided to go back to the north field where he knew Midnight would still be working. He cut across every field he could to get to the far northern part of the plantation near the Indian Wood. At first he walked quickly but the closer he got to the slaves working in the fields, the faster his pace until finally he was running. He tripped in the furrows and ditches a couple of times but, though muddied and scraped, he kept getting up and running toward Midnight. There was so much going on in his head, a reflection of his life. He just had to talk to Midnight.

When he reached the bluff where he and Richard had sat on horseback earlier in the day, he saw the group of slaves still toiling away. Instinct told him not to run into a field guarded by men with guns. Instead, he sauntered slowly to the edge of the field so the white guards could see who he was. He grabbed an empty sack, entered the field, looked around, and meandered his way toward Midnight.

"Cat, whatcha doin' out here, ya fool." said a surprised Midnight. "It's too dang hot; you oughtta git your lilly-white backside back home."

Nate ignored him and started picking cotton.

"I talked to Rubideaux today," he said at last.

"You did?" There was some excitement in Midnight's voice.

"Uh-huh." Nate stopped picking and looked at his friend. "He looks bad, Midnight. Monsieur Eduard doesn't think he'll live." His voice trailed off sadly. This was new territory for Nate.

"Ah, he be fine. He's a young buck; what's a whippin' to him," Midnight lied. He was still hurting from his own the day before.

"They dragged him on horse quite a ways. Mama said it damaged somethin' inside. Mallock won't let her fetch a doctor."

"You surprised? Massah ain't gonna spend good money on no runaway."

"I think he's just tired, and knows he ain't ever gonna see his wife no more. Monsieur Eduard says she was carrying his baby."

"It ain't right, is it Cat?"

"No, it ain't." Nate stopped picking cotton and looked at Midnight. "But there's more."

Midnight, more used to the watchful eye of the guards, kept working, but at a slower pace. "What more could there be?"

"It's my fault he got caught."

"Yours? How can that be?"

"Remember the book inside the Wood? I picked it up and took it with me. Rubideaux went lookin' for it and stumbled outside the Wood."

Midnight's eyes got bigger as if he had just remembered a forgotten secret. "Ah, you see, there it is! The Curse. I told you it was cursed." Midnight whispered fiercely at Cat under his breath. "You said there's no such thing; said it brought good luck—an' my freedom. But what about him, Cat? He was free in the Wood; shoulda never come out. Man could live in there for a lifetime an' never be found. But we went in and opened the curse. We done opened the curse and let it out to kill a man."

Nate said nothing; he knew Midnight was right. Midnight watched his friend pick cotton silently and began to feel bad for lashing out. He knew there wasn't another white boy in Louisiana who'd pick cotton in a slave's field.

He put his hand on Nate's shoulder. "I'm sorry, Cat. Wasn't your fault."

"No. It was my fault. I gotta go tell Rubideaux. I have to." He threw down his sack of cotton and started to leave.

"What good'll that do, Cat? It'll just make Rubideaux mad an' send another curse."

"I have to tell him; else I won't sleep at night."

Unlike when he went into the field, Nate ran out in a rush, pushing his way past tired and sweaty slaves. He pulled himself up the bluff and dove into the next field. It was tough running in the steep humidity; in fact, by the time he entered the Cimetière, Nate was wheezing as bad as any kid with severe asthma. His intense gasping outside Monsieur Eduard's cabin brought out the elderly pastor.

"Cat, what's da matter? You'se as white as a ghost and breathin' like a man brought from under da water."

Nate was doubled-over, his hands on his knees for support. His chest surged and deflated disproportionate to his size. "I—I-ran—all the way. From—the north field." Spit dripped from his mouth onto the dusty lane.

"Why da hurry? You gonna kill yourself."

"Need to see—Rubideaux." His breathing was still well labored.

"You come to da porch an' sit a spell. Then you see Monsieur Rubideaux."

Monsieur Eduard led Nate up the stairs and into his rocking chair.

"Here's cold water, son. Drink it slow-like."

Nate gasped as he drank, spilling much of it down his already-soaked shirt. "Merci, pastor."

He wiped water from his lips, and closed his eyes. For a moment he was back at Dexter Middle School, sitting in the office on his first day of school. His palms sweaty, and his stomach in knots. Only now, his mothering mom was not sitting next to him, and would not soon be doing all the talking. He would have to muster the courage all on his own and tell Rubideaux what he had done.

He was in many ways glad for the difference. No matter the physical hardship or emotional turvy, he liked being in charge of himself now. He liked running barefoot in the fields, climbing the oaks to where the branches were no rounder than his leg, swimming naked in the creek in the early evening. But, mostly, he liked being part of a group—both a family and a group of friends. Here, at Vieux Saules in this time, he truly belonged and had all the self-confidence he ever needed.

He stood up and went into the cabin. The pastor kept the windows covered so that Rubideaux could rest in darkness. It took a moment for Nate's eyes to adjust. He stood just inside the doorway waiting for the distant body to materialize and become Rubideaux.

"Monsieur, are you awake. Monsieur Rubideaux?"

"I am, Master Hennessee."

"Please call me Cat."

"Come and talk, Cat. Pastor says you have somethin' on your mind you need to lift." Rubideaux's voice was clear, but Nate could hear the pain mixed in with the words. He was breathing as hard as Nate was when he had first arrived. Only Nate had a chance to recover. He knew Rubideaux was not going to be as lucky.

"How are you?" the boy felt obliged to ask.

"Mizz Jenna say I'm most likely bleedin' inside. Not much hope 'less I git to a doctor, and that's not likely."

"Maybe we can find a doctor to come here. I got a twenty dollar gold piece Master LeBeaux gave me."

"Means a lot you'd do that fo' me, but save your money. I be goin' home soon; I can hear the Lord callin' me, Cat. An', as my Mama taught me, when the Lord calls, you best answer."

"What about your wife?"

"I know I'll nevuh see Mary on this side of Heaven. She'll be long gone an' not even my master knows where she is."

"But you went lookin' for her. How did you expect to find her?"

"Prayer. Lots an' lots of prayer. The Lord was leadin' me; He led me to that dark forest. Fo' the short time I was in there, it was a garden of Eden. Saw the Lord's work with my own eyes. Saw the Lord Himself. Walkin' in the cool o' the morning. What a sight He was Cat. An' He knew my name. Imagine that! The Lord knew me by name!"

"So why'd you leave? Not for the book." He hoped desperately to get rid of his guilt.

"Love's a might powersome thing, Mr. Catfish. It leads you to places you never thought were there."

"Rubideaux—I need to tell you somethin'. It's sittin' heavy with me."

"Cat, even in this light, I see it in your face. What is it?"

Suddenly, the words came faster than Nate expected. "I'm the one who took your book out of the Wood. I didn't know you were there in a tree. I shoulda left it there; then you woulda stayed in the Wood. You'd be there now, or maybe up north already. But now—"

Rubideaux laughed weakly. "Is that what's holdin' ya down?" He laughed again.

"You said that's why you left the Wood—to find the book. Then the overseer saw you. And here you are waitin' to die."

"I'm waitin' to die cause the white man can't stan' to see a black man free. But I was runnin' free in the meadow before they roped ol' Rubideaux." His voice lifted and he seemed to be back in the meadow then running as free as his African fore-fathers centuries before. At that moment, everything was possible, including finding his wife and seeing his child enter the world free.

"But, Cat, don't blame yourself cause I went lookin' for the book. Back in the Wood I was truly free, an' I moved where I wanted an' I—Rubideaux—left Eden to get back my book. It ain't your fault; it ain't my fault. It's just what it is. And I know, sure as I layin' here, dat the Lord needs ol' Rubideaux in Heaven. So I'll go, an' happily. This is a mighty tiring place you know."

Nate's face was awash in tears. Rubideaux, despite the pain, lifted his hand and put it on Nate's shoulder.

"All my life, I asked nothin' from a white man but now I have to ask you fo' somethin'."

"What? Anything." Nate leaned in closer to Rubideaux.

I never did fin' the book. I want to see my Mary's face 'fore I die. I want to touch the paper she touched. Maybe you remember where you dropped it."

"I'll do it, Rubideaux. I mean, I'll try. No tellin' if I'll find it." He could see Rubideaux smiling.

"You're a good man, Cat. You best go so I kin rest."

Nate put his hand on Rubideaux's. "I'll come as quick as I can find it. I'll do my best."

"I know you will. God bless you, Cat."

Nate went back to the other side of the cabin where Monsieur Eduard was standing. The two left the dark room and went out to the porch. By now, the sky was beginning to match the color inside the pastor's cabin.

"The man don't have long. Soon he'll be in the promised land, and know for da first time what it feels to be free.

"I feel sorry for him right now. He's all alone. His poor wife doesn't even know he's gonna die."

"He ain't alone. No, suh. God is everywhere but sometime he is stronger in one place than da other. He be mighty strong here now. I feel him powerful here. He's in there with Monsieur Rubideaux. I tell you Cat. He, da Lord himself, is in dat room. You wants da feel sorry for someone, you give it to ol' Massah. He'll need it somethin' powerful when he gets to Heaven's gate. Yes, suh, he'll be gnashin' his teeth when the Gate closes on his sorry soul.

Nate was now anxious to go to the Wood and find the book for Rubideaux, but it was already too dark. He felt like it was right before final exams, waiting impatiently for the sun to come up so he could head off to the library to study. Only this time, it was just one book he needed. Just a simple blue book.

Before going to bed, Nate pulled out Cat's journal and wrote about his fight with his parents, his talk with Brett, working in the field with Midnight, and his talks with Rubideaux and Monsieur Eduard. Nate looked at the words he had written and was surprised by how involved he had become with others on the plantation. Back home, he spent most of the school day buried in books and the afternoons secluded in his room, either on the internet or with his Game Boy. He had never done so much in a single day. And, despite all the sadness around him, he had never felt more alive.

He thought about Tiddy—he was still in shock at the news—and how uncomfortable her cabin was compared to his home. He looked over at his bed and pillow—simple things that he knew she didn't have.

He also thought about how odd it was that her father was allowed to be a father to him, who was not blood, but not to her, who was. He wondered most of all how he would be able to keep this a secret from her. He could no longer look at her and not feel a special bond to her. She was, after all, Cat's sister.

Before he put his pen down and closed the inkwell, he thought of his new best friend, and how hard he worked and how little freedom he had. Midnight and Cat had been born only a month apart but because he had light skin, he was allowed to keep his freedom whereas Midnight's was taken before he could know what it was.

He remembered what Midnight had told him as they stood in the shade yesterday. He was still crying from the whipping the Overseer had given him. It was his first, and a taste of what he could expect for the rest of his life—or at least for the next ten years. All Midnight wanted to do was crawl up in a corner and go to sleep. He couldn't wait for the night to arrive.

Jenna saw the light on under her son's door. "Cat, you need to go to sleep. It is very late already." He glanced outside his window and saw the moon and its stars. Most likely, everyone in the Cimetière was on their way to sleep by now, including Midnight, Tiddy, and the dying Rubideaux.

"All right. I just need to finish in my journal."

"Not too long." She walked away and then he heard her say "Rêves doux." *Sweet dreams.*

Nate dipped his pen and wrote his final thought of this emotional day, remembering what young Richard had said about Midnight and the other slaves being spots of ink in his father's ledger.

And so he wrote:

The Song of Midnight:

The Myst'ry begins.
'Tween the blue moons,
on the rhythm
o' the strings,
I sometimes
fly at night—
While others
want to sleep,
to firs' wash away
the dirt o' the day
then lumber to bed,
close their eyes
to the white world
an' drift away
to nothingness.
Like children,
they still pray
to God
for 'no bad dreams.'
Only slumbering snores,
their demons now
safely tucked away.

Life passes by— Quickly.
In a snore and a sneeze
A third of the day is bye.
Both the free
an' the homeless
wish the night
to quickly pass,
to bring around
the sleeping sun—
its famous heat
and golden light.
But not the slave.
Night is his ration.

While I am
snug in my bed,
for flittering
seconds it seems,
I fly as far
from the Old Willows
as the good Lord
will take me.
& leave behind
the heaviness o' color
an' soar beyond
the mark o' my birth.

He looked back at what he wrote, and there was nothing more
to say.

Friday

August 28, 1857

16 THE FISHIN' HOLE

Nate could not sleep at all. He couldn't get Midnight out of his mind. He kept seeing him there in the shack with the devil Mr. Mallock.

'Il est sûrement le diable.' *He is surely the Devil.* The phrase haunted his mind all day yesterday and now into the night.

He got out of bed and put on his clothes. Tip-toeing across the room, he slowly opened the bedroom door and listened. The house was quiet; unlike his home in Whittier, there were no electric gadgets creating white noise. It was a simple house, one without even a ticking clock adorning its mantel or far corner.

After listening intently for a minute or so, Nate was sure his parents were still asleep in the other room. The dawn was an hour or so away from Vieux Saules. He knew now was the time to leave if he was to go unnoticed. After walking back across the room, Nate stood still one last time and listened. He leaned out of his window and slid into the bushes headfirst.

The boy looked around, particularly in the shadows, for any signs of the overseer or the Master himself. From Cat's Journal Nate knew that the two men sometimes liked to rise early to keep the slaves on edge, and keep them guessing. For Mr. Mallock, especially, half the fun of his job was the power he had to make others' lives simply miserable. For Master LeBeaux it was pure business. Every man, woman, and child on Vieux Saules Plantation was an asset, a working, breathing asset.

If caught, especially in the Cimetière, he would be hard-pressed to give a believable reason for being there before the sun. Either man could come down hard on him; neither understood or appreciated Cat's affinity with the slaves.

The boy could also put Brett at risk of never seeing Tiddy again. His dad had spent the last fourteen years as a frustrated artist just to be able to watch her grow up from a distance. And, if booted off Vieux Saules, Cat would have no chance to see Midnight anymore. They would lose touch forever.

But Nate had to talk to Midnight; he had to tell him about Rubideaux. He had to know what he thought. He also wanted desperately to tell him about Tiddy, but knew he couldn't. *How would Tiddy react if she found out who her father really was? And to know that he had done nothing to get her to freedom?*

Nate kept turning that phrase in his mind: '*he had done nothing to get her to freedom.*' For fourteen years his father lived on the same plantation so he could be near her but, as far as Cat knew, he had done nothing to save her. He had always thought of Brett as a bold Irishman; now, he wasn't so sure. The pedestal he had put him on was sinking in the Louisiana muck. And, that, perhaps made Nate saddest of all. He knew Cat had also looked at his father with large eyes. Such awe and pride. Now, he wasn't so sure.

As Nate walked down a side path, the one less traveled, an owl swooped low toward the ground. A spooked Nate dove into a ditch half-filled with mud and dirty water. His entire front was covered with the smelly ooze. When he freed himself from the muck, he was dark as Midnight.

'*Boueux enfer.*' *Muddy hell.*

He scraped the mud off his hands and continued toward the Cimetière. As he walked, he smelled a strong odor in the air. It followed his tracks.

When he got to Midnight's cabin, Nate poked his head in the unframed window. The room was a heap of blankets and bodies.

"Minuit. C'est moi. Réveilles-toi." He had to whisper over the snores of a tired lot. "Minuit." He said it a little louder.

"Réveillez-vous. Wake up, sleepy head."

Midnight stirred a bit. He was flying on the back of a large bird when he heard his name.

"Midnight." Nate paused. "Midnight!" Nate looked over his shoulder, nervously. It would start to get light in another half hour.

When he turned back to the window, Nate came face to face with a yawning Midnight. Poor Cat. The unexpected appearance gave the boy's heart a jolt and knocked him on his bottom. Midnight laughed loudly; his voice carried across the way by the bats overhead.

Midnight stuck his head further out the window. "What is that awful smell?"

"Me, I'm afraid. I fell in a ditch o' mud."

"Some cat you are." He climbed out the window to join Nate and then quickly took a step back. "Phew!" He took an exaggerated step back. "Why are you here so early?" he asked, holding his nose, which made his French even more nasal.

"I couldn't sleep. I kept thinking about you and that devil of a man."

Midnight brushed him off. "Don't lose your sleep, Cat. It ain't worth it."

"How can you say that? He—"

"—Forget it. I know what he did, but it ain't worth it."

"Midnight. It is."

"No, Cat. This body ain't mine. Never was. Even when I was inside my Mama, it wasn't mine. But this—" he thumped his chest—"my soul, God gave me that. Can't no one take that away, not even the Devil."

"But, Midnight, it still ain't right."

"It ain't right, but that's what it is. A black dot of a boy ain't gonna change that, Cat and you know it."

Nate stared at the ground. When he looked up, his eyes were moist and his jaw was tight.

"Midnight, how ya gonna git through the next ten years? That's a powerful long time."

"I dunno Cat. Some days I ain't sure how I made it this far."

While they were talking, the boys didn't notice the sun rising. They were now surrounded by clear blue light.

"Catfish—Minuit! —is that you standing outside?"

Midnight's Mama came over to the window and looked at the two in a mixture of surprise and suspicion. She knew her boys didn't get up on their own unless something was afoot.

"Oui, Madame." they answered in near unison.

"Come inside, both of ya. It's barely light out."

Midnight's Mama came over to the window and put her hand on Cat's and kissed her son's forehead. She stopped and smelled the air and looked at the now dirtiest boy at Vieux Saules. She smiled.

"Minuit, you bes' take Catfish down to the creek 'fore break-fas'."

Within minutes the two boys were running down the path toward a grove of trees that marked the creek. While all around them was the collective, unspoken groans of a tethered folk. It was a summer morning in Louisiana.

Midnight swung the rope over to Nate, but he stared into the water as if he were in a dream.

"C'mon, Cat." When the rope swung back to Midnight, he pulled it and threw it harder to Nate, startling him so that he nearly lost his balance and fell in the water.

Midnight laughed, softly—almost to himself, but it was a laugh, his first since his encounter with Mallock yesterday in the shack.

"You're a mopey cat. No one likes a mopey cat." When the rope returned, Midnight grabbed it. "You ain't gonna git clean standin' on the dirt. 'Sides, it be eatin' time soon. You be wastin' time." With that, he took a couple steps back and, holding tight to the rope, jumped off the bank. At the right stroke of Midnight he let go. He was at the highest point possible.

Nate watched his new friend who now seemed to be frozen in the air. He could see the bruises and welts, and it reminded him that he had done nothing yesterday to help him. Standing there on the bank over the water he felt totally useless and unfit to be his friend. Just like *That Day* with Ryan. He could feel the redeeming feeling from the River ebbing away. Quickly.

In almost slow motion he saw the splash envelop Midnight and take him under. And then he was gone, and Nate was left alone to watch the water for signs of life.

For any sign, but the water was relatively calm. Nate forgot his own problems for a moment and scanned the creek for his friend. It seemed long enough for him to have shot back up to the surface. 'Maybe he had hit his head.' He could hear his mom Diana talking. 'Maybe she was right.'

Nate bent his knees and tried to peer into the dark water, but the fishin' hole was a large, deep pool. He could feel panic starting to set in. His mind was getting fidgety, and racing to find a trace of Cat, who might know what to do.

For Nate, it was déjà vu, and he was again on the porch looking through glass, not knowing what to do. Again, he was at the edge of the pool at the Y. Only this time, he couldn't see anyone in the water at all.

He cupped his hands. "Mid-night!"

He could feel the sweat pooling all over his body. "Minuit, damn you! Where are you?"

Nate knew what he had to do. He had to save his friend; he just had to this time. He took a deep breath, hoping Cat's love of the water would kick in, held his nose, then bent his knees, and—

—Miraculously he felt himself lift off the bank in a high arc over the water. But he wasn't alone in the jump. Midnight had somehow snuck out of the water and circled around behind Nate.

"Minuit! You son of a—" The words trailed him underwater.

In an instant he shot up out of the water, choking for air, and spitting words out at the same time. All to a now-laughing Midnight.

"I thought you had hit your head, dang you! I thought you had drowned!" He splashed water in Midnight's face. The laughing boy was now choking on water himself.

"Sorry—Cat" Midnight burbled. He continued coughing up more water while still half-laughing. "You was jus' too down on yerself. Like a mopey cat. Can't have that, can we?" He sent a wave back to Nate.

"Dang it. I thought you was dead. What would I have done, then? Huh?" Nate shot a bigger wave back.

"How could I be dead? You did what I knew you'd do. You jumped in."

"You pushed me in." Nate started to swim back to the bank.

"You were in the air already, brother."

"It was a dumb trick."

"Jus' havin' a little fun, Cat. What's wrong with you anyways? You have a long face."

"I'm just mad about yesterday. Mallock had no right. And you—you don't even care."

"Oh, I care, but I know I can't do nothin'. Not now. But in ten years—" a smile started growing across his face—"in ten years, you and I we're goin' out west. I'll be free then, and ol' Mister Mallock can rot away here."

"Midnight. I shoulda gone in the shack yesterday and saved you."

Midnight laughed and shook his head. "No. You did right. Some things you jus' git through. It passes."

"But I was there. I should have saved you."

"I'm already saved, Cat, you know that. Thanks to your Mama, and to God for sendin' her here. And, you've saved me too."

"Yeah, in ten years. That's too long."

"Nah, every day, Cat. You save me every day. Jus' being my friend. That—" he thumped Nate's chest "—that saves me. That's all I need to keep me goin'."

Midnight grabbed Cat's arm and pulled him toward the deeper end of the pool.

"Now I'm gonna baptize you in the name of Midnight." He jumped up, grabbed Cat's shoulders, and pushed the two down under the water. Midnight counted to five, let go, and surfaced.

Nate stayed under, and this time it was Midnight who was left to wonder where the other had gone. With his arms and legs keeping him afloat, Midnight turned in a circle scanning the surface.

"Ok, Cat. Rise and Shine!"

The water seemed to bring the clever Cat out of Nate. He surfaced quietly behind Midnight, took a deep breath, and slid back under.

For Midnight, these moments to play were the only shivers of freedom known to his fourteen-year-old spirit. Just he and Cat at the fishing hole where they generally swam more than they fished. Here, in a pool beneath a canopy of trees, he was owned by no one.

He often imagined he was an African warrior still in his homeland and it was hundreds of years before the first slave ships would arrive. He would fear lions and the other beasts, but not the white man.

"If you are in Africa, Midnight, what am I?" Cat would ask.

"What d' ya mean?"

"You say this is a sacred pool for the African warriors. What am I?"

"You're my brother."

The three words Cat loved to hear.

"You can't stay under the water much longer," Midnight said aloud but in an almost hushed voice. "You are a cat, not a fish. Dang, where are you, Cat?"

Underwater, Nate had eyes of a fish and swam in an arc around Midnight. He reveled that he could now swim. Running out of air, he approached Midnight's back. The water was a little shallower at that spot. He crouched on the bottom and, shooting out of the water, he grabbed his buddy from behind and brought him back under. Then he swam quickly into the deeper middle where he would be safer.

Both heads bobbed in the cool water. And both were now laughing; they were even.

It was starting to get lighter and Midnight would need to get home soon to be ready to go to the field. Midnight knew he'd soon be in the hot sun working for the Master. His jaw tightened and, cursing under his breath, he shot a wave of water in Nate's direction and headed back to the bank. A rare cool breeze brought bumps to his skin.

"Come on, Cat. It's time." Midnight started back to shore. While Nate floated in the cool water, Midnight's feet settled in the thick muddy muck of the creek bed. The water seemed heavier to him than just a moment ago, as if he were now wearing clothes filled with sand. He struggled out of the water.

"Come on, Cat! If you want to eat..." his voice trailed off as he turned away, got dressed quickly, and then started up the path toward the cabins in the far distance.

"Midnight, wait." Nate climbed onto the bank and scrambled to get dressed while he ran after his friend. But his feet kept getting stuck in the legs, knocking him back to the ground. He got up and chased after his friend, shirttails flying, while also hopping like a wounded rabbit. "Midnight, what's the hurry?" he said, catching up to him at last.

"I'm hungry, an' I don't feel like goin' to the fields today. I'd rather be runnin' in the jungle, and swimmin' all day with you."

"Some day, right? We'll do it, some day. Whatever you want, every day."

"The only thing worse than a boy slave is a man slave."

"But—"

"How many dark men do ya see swimmin'? My brother Samuel was almos' a man when Master sold him."

Nate held Midnight at his arms. "That can't happen now; you'll be free in ten years, remember. I have the papers."

"Ten years is a long time, Cat. A mighty long time."

"But that's not what you said back there. It'll go like a snap. You'll wake up and you'll be free. And all of this will be just some bad dream. Like it never happened."

Midnight broke away and continued up the path, with Nate following behind him a bit confused. He turned around again.

"Cat, when you start to be a man, I'll be happy for you. It'll mean somethin' good. Fo' me, it means the end of my African dreams, and the beginnin's of a life harder than I already know. Life my pappy knows."

He turned and left his bewildered friend to linger longer in the shadows of the canopy.

17 RAISING CANE

Nate knew enough not to follow Midnight back to his cabin. Some things were best left to a person to dwell with on their own. He looked at the sun, and knew the morning was getting away. He had to get over to the Indian Wood before Mallock and his men were out with the slaves in the large field.

He cut through the backside of the Cimetière and headed on a small path that he and Midnight sometimes used when they didn't want the grownups to see them going toward the River. He followed the path through a small grove of trees. At the other side, he walked around a small marsh and rejoined the main path that both white and black used to get to the north side of the plantation.

Nate looked to the south and the road was empty as a field on Sunday. '*So far, so good,*' he thought. Up ahead was a sugar cane field and the large meadow that spooned the Wood.

Nate reckoned he had about a half hour to look around in the meadow before the field would be worked. After that, he would have to duck into the Wood and follow nearly its length before he could exit between two cotton fields in the northwest section. It would then be a long, roundabout walk back to the Cimetière.

It would be worth it though if he managed to find Rubideaux's precious book.

The green cane in front of him was several feet over Nate's head. Once he entered the field, he could no longer see the Wood on the other side. He had to navigate from instinct and hope he was heading in the right direction. It was a natural maze and a couple of times he had to stop and think before moving on.

As he parted the cane, groups of rats scurried away. Nate looked down at his bare feet and hoped—no, prayed—he would not step on a tail or two. The last thing he needed was a mad rat taking a bite out of his big toe.

The air in the cane field was stifling. The humidity was high, and the airflow was constrained by the abundance of the tall stalks. In his head, Nate tried to measure how far he had gone, and how much further he had left to go. He knew the clock was ticking.

Up ahead he saw slits of blue; he was getting close to the meadow. '*Thank God,*' he thought. As his left foot left the field, he heard the gospel singing of the slaves coming down the Northern Loop, the stretch of lane that came closest to the River.

Nate pulled his foot back quickly and then peeked his head out. The large group of slaves were on the Loop even with the edge of the field. He pulled his head in and sat down just inside the field, out of view from the guards. He would have to change plans and go straight for the forest.

The ten minutes it took for the group to pass seemed like an hour to Nate. At the end of the parade were the elderly and those less able to work. From Nate's point of view, they looked tired already and the long day had not even begun. He wondered how they would outlast the guards' attention.

When he was sure that the guards would not be turning back to check for stragglers, Nate dashed out of the safety of the cane and into the meadow. He crouched as he ran, which made running awkward—and slow. In the final fifty yards, he straightened up and sprinted into the forbidden Wood.

The Indian Wood seemed darker this time around. Before, when he was with Midnight and Tiddy, he had no fear. They were looking for a runaway who was more afraid than they were. It seemed more of an adventure. They were in a restricted place, which, for fourteen-year-olds, made the venture all the more exciting.

Now Nate was on his own, looking not for a black man but a small blue book. Every step he took, he was on his own. There was no one to ask whether or not he was going the right way. To Nate, each spot of the Wood looked pretty much the same. But was he really on his own? What Nate didn't know, his alter ego Cat did, and vice versa.

Back in Whittier, Nate would have looked around the forest and said all he saw was a bunch of trees. Cat, though, knew the names of each. He could tell a white oak from an overcup oak; a beech from a birch. He knew which plants were poisonous and where the snakes liked to hide. It all seemed instinctual to him.

Nate stopped in his tracks and looked around for a landmark from Tuesday. He thought *'Wow, have I really been back in time almost a week?'* His dream—or nightmare, depending on the moment—seemed to have no end.

"Ow—dang it!" He slapped the back of his neck, but the deer fly got away. Nate looked at his blood-smeared hand. It was a painful bite. He knew he was better off to keep moving if he was to get home unscathed.

Fortunately, humans entered the Wood only about once every generation—this week seemed a rare exception—so the clever Cat was able to find the trail. Three kids running from an ancient ghost cut a wide swath in the forest floor.

He then went further into the Wood to the tree where Rubideaux had 'disappeared' and he had first seen the book. Nate looked around the base of the trunk to make sure he hadn't dropped the book before he had even left. There was no sight of it anywhere.

Nate kept rubbing the bite on his neck. It still smarted. The only thing that would have made Nate feel better was if he had gotten the blasted fly. He tried to keep alert for anything else that coiled, bit, or stung. But this was a wild Wood ignored by man, and the animals within it were bolder because of their ignorance.

The boy watched a small herd of deer graze in a clearing a short ways off. They watched him briefly but soon returned to the young grass. Nate was taken by their raw beauty and so focused on them he didn't hear the grunts and sound of the wild boar rushing through the foliage straight at him!

Nate saw the blur of dark brown as the animal cleared the last bush between him and serious injury. In a rush of adrenalin, he looked above his head and jumped to a branch he could only describe afterwards as a God-send.

The branch was strong enough to hold his hundred and ten-pound frame but thin enough that Nate could get his fingers around and keep a tight grip. As the boar raised his head toward Nate's bare feet, the boy swung his legs up like a struggling gymnast. His soles could feel the rush of air as the high-pitched boar passed by.

Rather than returning to the ground, Nate swung his feet up and pulled his entire body onto the branch. Rubbing the bottoms of his feet, he thought '*A direct hit and a close shave in the first ten minutes. The quicker out of the Wood, the better.*' He sat on the branch for what seemed to him an eternity, straining his neck and ears to see or hear the boar or any of his kin. He knew they generally traveled with others of their kind.

Of course, Nate wondered how long he should sit up there looking like a poor boy who'd been '*tree'd.*' The boy knew time was ticking away; it was times like these that he wished he still had his watch, or his step-dad's cell phone. *Of course, who would he call? Could someone stuck in 1857 with a cell phone actually call someone in the present?* The question intrigued Nate, but the Cat inside knew he had to suck up the courage and get back to the ground. Rubideaux did not have much time.

In a thud, his bare feet were back on firm soil and he began following the trail out of the Wood, looking closely for any sign of the blue book. By the time he reached the edge of the Wood, his eyes were tired and watery. The only blue he saw was in the sky.

Nate sat down in the fringe of the meadow depressed. '*What would he tell Rubideaux? The poor man was going to die without ever seeing his wife one last time.*' And Nate knew it would be all his fault. Sometimes his curiosity got the best of him and, this time, it hurt someone else. Despite what Rubideaux told him yesterday, Nate knew it was his fault that the man had walked out of the Wood and gotten captured.

Secretly, Nate had hoped that he would find the book inside the Wood, rather than the meadow. Then, at least, he could ease his guilt a bit knowing that Rubideaux didn't have to leave the

Wood itself to retrieve his book. Small comfort, he knew, but at this point, any bit of comfort would have been a help to Nate.

He threw his hat down and stomped on it.

"Aaargh!"

He leaned back against the meadow floor and stared at the cloudless sky. '*Where could it be? Nobody, nobody, goes into the Wood and unless that bloody boar ate it, it has to be there. Or here.*' Nate sat up and surveyed the wide meadow. Unfortunately, unlike the protected Wood, the meadow was open to the rain and wind. Their trail from last Tuesday had long since been erased.

If it was in the meadow, it could be anywhere. The grass and flower stalks were half his height. The book could have fallen between the grasses anywhere. It was hopeless, he knew. There was no point checking the meadow and he had had enough of the wild boar and the deer flies. There was nothing to do but go back home. He was kicking himself inside for his recklessness the other day.

As Nate reached the dirt road, he saw a rider approach. He strained to see ahead in the sunlight. It was Richard. '*Oh, great.*' Nate moaned.

"Bon jour, Peter." Richard, to the contrary, seemed excited to see him.

"Morning, Richard."

"You look beat up."

"I'm all right."

"Did you dry off from the other day?" he started to snicker, remembering Cat's flight off his horse and into the pond.

"I'd have beat ya, if you hadn't pulled that stunt. And you know it!" Nate shot back.

"Easy to say when one is barefoot and horseless."

"You set the race and I'll be there. Only no funny stuff."

"Sunday night?"

"You're gonna lose." Nate was feeling particularly brave. Cat was rubbing off on him.

"All right, then. Sunday."

Richard started to turn ride away and stopped.

"What are you doing out here anyway?" he asked. "Do not say you are picking cotton with the slaves?" That always seemed to annoy Richard. He could never understand why a white boy would work side by side with the Negroes in the hot sun. Especially when he could be fishing with him instead.

"Just explorin', that's all."

"In the Wood?" Richard looked beyond Cat to the tall trees that marked the edge of the Wood.

Nate blew a grunt. "That'd be foolish, wouldn't it? It's haunted and all."

Richard wiped the sweat from his forehead. "It is much too hot to be sitting out here. Do you want a ride back to your house?" Richard extended his arm.

Nate thought about it, and about the sweat pouring down his back. *'Why not,'* he thought. *'I could use some of Mama's cider right now.'*

"Sure."

As Nate strode toward Beaumont, he noticed a blue book in Richard's other hand. His heart quickened considerably. *'Maybe that's it! What luck! Thank you, God.'*

"Where d'ya find that!" he said excitedly, too much so.

"What, this?" Richard said, holding up the book. The look on Nate's face told him he was holding something he wanted. "Were you out here looking for this?"

"For that? Naw, I don't even know what it is."

Richard flipped through the pages quickly. "Just a bunch of high-minded poetry." Richard started to hand him the book but as Nate reached up for it, Richard yanked it back.

"C'mon, Richard, let me see it."

"You want to see it?" He leaned from his saddle until the book was just a few inches from Nate's face. Nate moved his hand up just as Richard sat back in his saddle.

"See it? Watch it fly."

With a quick flick of his wrist, Richard threw the book up in the air toward the cane field. Nate's eyes widened as he watched the blue speck sail into the sugar forest. His eyes locked on the target and fixed its exact point of entry into the cane field.

Richard stared at Nate's face.

"What is wrong with you, Peter? You look like you were watching a ghost fly. Peter?" The planter's son lifted his foot out of the stirrup and pushed his foot against Nate's shoulder.

"What?"

"I said 'You look like you were watching a ghost fly. Come on, I will take you home and get you out of this sun." He reached out his hand for Nate to grab.

"Uh, I just remembered—I'm—" Nate's eyes were fixed on the spot where the book had disappeared into the cane field.

"What?" Richard leaned in closer.

"Um, I'm supposed to help Brett. I should go." Nate pointed in the opposite direction. His pulse was rising quickly.

"Then I will take you there. Come along. It is better than walking on the hot dusty road."

"That's all right. He's not far."

"I thought he was painting an outhouse near the sugar mill?" Richard grinned. He liked pointing out to Cat every time his father was assigned to paint a disgusting outhouse. 'It's necessary to paint the Necessary,' he would say, mimicking his father's own mocking words to Cat's dad. It reminded Cat where he stood in the pecking order at Vieux Saules: a half-inch above the nigras, in Master LeBeaux's view, though Cat had risen considerably since last Tuesday's heroism on the Mississippi.

"Sugar mill? No, he's um—"

Richard was getting impatient with Nate. "The sun has baked your brain, Peter. Go ahead and walk, if that is what you want." He prodded Beaumont and was down the road in a flash, the rising dust clouds swirling back toward a very relieved Nate.

He waited for Richard to disappear around the bend, and then a little longer to make sure he wasn't circling back. When he thought it safe, Nate ducked into the tall cane and headed straight for the spot he had memorized in his baked brain. He hoped that he would not soon find himself on another wild goose chase.

Like north and south poles of two magnets, Nate headed, or was led, straight to the blue book. He picked it up and dusted it off. He could tell just from holding it that it was the same book he had found in the Wood. He opened the book and saw Rubideaux's name.

Unlike the first time, he skimmed through the book until he found the small papers folded halfway through. He took one out and unfolded it. There, in his palm, was the beautiful self-portrait of Mary, Rubideaux's wife.

Rubideaux had told Nate that he and his wife had worked in their Master's Main House and that the two of them would sneak into the library late at night and read. Mary, at times, would borrow the Master's pen and ink to draw for her beloved husband.

These were the 'crimes' of educated slaves and serious enough when discovered to prompt the Master, in a fit of fear and panic, to sell Mary as far from Rubideaux and the other slaves as possible. The poor white man couldn't sleep for fear of a midnight rebellion. He now had fodder for his regular nightmares of underground classrooms where his slaves learned to read maps, forge passes, and plot revenge.

Some folks around New Orleans say that the spooked Master was actually relieved when he learned his Rubideaux, the smartest of the bunch, had run away. It gave him the moral right to have him hunted down and killed.

From the sketch, Nate could see that Mary was a young woman. Her features were pleasant. Nate was drawn especially to the eyes, which seemed to be staring at him. Even when he shifted the paper, the eyes remained focused on him.

Nate wondered where she was now. She couldn't possibly know that her dear Rubideaux was on his deathbed. Or that his only wish now was to see the sketches she had made in the tense quiet of the night beneath a light that gave her the chance to draw but also the risk of punishment.

Grabbing a stalk of green cane, Nate crushed the leaf between his fingers. The green smear on his skin was real. He could pinch himself now, and he would still be here.

He looked around. A light breeze, a relief for him, was moving the cane like an invisible hand. The bees and the butterflies were busy on the flowers, and there were birds all around him adding their voices to the rustling of the cane.

It was peaceful; not a modern convenience anywhere. But he knew what was just on the other side of the field—forced to be slaves to one man.

He looked again at the sketch. If he hadn't been here at Vieux Saules this week and seen it with his own eyes, he would not have believed that less than 150 years ago, humans could have been treated this way. That they could be owned and sold;

grown men whipped; women at risk to the whims of white men. Jenna had told him about the Israelites being slaves in Egypt, but that was thousands of years ago. This was 1857 and America.

The native Californian shook his head to no one because he was alone. Perhaps, subconsciously, he was trying to knock these new memories out of his brain and onto the ground for the rats to take away. He knew he was in a nightmare and that he was alone. There was no one on Earth at that time who knew what he knew. There was no one who could help him get home.

His stomach began to gurgle, reminding him that he was indeed mortal even in 1857. He put the book in his back pocket and walked toward the road. Now he wished he would run into Richard again and take him up on his offer of a ride home. It would even be worth listening to his insults and haughtiness.

But no such luck. He was on his own and it was for him to find his own way home. Come hell or high water.

TIMOTHY PHILLIPS

18 The Wicked Ways

Until now, Nate had seen little of Mr. Mallock. He had managed to stay out of his way for most of the week and saw him up close only yesterday when he watched him whipping Midnight in the shack.

That was all to change today. As Nate walked toward the Cimetière to give Rubideaux the book, he was set for a collision course with the dreaded overseer.

Nate's mood was a bit more light-hearted since those moments in the cane field. He had gone home, eaten, and listened to Brett play the fiddle. Brett tried to coax his son into joining, but Nate knew that Rubideaux had precious little time. As soon as the boy had caught his second-wind, he was off for the Cimetière.

He crossed the footbridge excited about having found Rubideaux's book. He knew how badly Rubideaux wanted to see his wife's picture again. If Nate hadn't been whistling with his head in the clouds, he would have noticed Pouty Robert's pained expression.

Most of the other boys, including Midnight, and the men were still out in the fields. Robert had somehow managed to get left behind and had seen the overseer take young Tiddy into the cabin across from his. He heard Tiddy scream, but there was nothing that he could do, other than voodoo. That seemed powerless against the white man.

"Cat!" he yelled at the risk of being heard.

Nate stopped in his tracks.

"Pouty Robert? Why aren't you in the fields?"

Robert motioned Cat over to the porch. "Forget that," he whispered. "Mr. Mallock be in the cabin there," he said pointing across the way. "—with Tiddy."

Nate's eyes widened, and his face immediately flushed, and his jaw set. He turned toward the cabin, but Robert grabbed his arm.

"Cat. No! You can't."

"Then why did you tell me!" he shot back. He brushed Robert away and stormed across the lane and up the steps.

Without knocking, he barged into the cabin, catching the surprised overseer in an odd state.

Anger overcame Mallock as quickly as it had Nate.

"Get out!" he screamed. But Nate stood his ground. "Get outta here, I say!" He was not at all comfortable or pleased to be seen in this situation by another white person.

He reached toward his baton, which was on a chair a short distance away, but his feet were caught in his trousers. Unable to catch his balance, he fell sideways in a clumsy way.

Through gritted teeth, Mallock ordered Nate a final time to leave. Nate stood his ground.

"Leave my sister alone!"

"Your sister?" he mocked.

"My sister—uh, yes—in Christ." The last words came to him without thinking, from that part of his mind inhabited by Cat.

Pulling up his trousers, Mallock got back up and took a step toward Nate. He was a good foot taller.

"I don't care if she's your sister in blood and spit, she be the property of Master LeBeaux and under my care!" The agitated man thumped Cat's chest hard as he made his point. "And I will do what I damn well please with that property."

Nate peered around Mallock and for the first time saw Tiddy crawled up in the corner of the bed, her clothes bunched up in front of her. Her face was runny as she looked to Nate for help.

"You have to the count of three to get your sorry backside outta here!"

"Or what?" Nate tightened his fists at his side.

"I'll give you what I gave your best boy yesterday."

"I ain't sure Massah LeBeaux would take kindly to that, seein' as how the bandage is still on Richard's head. I know I sure wouldn't—nor would my daddy. He killed a man in Ireland once—did you know that?"

The uneducated Mallock couldn't tell if Nate was bluffing. But he wasn't sure he wanted to take the chance. With the slaves, he was the absolute tyrant and he had no fear. With other whites, even children, his inner sense of inferiority was a hard enemy to overcome.

Mallock had always been intimidated by the handsome and charismatic Cat. He was the son of one of the most beautiful and moral woman in the New Orleans area. He was also fearful of her temperamental Irish husband.

"This ain't the end of it, boy! Not by a long shot!" He pushed Nate's chest hard as he strode to the door and left.

Nate took a deep breath. He was lucky and he knew it. He also knew that Mallock was right; this wasn't the last of it.

Mallock fumed on the other side of the door. He looked out from the porch at the other cabins and down both ways of the alley. Not a soul in sight to see the look on his face that moment. A look that Nate would describe as '*postal.*'

Beneath the porch a petrified Pouty Robert stared at the heels of Mallock's mud-crusted boots. A small sneeze and Robert would be the sacrificial lamb for Tiddy's reprieve.

He watched in fear as Mallock descended the steps and headed back to the fields. Like most slaves, Robert was convinced that Mallock had eyes in the back of his head. He somehow seemed to know everything that went on in the Cimetière. Robert was sure that at any moment Mallock would turn around and seek his doe eyes between the steps.

Pouty Robert decided to stay put until long after the overseer was gone. He was curious but had no stomach to go inside the cabin. He had heard the argument through the floorboards and knew that Mallock was not at all happy and could come back with some of his guards.

Inside, Nate rushed over to Tiddy who was crying and in a daze.

"Tiddy? Are you OK? Did he hurt you?" Nate grabbed a nearby blanket and wrapped it around her.

"It'll be OK, you'll see," the boy told her, though he was less convinced inside. Nate had been lucky to be nearby, but he wouldn't always be there. He had to figure a way out.

While Nate sat with Tiddy and comforted her, he tried to find a solution. Unlike anyone else at Vieux Saules, he knew the future; he knew what would be invented and when; when the War would start and when it would end; when the slaves would be freed. He was smarter than Mallock and there had to be a way to put that to their advantage.

As Nate and Tiddy sat on the edge of the bed, they heard excited voices just off the porch. They were getting louder.

"Wait here, Tiddy. I'll be right back." Tiddy clutched his arm and tried to keep him near. "I'll be right back. I just need to find out what is happening outside."

Nate rushed across the room and opened the door to find Robert and Monsieur Eduard. The pastor was relieved to see Nate.

"Cat, you must come quickly. Monsieur Rubideaux is near his end. He's asking for you."

Nate motioned the pastor up the steps. "Can you stay with Tiddy until I get back?"

Monsieur Eduard looked over Nate's shoulder at the tormented Tiddy and gave Nate a perplexed look.

"Mallock" was all he said, but that was enough. Monsieur Eduard nodded and went into the cabin to minister to one of his newest sheep.

Nate ran down the alley to the pastor's cabin. As he walked into the room, a distinct smell overwhelmed him. Death was already present in the small cabin.

"Monsieur Rubideaux! I found your book!" The curtains were still drawn so it was impossible for Nate to see Rubideaux's pleased expression.

But he heard it in his voice. "Open the curtain, Cat. Let me see my baby one las' time."

Nate handed the precious book to Rubideaux and swung back the tattered cloth that had shielded Rubideaux's open back from the blistering sun these past few days.

The young man was still confined to lying on his stomach, so he lifted his head as high as he could. For a moment, he just held the book and closed his eyes.

Nate couldn't tell whether he was praying or thinking or a bit of both. It was almost as if he was willing the words and pictures into his hands and to his heart and mind.

At last, he opened the book to a specific page and read a few lines aloud:

> She sits there in the blue of night
> beneath the dome of starry light.
> Day's end has shown a dazzling sight
> divinely placed in Heaven's height.
>
> She wears her heart upon her sleeve,
> though cold and weary on this eve.
> She sits alone upon the stone
> and listens to the Whistling Swan.
> One day she'll find a goodly man
> whose name right now to God is known.
>
> She shyly dreams romantic tales
> while shooting stars leave speckled trails.

Rubideaux stopped reading the poem and let the book open itself to the sketches tucked inside. He pulled one out and unfolded it to reveal his bride. It was the same picture that had stared at Nate earlier that morning.

"She's beautiful, Monsieur."

Rubideaux nodded. He seemed overcome with emotion. "We were children together," he said. "Grew up near each other. She was always in my way, bossy like my mama," he laughed. "She was like a kitten following a piece of string. Made me as mad as a beehive rolled down a hill." He laughed again.

"Then one day I open my eyes an' I see this mos' beautiful girl in fron' of me. I didn't know where she came. The Massah hadn't bough' any slaves that year. But there she was for my eyes to see. My daddy laughed—says I was growin' up. From then on, I was the pup chasin' the string. An' pretty string she was, Cat. Prettiest I've seen to this day.

"Now, all's I have is this. Pictures of a pretty kitten."

Rubideaux looked over at Nate who was sitting, his hands resting on his knees.

"You're still a pup yourself, Cat, so I don't 'spect you to know what I'm sayin'. Some day you'll know an' you're gonna remembuh ol' Ruby here."

Rubideaux was silent for a moment; it was quiet outside the window as well. Nate could hear the gates and windows inside his mind opening and closing. In the periphery of his brain he rummaged through drawers like a cat burglar looking for an emerald or two. There had to be an answer picked up over the years and stashed away somewhere amongst all this grey matter. But in this particular mind there was too much Cat and not enough RAM.

"Cat! Cat!" Rubideaux painfully stretched his arm to nudge Nate back to earth.

"Sorry, Monsieur Rubideaux. I was thinkin'."

"I could see. Even when you're restin', you're movin'." He chuckled. "Cat, you're a good white boy; you an' your Mama are the bes' white folk I've evuh met. You're never gonna know how much you bringin' the book back means to Ruby. No suh. I think the good Lord was testin' ya, Cat.

"Findin' it wasn't the test—God put it in your hands—goin' for—that was the test. You put yoursef at harm for someone else, someone mos' of this world says is not a man but a thing." Rubideaux declared.

"Yes, suh, you're lookin' at a once-walkin', now talkin' thing. Not even a full person, accordin' to Massah's law. But I am special all right. No mechanical thing can think like me." Rubideaux looked back at the picture of his Mary. "Or love like me."

Rubideaux began a coughing fit. When he had recovered from it and took his hand away, Nate saw the bright red blood.

'Rubideaux!"

The man looked down at his hands. "My time is comin', Cat. I'll be free by supper, that's for shore."

"No! God! He can save you."

"God already has, just like He did your friend Tiddy. Trus' me, Cat, for a slave to leave the world for Heaven, it is a happy time. An' from Heaven's height I'm gonna see my Mary and I'm gonna watch God's own angels lookin' out for her. So don't cry for Ruby—this be his Jubilee day."

Rubideaux slowly turned on his side and with his weight on one arm, forced his numb legs to swing down to the floor until he was sitting on the bed face to face with a distraught Nate.

"I said before I ain't ever ask a white man for anything 'til I askd you. So now I want to give ya somethin'. Firs', remembuh this—until you are with God in Heaven—" his hands grasped both of Nate's "—this is only one master worth servin', an' He sits on the highes' throne there will ever be. Listen only to God. That, I say to your soul. Seconds when I'm gone, I want you to haves this book. It is the only only thing Ruby ever owned."

He eased himself slowly against the cabin wall. His final message to Nate had consumed most of the remaining life within him. His breathing was now shallower than before, except for bursts of coughing. The tortured man kept his eyes closed and, to Nate, it looked as if Ruby was watching a dream playing in his mind. Then he was gone, and the only thing left moving in ol' Ruby was a thin trail of blood down his chin and onto his open book.

The door creaked open. Nate turned to see Monsieur Eduard with Tiddy at his side. Tiddy wanted to run to Nate, but Monsieur Eduard kept a firm hand on her shoulders.

"Monsieur Rubideaux is gone, Tiddy," the pastor said softly.

Tiddy burst into tears and buried her face in the elderly pastor who had over his many years seen a hundred or so slaves die in every conceivable way, and some not so kind. He was glad in his heart for Rubideaux. He knew he was a believer, and knew to the core of his soul that Rubideaux was now being comforted by the one true Master of all.

"Cat!" He motioned the boy to join him.

Nate gently pulled the book from Rubideaux's hands. The boy looked down and re-read the verse that a man—not a thing— had read aloud no more than ten minutes ago. A moment passes, and that life is gone. Such a simple truth but so hard to fully understand. Especially for a fourteen year old boy.

"He killed him, pastor. Mallock killed him."

"Oui." he answered softly.

"For no reason. He could have sent him home."

"He did. Now the young man is truly free."

With a child in each arm, Monsieur Eduard hugged them both tightly and stared across the room at the peaceful countenance of a mortal man lifted into eternity.

That night before going to bed, Nate set Cat's journal on his desk and opened his ink well. He wrote, as much as he could remember, about the busy day, especially his search through the

Wood and the wild boar, his tense encounter with the evil Mallock, and his final conversation with Rubideaux. And, of course, Ruby's death. He also wrote down the advice that Ruby gave him. Maybe one day, when he was older, he could read it and it would make more sense.

Something Rubideaux said about God intrigued him. Nate was not a believer like Cat; his mother never had the time, and his step-dad usually went to the golf course on Sunday mornings. From Nate's point of view God was not at all a part of his family's life, and Nate never noticed anything was missing. He was, in most ways, left to himself and had gotten used to it. It was just the way it was.

But this week, God seemed to be everywhere and in every thing. From Tiddy's baptism last Sunday to the terrifying ordeal on the River on Tuesday, to Rubideaux.

Cat's parents believed and—strange to Nate—a good number of slaves believed in what Nate thought of as a white son of God.

Even the Indian Wood seemed close to God. Rubideaux had described seeing God walking in the forest the way the Bible described Him in a garden called Eden, which Jenna said was where the first man and woman lived.

When Nate had gone back into the Wood looking for the book, he had kept an eye open for God. But all he saw were the animals and the bright flowers and towering trees. Unlike Rubideaux, he never saw God walking on the forest floor. If God was there, why didn't he see Him?

In a chair by an open window Nate flipped back to earlier pages in the journal, before Nate had ever set foot on Vieux Saules. It was late and except for the lamp at his desk, the rest of the house and all of Vieux Saules was dark. It was Midnight's favorite time of day and no doubt Cat's best buddy was flying free in his dreams right now.

But Nate couldn't sleep. He had to know more about God. He was certain, as sure as the date on the gold coin on his desk, that God was his only way out, just like it was for Rubideaux. From the time he walked down the back stairs into the past, his life was in the hands of someone else. And it wasn't Mallock or LeBeaux. It was someone good; he knew that for sure.

Nate had walked—or was led—out of a house of wealth and questionable morals to a small house of believers. It was becoming more and more clear to Nate that stepping back in time was no accident; sharing Cat's life wasn't either.

TIMOTHY PHILLIPS

Saturday

August 29, 1857

TIMOTHY PHILLIPS

19 HEARTSTRINGS

It was now nearly two in the morning. Nate had stayed awake, far longer than Jenna would have approved, reading the early entries in Cat's journal. As he read, the memories fastened to the pages flooded into Nate's consciousness as if secret vaults were suddenly being opened.

In one short week, Nate had become attached to this life and despite wanting to go back to his real life, he knew he would miss these days. Every morning when he woke up, he was sad and worried that he was still in the past; he was beginning to miss his real mom. He was starting to see her in a different light.

Perhaps more importantly, the slavery issue was becoming more than he could bear. Its reality was far more oppressive and de-humanizing than the history books could hope to capture or express.

But every morning he was also sad at the thought that he might open his eyes and find himself back in Whittier, with Ryan and Patty just down the hall. He knew he would miss Midnight and Tiddy terribly. They were like a brother and sister. They were what Ryan and Patty should have been.

This week had in many ways been a dream brought to life. From his first days in kindergarten when the other kids had doting moms and dads at their side, he had only a mother without confidence. His wish at every birthday was always the same: that he could have both a mother and a father. Now he had Jenna and Brett. Firm but fair; good but not preachy. Giving, and humble. His birthday wish had come true after all.

He had spent lots of side-by-side time with Brett; it was such an incredible feeling for Nate. Brett was a true father to Cat—and Nate.

Nate stopped reading the journal. An idea had been dropped on his porch. *'If reading Cat's words brought his past to Nate, then the opposite should be true. He could leave messages for Cat in the journal, words to help him in the coming years. Then, if Nate should ever make it back home, and Cat was again on his own, maybe Nate would be able to help his* 'twin' *out over the distance of time.*

The boy thought carefully before grabbing the pen, and he worked feverishly to get it right. Though tired, he pushed himself. He wasn't sure how many more nights he had left at Vieux Saules. Depressingly, this could be the last, or the sign of a thousand yet to come. Nate's emotions were topsy-turvy. He felt constricted in so many ways.

Finally, he put the pen down, got undressed, and fell into bed. In the minutes before he fell asleep, he re-read in his mind his journal entry. He was pleased.

Now, if he could only understand God and how He fit into all this, maybe he could be at peace in his bed at home.

While Nate slept through breakfast, Jenna and Brett had a spirited discussion about Mr. Mallock. Brett was in a fit of rage after learning what the depraved Mallock had done to his Tiddy.

News of this type traveled quickly through Vieux Saules. Cat, the hero of the day, was still asleep.

"He's a monster, Jenna." Brett's voice boomed to the ceiling. "A monster who has no right being in charge of a pack of dogs, let alone decent, hard-working folk."

"You are right, of course. But what—what, can you do?"

"I'll talk to Master LeBeaux and tell him the kind of man he's hired on as his overseer."

Jenna smiled. "Brett, now you sound like me. Don't you think he knows what Mallock is like? He has been here nearly fifteen years. Master LeBeaux knows what he is."

Brett began pacing in front of the kitchen table and moving his hands every which way. He was on Rage's doorstep.

Jenna continued. "Mrs. LeBeaux, especially, has an extreme fear that the slaves will revolt in the middle of the night. So any overseer Master LeBeaux hires is going to be ruthless."

"He's beyond ruthless. Use of the whip to get more work is cruel. Dragging a man behind a horse for a mile is evil and depraved." He stopped pacing. "Attacking a little girl—" Brett's voice broke mid-sentence, and Jenna rushed to his side and embraced him.

"I know, dear."

"God must protect her, Jenna. I can't do it."

"He will, in His own way. He sent Cat into the Cimetière at the right time, didn't he? He kept Pouty Robert behind so he could tell Cat."

"That was this time. What about the next?" He began his nervous pacing again.

"I don't know," she sighed. "Tiddy is getting older, and she is going to face situations we can not imagine. I don't know the answer."

"I do." Brrett stopped in his tracks at his epiphany. "I will go to Master LeBeaux and, one way or another, get her out of this hell."

"You tried that before, when you first got here."

"That was almost fifteen years ago. I was seventeen, and I had the voice of a boy. I was too easily intimidated by the man and his wealth and power. I have been a wee milquetoast for too long. "Not now! I will not watch my daughter live another day as an animal. She is a human being, and a follower of Christ." He grabbed his hat from the peg and opened the door with such force Jenna thought it would come off its hinges.

"Oh, Brett! Don't be rash. We need to get Tiddy free, but we have to be careful. If you anger Master LeBeaux, the door may be shut completely."

"I have to go. I cannot allow this to stand." He kissed Jenna quickly on the cheek. "God is on our side, isn't He?"

Jenna nodded.

"Then this is the right thing to do. The time is right."

She watched her idealistic man walk briskly down the lane toward the Main House that was most likely still asleep on the second floor.

'Oh, God, please be with him now. Help him to find the right words and help Master LeBeaux to have a softened heart.'

Jenna was nervous for Brett. She knew it was something that he had to do, but she worried that his Irish would get the better of him and he would not do well against the refined French of the rich planter. She wished she could be at his side to be a support, but she knew it was something he had to do on his own.

She chided herself then for leaving God out of the situation. She knew God would be at Brett's side—and at his feet and his head and in his heart the whole time. She kicked herself for showing such little faith, just when it was needed most.

Brett rushed up the Twin Stairs. The Irishman and his temper pounded on the mahogany door. He shoved his impatient hands into his pockets and a second later they were clutching the white rails. Then back in his pockets they went.

"Oh, come on! It's bloody nine o'clock in the marning!" He pounded even harder on the door and continued pounding until the dark wood was replaced by the dark face of the LeBeaux's servant, Benjamin. The sight of the agitated Irishman threw the low-key Benjamin off-keel.

Brett shoved Benjamin aside and entered the House.

"Where's Master LeBeaux?" he demanded.

Benjamin hesitated. He was not used to visitors being so forceful and, in his opinion, disrespectful of Benjamin's fine uniform. Mrs. LeBeaux had bought it up in Natchez last spring to, in her words, '*give the plantation some sense of decorum.*' Benjamin wasn't sure what all that meant, other than he got to trade in his ordinary clothes for a bright uniform of scarlet, white, and gold. Even Benjamin's wife found it difficult to get him to part from it at the end of day.

"Where is he, Benjamin? I have urgent business."

"Uh, he is not here."

"Don't give me that bloody lie. Now go get him."

"He be in his study."

"Then get him, dammit."

Those were harsh words flying onto Benjamin's jacket, and he felt the importance of the cloth shrinking on his very body. As he left to get his Master, he shrank an inch or two.

Brett looked around at all the wealth nailed on the walls. Art and tapestries from the great powers of Europe. Italian marble sculptures in the entry way and by the mantle. Gold candelabras. Mahogany floors and doors. And, of course, the infamous drapes that had been purchased by Samuel and Ruth.

He stared at one particular painting and was drawn close to it. In the past ten years he had been reduced to slopping paint on various out-buildings, with only his nighttimes to create true art. No lessons or mentors or guidebooks. Just his artistic instinct.

Yet here, just a couple hundred yards down the road, hung works from masters on the Continent. Some were copies, to be sure, but what works they were. It reminded Brett of all he had given up over these years and for what? To see his daughter grow up in poverty and humiliation. Sadness was now tempering his earlier rage.

Brett heard the heavy boots of LeBeaux coming down the hall, followed by the soft shoe of the servant Benjamin. The planter, in his riding gear, swept into the hall and with his hand waved Brett to follow him into the front parlor.

"What is it, Mr. Hennessee? Benjamin says you have urgent business." Benjamin, still lurking near the doorway, stiffened at the sound of his name.

LeBeaux had two speeds: '*slow, genteel, we'll-get-there-when-we-get-there*' and '*you've got five seconds to spit it out.*' There was no in-between, and the problem is no one could ever predict which speed he would be. He liked to surprise the other party to his conversation; for him, that was half the fun of being the wealthy landowner. He got to watch weaker men squirm.

LeBeaux walked over to a table and pulled a cigar out of a box. He didn't bother offering one to Brett. As he lit the cigar, he thought better and shook the light out. Chomping on the cigar, he asked the question again.

"What is it, man? I don't have all morning for you to gather your words in your Irish head."

Brett had to dig his heels in to avoid spouting off. LeBeaux could see his opponent tense up. He too had heard about Mallock's incident with Tiddy, and Cat's chivalrous rescue. He could guess what was on Brett's mind.

LeBeaux sat down on a small sofa so that the worker was left standing in front of the feudal lord.

"Master LeBeaux," Brett checked himself to make sure the words that came out were the right ones. LeBeaux could almost imagine Brett scraping his cranium to find his next word.

"—I—"

'Ah, there it is,' LeBeaux smiled to himself. "Yes?"

"I have worked hard for you these last fifteen years and—"

"And, and what? Do I owe you something? Have I not paid you? Not given your family a house to live in?" He raised his eyebrows for effect.

"No—I mean, yes, sir, you have paid me. But, it seems to me, that—perhaps—because of my service, to you, that we—I mean 'you'—could—"

"Could what, Mr. Hennessee? Give you something?"

"Um, well, yes, sir."

"And what would that something be?" He looked around for an ashtray but realized, as always, that he was still in the Mrs' smoke-free zone. *'Blast it!'* he thought. *'If only she knew how much better I worked when I am in the clouds of a cigar.'*

Brett knew he had to choose his next words carefully.

"We spoke. Fifteen years ago." He measured his breathing and watched his tone. "When I first came to Vieux Saules. I asked you then for Tiddy, my daughter."

"I remember. And I remember that I told you how valuable she was to the plantation. And I also remember that I gave you the generous offer of working and living here so that you could be near her. Not many men around here would have done that."

"I appreciate that, I do."

"Look what it got you. A beautiful wife, and a son who trips over your heels."

"Yes, sir, I am grateful to God for that."

"—To God?" LeBeaux laughed heartily. "My dear, Irishman, God had nothing to do with it. I needed a white painter and you fit the bill. God can have credit for many things, but not this one, I assure you."

"Nevertheless, sir, it has been a long time years—and I have worked hard for you."

"Maybe when you are old enough to retire, I'll buy you a watch. But painting fifteen years with room and board doesn't buy you your daughter's left foot."

"She shouldn't be for sale at all," he said in a raised voice. *'Careful,'* Brett thought. *'This is how I get myself into the briars.'*

"But by the cruel facts of life, she is."

Brett stood there, dejected. He had used as careful words as he could, and had prayed in every space between them. But LeBeaux was not budging. He was giving the planter his best shots, but to no effect.

Leaning comfortably back in the sofa, LeBeaux watched every slight itch and twitch of the Irish man. He focused on the eyes, which seemed glazed and staring off into the distance, into a field of wildflowers where a man held a girl in his arms watching the sunrise. It was the picture that mesmerized Brett when he was standing in the foyer by himself.

Brett could feel the rage building inside, as he thought about all the days that had passed for him and Tiddy, and this rage paralyzed him. The only movement on his face was a parallel line of tears down both cheeks. A silent roll of emotion, remnants of powerful prayers to the Almighty.

The sight made the manly LeBeaux uncomfortable for the first time in many seasons. "All right, Mr. Hennesee, you have caught me in a generous mood. For your son's valor, I gave him a slave. I chose Minuit out of affection for your son. I know how close the two of them are, though I'm not sure our God would appreciate their friendship together." He took another sip of the bourbon Benjamin had wisely left him. "Nevertheless it is what is, isn't it?"

Brett tried to cut in but the Master had stepped onto his soapbox and he was not yet ready to relinquish it.

"As I say, Mr. Hennessee, you have caught me in a generous mood, and I am willing to alter my arrangement with your son. He being a mere boy, I'm sure you speak for him."

"What do you have in mind?" Brett asked nervously.

"An even exchange, Minuit for Tiddy-Beaux. He's worth more in the field, but I can't get any babies from him."

"Why, you're askin' me to choose. I am no King Solomon!" He took a step toward LeBeaux.

"You can take it or leave it; I don't much care."

"You have put me in the Devil's position."

"I suppose I have. Do you deny your son's best friend's freedom in ten years, or your daughter's now—and forever."

"How do you bloody well sleep at night?" he demanded, his fist punching in the air.

"Oh, I sleep fine, Mr. Hennessee, and in the finest of sheets and pillows in the entire South."

"But you're damned for hell!"

"In your book perhaps. In mine, I'll be walking on the streets of gold."

"How can I choose? How can I take freedom away from Midnight? Free them both! What would it be to you? One less mouth to feed."

"You mean, 'Two less hands that can work the fields.' Your problem, Hennessee, is that you and your wife worry too much about their feelings. Midnight's a slave, for Christ's sake; he's used to disappointment."

"He is not a slave for Christ's sake, but yours!"

"Take your daughter and leave Vieux Saules. Make yourself happy dreams in the north and don't give Minuit a second thought."

"You're a bloody—"

LeBeaux held up his hand, which stopped Brett cold. The sharpness of Brett's words and tone didn't please the aggressive but genteel Mr. LeBeaux. "Watch your language in this House. My wife is in the other room."

"You know I cannot choose."

"Talk to your son. He's a level boy. I'm sure if you shared all the pertinent facts with him, he'd understand."

"They are like brothers."

"Indeed."

LeBeaux rang the silver bell on the table and Benjamin appeared seconds later.

"Mr. Hennessee is ready to leave. Show him the way out. And—" he grabbed Brett's sleeve—"the next time you want to see me, make an appointment first. I do not much care for anyone disturbing my privacy."

Brett freed his arm from LeBeaux. "I know my way out, thank you."

"Mr. Hennessee, my offer is good for twenty-four hours. If you decide on Minuit, you give up any moral rights to Tiddy. Any subsequent thoughts about her you might want to share with me, you can leave them in your own bloody head. Am I clear on that?"

"Quite." Brett stormed out of the room, down the hall, and out of the house. He stood at the top of the Twin Stairs and looked around. In the far distance he could see the copse of trees that marked the Cimetière. Somewhere under those trees the lives of two youngsters depended solely on a decision LeBeaux had now left at Brett's feet.

'How can I choose my daughter and take away a freedom just given? On the other hand, how can I not? She's my daughter.'

Brett returned home more pained than when he left. When he entered the kitchen, Nate was sitting at the table with Jenna having breakfast.

"Brett? What's wrong? You don't look well."

"I feel—"

He started toward the other room, but Jenna caught his arm.

"Sit. I'll get you some tea. We're both dying to know what Master LeBeaux said."

Brett obliged and, grabbing the back of the chair, swung it around and sat down. He looked into the expectant faces of his wife and son.

"He's turned me into a bloody Solomon."

"I don't understand."

"Cat, he's given you Midnight in ten years time. Well, he's willing to let me exchange Midnight's freedom then, for Tiddy's now."

Jenna put her hand up to her mouth. "He can't be serious. How could he expect you to choose? They've grown up like brother and sister."

"And I've already told Midnight," Nate added.

"I know, and I told LeBeaux that. But he doesn't care. The scourge of slavery is on his hands, and he wants to bloody well put it on mine. He wants someone else to carry the guilt to their grave."

"What do we do?" asked Jenna.

"I don't know. I honestly don't know. Either way, how can I look the other in the eye knowing I am the reason they will be in chains the rest of their life?

"LeBeaux's given me twenty-four hours to decide. Then it's off the table and, in his mind, I forfeit all 'moral' rights to her as me daughter." At those words, Brett began to weep, though not as silently as in the Main House. He was among family now.

Nate sat silently. There was nothing he could say, one way or the other. It was an impossible position for anyone to be in.

"If we don't do something, how do we protect Tiddy from Mallock, or any other white man?

Brett shook his head in futility.

Then Nate spoke what had been in the back of their minds for many years.

"What if we just leave and take them both with us?"

20 BROKEN WINGS

Nate walked between the rows of trees in the peach orchard. Just a short week ago he would never have pictured himself in this situation. He had been a loner at school, detached from anything of interest within the family. Most days he barely grunted to his mom's questions, while he listened intently to his headset.

But now, Nate was in the thick of things. He was a key player—a captain, rather than one of the kids on the sidelines waiting to be picked. Fate had now chosen Midnight as well, or so he thought. Now Brett would have to choose. Tiddy was family, but Midnight was like a brother.

Nate cursed Master LeBeaux for putting Brett in this spot. It was a cruel thing for him to do. But, then, keeping nine hundred souls in life bondage was already over the top in Nate's mind.

Picking up a stone and throwing it toward one of the peach trees, Nate thought seriously about his idea of all of them escaping north. They could go all the way up to Quebec where Jenna's relatives lived. He knew his geography. North into Missouri and cross the Mississippi into Illinois. A day by car.

He was nearing a white fence that marked the plantation's western boundary. The fence ran along the famous River Road that connected the vast and wealthy estates, each possessing at least a modest strip of land along the River. From a satellite photo they would look like wedges of lime straddling a glass of Mississippi Mud. Vieux Saules was one of the few fortunate enough to sit on a small peninsula formed by the River's curvy whims as it wound its way down to the Gulf.

Nate hung his arms over the white fence, which Brett had painted only a month or so ago. The River Road was unpaved and empty. Staring to the north, he wondered what really lay ahead around the bend. If he left Vieux Saules and walked along the Road, would it really take him to other parts of the country in 1857?

If they all made it north, was there really the chance he could bump into a living, breathing Abraham Lincoln on the streets of Springfield? Was the world out there still asleep in the pipe dream that a terrible war would never come?

Yet here he was in this sleepy world, the only one wide-awake, the only one who knew the real dangers yet to come. The only one who knew the ultimate fate of slavery. This knowledge, though, was not helping him when it counted most—getting both Midnight and Tiddy to freedom.

'And, if we did get them to freedom, then what?' he wondered. Could he get back home to Whittier from anywhere in 1857 or did it have to be from Vieux Saules? If he left, would he be destined to stay in the past? Would he then become one of those farm boys caught dead in the fields of battle?'

All these questions crowded Nate's mind and didn't bring him any closer to a smart solution.

He turned back and looked at the Main House, glistening in the late morning sun. Nate, the Whittier boy, had to admit the House was a majestic sight, with its columns and Twin Stairs, and old oaks in its wings. All the sterility of the museum was missing, and it was the crown jewel of a living estate.

The noise of an approaching carriage pulled Nate's attention back to the River Road. Inside the carriage were Mrs. LeBeaux and the Princess Elizabeth. Mrs. LeBeaux smiled politely at the barefoot Nate, but Elizabeth stuck her tongue out instead. She had been ill tempered to him since she had met the skunk in the Necessary. Richard had convinced his sister that a cat was behind the skunk.

'That's ok,' thought Nate, and he stuck his tongue back out to her, that is, until her mother glanced back at him. Like her husband, Mrs. LeBeaux had lifted her estimate of the carefree poor boy since the rescue on the River.

Nate watched Mrs. LeBeaux put her arm protectively around Elizabeth and then he made his move. Climbing through the slats in the fence, the boy ran after the carriage. When he was close enough, he grabbed hold of the back of the carriage and lifted himself up into its open trunk. He smiled at his cleverness and watched the world pass behind him.

Princess Elizabeth turned around for another look at her nemesis, but he was gone. Vanished. She seemed disappointed, unaware that the boy she thought so cute, even if poor and bothersome, was much closer to her than she knew.

As the carriage approached the front circle at the Twin Stairs, several slaves dressed in fine French style clothing appeared out of the shadows. While they prepared for the arrival of the Royal Family, Nate jumped off his free ride and dashed between two of the oaks that lined the lane.

Nate looked toward the sun and saw it was getting close to noon when Rubideaux would be buried in the Meadow across from the Cimetière. LeBeaux intended to send Rubideaux's body back to his owner in New Orleans, but when he saw how brutally he had been treated by Mallock, he had second thoughts. He sent his regrets to the owner that his slave had met an untimely death, and gave the body to Monsieur Eduard to do with as he saw fit. Of course, for the black pastor, that meant a proper Christian burial in the Meadow.

Picking up his pace, Nate crossed the lawn past the pigeonnier and Richard's garçonnière. The hexagon-shaped playhouse was last year's birthday present. Some day it would become his bachelor's apartment.

Nate saw the backside of Richard who was peering through the bushes. The sight was too much to resist. Running up to the unsuspecting boy, Nate gave him a good boot with his foot. The force of the kick sent Richard lunging further into the bushes and smack on his face.

"Lizabeth—I am going to murder you!" He backed up and stood erect all at the same time, creating quite a shaking bush.

Nate took a step back and held up his fists in defense for what he knew would come.

Shaking leaves out of his head, Richard turned around and spotted a Cat poised for attack.

"What the dang hell, Peter!"

"That's payback for the Duck Pond!" Nate raised his right fist a tad higher to defend his face.

"Aw, put them down. I am not going to fight you." Nate was not believing him and kept his stance. "Quit it, Peter. I have more serious matters here." He tilted his head toward the bushes.

"Whatcha got in there?" Nate asked, still keeping his fists at the ready.

"A blue bunting. He is beautiful, Peter, but he has got a broken wing and needs help."

"Since when did you care about broken wings? Maybe your brain's still swollen from the bump it took."

"Laugh if you want, Catbird, but I am going to catch him and put him in the pigeonnier until he can fly again." He started to crouch down to go back into the bushes but stood upright again. "Look here, you kick me again and I will kick your backside all the way down to the River, y'hear."

Nate held up his arms as if to say *'Who me?'* but the smirk gave his thought away.

He watched Richard crawl combat style into the mass of bushes and once inside work his way to a standing position. But the closer Richard's hand came to the bird, the little fellow simply moved further out on the limb.

"Y're too slow, Richard. You gotta move your hand quick, like catching a fish. He'll die from fright before you get him."

"Easy to say out there, I should say. I can hardly move it is so tight."

Nate followed the rustling sound until he saw the profile of the bright blue bird emerging out of the green. While the hurt thing kept his eye on the intruder from within, he missed seeing Nate's sleight of hand. Nate had scooped him up and a second later had put his other hand on top so that only his little head could be seen.

"I cannot see him anywhere in this thick bush. He has simply disappeared."

"Maybe he flew away." Nate said as he nestled the bird against his chest.

"I told you. He has got a broken wing." Richard didn't hide his annoyance in his voice.

"Maybe you forced him to jump. Check the ground."

"I have, but I do not see him anywhere." He emerged from the hole, shaking the leaves and dirt off his white pants. "Peter, that beats all. I have no idea where the little fellow went." He looked up as he spoke and saw the blue spot against Nate's chest, close to his heart.

Nate stood there with a Cheshire grin.

"Funny Peter. You are very funny. Both clever and lucky."

"I told ya, Richard. A quick hand's what it takes. Here." He handed the blue bird to the other boy, but Richard was hesitant. "Come on, take him, I gotta git."

"I am not so sure, Peter. Maybe—maybe you should carry him to one of the cages. He seems calm in your hands. I would not want to rile him up and give him a heart attack."

"I was kidding. Now hold out your hands. As I put him in your one hand, cup the other one over mine and take its place."

Richard's hands were a little shaky. Taking care of something so fragile was a new thing for the rich, pampered boy.

"There, that's it. You got it. Just keep your hands cupped tight. Not so tight he can't breathe, but enough that he gives in and relaxes. See, it's not so hard."

Now Richard was the one with the smiles. "He is so small, isn't he? I wonder how it happened—I mean, how he came to break his wing."

"Don't know, but I'll ask my Mama to come over to take a look. She can fix him up."

"Thanks, Peter."

Nate watched Richard walk along the lane toward the pigeon-naire and it occurred to him that this was probably the first time in that boy's life that someone else was dependent on him.

As he crossed the footbridge a short time later, Nate saw his friends in the Cimetière gathering in the main alley. He headed toward Monsieur Eduard's cabin where his parents would be waiting for him.

Midnight was already standing at the corner.

"Tiddy says you were with him when he passed." He, of course, was referring to the now late Mr. Rubideaux.

"Yup."

"What was it like?"

"Whatd'ya mean, '*Wha's it like?*'"

"Pouty Robert says soon as a man passes, his ghost sneaks out—and you can see it. That true, Cat? Did you see the smiling ghost of a free man?"

"Nope. He jus' closed his eyes and passed on. That's all."

"Can't be, Cat!" He was clearly disappointed by his friend's lack of enthusiasm. He thought hard for a moment. In the silence Nate looked around the growing crowd for his parents.

"You sayin' a slave hasn't a soul?" Midnight asked.

"What?" Nate clearly wasn't paying attention.

"I say 'Do you think he didn't have a soul?'"

"He had a soul," Nate answered matter of factly. "Course he had a soul. Believed in God, didn't he?"

"Pastor says he did."

"Then, blast it, he's had a soul. Been gone nearly a day now. He's most likely sittin' in Heaven already. Or maybe walkin' on those streets of gold my Mama's always talkin' about."

Midnight was skeptical. "So, why didn't you see his ghost goin' by?"

"I don't know. Maybe it waits 'til no one's lookin'—then up! Up it goes, right through the rafters!" He nodded his head. "Bet that's it. Probably flew up just when I turned to talk to Monsieur Eduard."

"Why d'ya do that, Cat? You missed your chance to see the ghost. If I had been there, I'd have stared at Rubideaux until I had seen his ghost. Wouldn't have move or anything 'til then."

"I wasn't thinkin' about ghosts, you fool. I was thinkin' 'bout a poor man who ain't never gonna see his own child. I was too busy cursin' Mallock to think about a glaze of a man flyin' to freedom."

Midnight wasn't convinced by Nate.

"Ah, stop your poutin', Midnight." The white boy jabbed Midnight's arm, but Midnight just brushed him away and then walked away himself.

Nate followed him and put his arm around him.

"Midnight, why's this so important?"

"'Cause, I wanted to know."

"Know what?"

"If a black man smiles when he's freed."

"He does."

"How you know? You didn't see him fly away."

"True, I didn't see the ghost. But I saw his face as he lay on the bed and closed his eyes. And, I tell ya, he was smilin'. Biggest smile I ever seen."

Midnight stared intently into his friend's eyes.

"You tellin' the truth, Cat?"

"I wouldn't tell ya a lie on that. He's livin' in pure joy right now. He ain't never been happier."

The boys joined the rest of the Cimetière's believers into the Meadow across from where they all communed.

Some of the men had fashioned a crude coffin for the young man they had never seen before this week. And they placed his broken body gently into it. Before closing the lid, Monsieur Eduard removed the sketches from Rubideaux's book and placed them on his chest.

Six of the strongest men carried the coffin while the rest sang spirituals praising God for His mercy in caring for young Rubideaux and His care in watching over the rest of His dark flock.

Before they lowered the coffin, Monsieur Eduard spoke about the young man and the life he led. It always amazed Cat how quickly the pastor learned about people. A visitor in the field would have thought that the pastor had known him as a baby. He had ministered to Rubideaux well in just a few short days.

In Jenna's mind, God had led Rubideaux to this place. He does not control the will of men—the hatred in those like Mallock—but He did make sure there were good people around to take care of him at the right time. People like Monsieur Eduard and her son. And, Rubideaux himself would add the sweet Jenna to the top of the list.

Pastor Eduard stood at the foot of the open grave and read from 2 Chronicles, Chapter 7, Verse 14. *"If my people who are called by my name will humble themselves and pray and seek my face and turn from their wicked ways, then will I hear from heaven and will forgive their sin and will heal their land."*

"Sisters, brothers," he spoke in a hoarse but impassioned voice. "God hears our prayers an' Jesus Himself has done forgiven our sins. We look for Him here on this earth while we live." He looked down at Rubideaux's coffin now resting at the bottom of the grave.

"For brother Rubideaux, his searchin' is done."

"Amen! Amen!" came a chorus of voices, young and old, male and female.

"Praise be to God that he is now at peace!"

"And some day—some day—we too will join the heavenly host on those streets of gold!"

"Yes, suh! Yes, suh!" they shouted in unison

The 'Amens' were now infectious among the crowd, catapulted by staccato claps and swaying bodies. Monsieur Eduard was energizing his flock.

"Oh, brothers and sisters, I can see His glory sittin' there— there!" He pointed to the sky. "—on the right hand of the Almighty God!" His voice crackled under the strain of his passion.

"Glory, oh Glory!" shouted Princess Tawna.

Nate found himself clapping and shouting with the others. He had found the Spirit within the inner Cat. He too was captivated by Monsieur Eduard's words and, for the moment, had forgotten completely the circumstances surrounding him and the others.

He looked across the crowd and saw his mother with her arm around Tiddy. She was crying out of joy, so it seemed to Nate. He watched his mother for the longest time, far longer than expected from a teenage son. He was in awe of her and how she pushed ahead despite the barriers and the dangers. And, through it all, she enjoyed life, as God gave it to her.

Brett stood next to Jenna, but was without his usual buoyancy even though he was within breathing distance of his only daughter. LeBeaux's offer was clearly weighing heavily on him. He had a hard time even looking at Monsieur Eduard.

Nate wondered how Brett would choose between Midnight and Tiddy. Cat had known both since they were infants. He and his son were as tight as swamp briars.

A sharp elbow nudged Nate in the ribs, disrupting all thoughts currently on his mind.

"Ow. What the—!"

Midnight pointed to the edge of the Meadow with a slight movement of his head. Off in the distance in a patch of shade stood the overseer and two of his guards. All three were carrying rifles.

"These things always make 'em nervous," said Nate.

"Yeah, well, I git the shakes when I see an open hole and a white man. Wouldn't take much for 'em to throw a couple of us on top of ol' Rubideaux."

"Pray to the Lord!" shouted Monsieur Eduard. He had seen the three white men as well so Nate wasn't quite sure who the pastor was commanding at that point. "Pray to the Lord that He might deliver you as well! Pray that He would lift you, broken wings and all, into His beautiful sight!"

"Amen! Amen! Amen!" With hands raised the people gave praise singing a spiritual that rose with Rubideaux to the gates on the other side. Gates far beyond the reach of Mallock and his men.

TIMOTHY PHILLIPS

21   BLUNDERBUSS!

Nate sat under a large oak that straddled the distance between his house and Mr. Mallock's. It was early evening on Saturday, and he was desperately trying to devise a plan to save both Tiddy and Midnight.

He hated Mallock. He knew Jenna would be disappointed to hear him say that out loud. *'Hate' is the Devil's weapon,'* she told Mrs. Devereaux, the carpenter's wife the day before. He had actually heard her praying that Jesus would knock on Mallock's door and save his soul. *'Phooey,'* was Nate's reaction. *'Some people just aren't worth the trouble.'*

Nate wondered, though, what Cat thought about Mallock. Being a Christian boy, maybe Cat would agree with Jenna. Maybe he prayed for him as well. As he sat under the large oak, Nate wondered what he was missing. *Why didn't he see things the way Jenna and Brett and, most likely, Cat did?*

There was no denying his hatred for the man. Unhealthy as it was, the slow-burning hatred had been heating up all week from the moment he saw him whipping Midnight in the shack, dragging Rubideaux behind a horse, and attacking Tiddy. Deep inside, Nate knew that the situation couldn't continue. Something had to give, and if he had his way, it would be Mallock. The question before him was '*How?*'

The plain house where Mallock lived was dark and had been ever since Nate had sat down under the tree. '*Where is that Devil?*' he wondered over and over. He hadn't seen him since they buried Rubideaux in the Meadow.

In time, Nate found himself in the same darkness that enveloped Mallock's house. Fearing he had to do something soon, Nate stood up, stretched his sore, cramped legs, and snuck to the side of the overseer's house. Clinging to the wall, he walked toward the porch and up the steps. Even bare tiptoes couldn't stop the creaks of the old boards. Nate's face cringed with each new sound.

He glanced into the open window by the door. The house was quiet and devoid of life.

Nate reached for the knob and without much hesitation opened the door and stepped inside the devil's den. '*Why is it so dang cold in here?*' Nate wondered. '*It's hot as hell outside— and muggy to boot.*'

The boy looked around the walls. The room was as sparse as the outside. For a man who had lived in the house for more than fifteen years, there was little to show for it. A table and a few chairs and a hutch of sorts holding up a few bottles of liquor. That was all.

He crossed the room and went into the smaller room where Mallock slept. Like the first, this room had little inside. Just a bed and dresser.

"There's nothing here." Nate said softly. He wasn't at all afraid, which was unusual for him. He had always been the cautious one, the *Nervous Nelly of the Neighborhood.* In some ways, though, this week seemed to be one long, unexplained dream. And Nate knew the dreamer always woke up. Cold and shaken sometimes, but always alive.

But Cat knew better and was scared stiff inside. The two boys had never been in greater conflict all week than at that moment. Cat knew Mallock and feared him greatly. Yes, Cat knew this wasn't a dream; it was real. For him, this moment was a matter of life or death. His!

Nate heard the heavy sound of boots on the rickety porch and then the creak of the door opening. His now racing heart conjoined with Cat's. He inched his way toward the far, darkest corner of the bedroom.

Mallock was now inside the house fumbling in the dark for the lamp he thought he had left on the hutch. The sound of the clinking bottles lifted Mallock's spirits and he forgot about looking for the light. He uncorked one of the bottles and took a long drink.

"Ah!" There was base pleasure in Mallock's voice.

Nate could smell the alcohol from where he stood. *'Oh, Lord,'* he thought. *'I'm in a real jam. I'm as good as dead.'* He could hear Mallock nearing the bedroom.

Nate's hands felt along the wall as he inched further into the corner. Then his hand touched something icy cold. His heart stopped as if it were anticipating a sneeze of a sneeze. While his mind raced over what to do, his fingers felt around the cold metal. He had found one of Mallock's guns.

'What do I do now?' The scared boy wasn't even sure if it was loaded. *If it was, could he really shoot a man dead? Even*

a man as wicked as Mallock? What would Jenna say? Or Brett,
who was already worried to death over Tiddy and Midnight.

Nate wrapped his fingers slowly around the barrel and picked
up the blunderbuss. It was heavy, but there would be no way to
know if it was loaded.

A few more steps and Mallock would be at the doorway. Nate
could feel the sweat pooling under his arms and on the sides and
back of his head. His toes were frozen on the cold wood. His
stomach was somewhere near his voice box, and the butterflies
had gone south into his intestines. And, had the moon been out
fully that night, it would have shown his face as pale.

He knew he wouldn't be able to shoot, but he had a plan
anyway. He tightened his grip on the barrel like it was a baseball
bat and got ready to charge the unsuspecting Mallock. He'd swipe
Mallock on the head and get out of the house before the overseer
knew what hit him. Nate squeezed his hands tight again and
took one last deep breath. His moment of truth was coming.

Mallock, though, stopped in his tracks. Nate stayed frozen
and tried to swallow but his mouth was dry as cotton. Mallock
was known for his sixth sense, his ability to know when a slave
or lesser soul was up to something.

Nate's mind raced while the rest of his body stood still. *'Go!'*
his brain screamed to his legs, but nothing was moving. *'Don't
wait for him to strike! Go!'*

A second later Nate heard what Mallock had heard. A man
on horseback had arrived at the front of the house. Mallock
walked quickly to the front door.

'Whew!' Nate breathed a sigh of thanks. Without further
thinking, he ran to the bedroom window and hurled himself outside.

The ground was harder than it looked in the movies. Nate lay
there dazed for a moment until the voices on the porch became

louder. He crawled to the side of the house and leaned against it while he waited for his heart to slow down.

Mallock was talking to Micah Jespers, one of his foremen. Nate didn't pay much attention to their conversation until he heard Tiddy's name. He immediately sat up and leaned toward the porch.

"Where she now?"

"I got her straight'nin thangs up in the shack."

"All right. Take the rest of the night."

"Thank you, Mr. Mallock." In a flash, before the overseer could change his mind, Jespers had prodded his horse and was half a furlong down the lane. Mallock also didn't waste any time heading out for the Cimetière. There was a definite quickness in his step.

Once Nate was sure he was gone, the boy went back to the bedroom window and hoisted himself inside. He quickly grabbed the musket and crawled back out the window. Tiddy was in danger and he had to help her.

The night was dark without a moon as Nate ran full-speed toward the Cimetière. Running with a gun in his hand was awkward but Nate pushed himself. It was a surreal moment for him. Hound dogs were yelping in the background, and the Main House was bathed in lights. The LeBeaux's were having a dinner party. He could hear the strings competing with the dogs.

Brett was at the House playing, though he was not happy about it. Brett had tried to get Nate to play as well, but Nate wasn't interested in doing anything that helped the LeBeaux's. Not after all that had happened this week. *'That's the difference between a man and a boy,'* Brett told Jenna. *'A man doesn't have near the choices.'*

While ladies and gentlemen danced, Nate ran to save Cat's sister from a fate he couldn't imagine. The gun was a sign of desperate times. The air going into Nate's lungs felt cold despite the hot and humid night, and it seemed to be without any oxygen. He was winded and wasn't sure he could make the final hundred yards. Despite Cat's physical shape, Nate was exhausted and ready to fall into a ditch and sleep for a day. *'That's not an option,'* he told himself as he pushed harder. *'Tiddy needs me.'*

Finally, heart pounding, Nate was only twenty yards away. He wasn't sure what he would do when he came face to face with Mallock, and what Mallock's reaction would be when he saw his own gun in Nate's hands. But Nate knew he had no other choice.

There was light coming from the window in the shack. Nate's stomach was getting queasy thinking about what was likely going on inside right then.

A loud scream pierced the night air. It was Tiddy.

Midnight was running toward the shack as well, but was further ahead than Nate. His friend bolted up the steps and into the shack. Nate quickened his pace; he was running now on adrenalin mixed with a lot of prayer coming from Cat.

Another scream came out of the cabin, this time higher pitched, followed by a loud crash. Nate knew that both Tiddy and Midnight needed him now.

'Oh, no!' Nate thought. *'This can't be good at all.'*

Nate was by now running so fast he couldn't think to slow down as he raced up the steps.

Inside the shack, Midnight knelt down over Mr. Mallock. A bloody board lay at his side. A large lump was beginning to form near Mallock's temple where Midnight had hit him with the board. Blood was flowing from the deep puncture wound left by a spent nail.

"I've done killed him," Midnight muttered in disbelief.

The boy's heart was pounding. He knew he would be dead by morning as well. White folks, even French ones, didn't take kindly to slaves striking back. His mind began to race with his heart. It was quickly becoming a dead heat.

Suddenly, the door burst open followed by a blur in blue overalls. Midnight's heart jumped and touched his mind.

'*Oh, Lord, help me.*'

Nate had run into the shack so fast, though, the only thing left to stop him was a rack stacked with flour. The force of hitting the shelves knocked the blunderbuss out of his hands and reeled him backwards onto the floor. Breathless, Nate looked up as several sacks of flour, now opened, dumped their contents right on his head like a broken hourglass.

"Midnight?" he asked, coughing up a dust of flour.

'Thank you, God.' Midnight's heart dropped back down to its cradle as he looked over at his crazy friend. "You beat all, Cat. You know that?" Midnight started laughing nervously with relief as he took in the sight of Nate covered all in flour. "Can't no one say you ain't white!"

Nate wiped his arm across his mouth and spit. He was still a bit dazed as he rubbed the flour away from his eyes. He could now see what was before him. He crawled over to his friend.

"You're bleeding." Nate wiped the blood near Midnight's mouth with his shirtsleeve, leaving a white trail on Midnight's cheek.

"I've done killed him. Cat, I've done killed myself."

Nate looked at Mr. Mallock and noticed a small movement in his chest. A slight rise and fall.

"Worse, Midnight. You only winged him. He'll wake up tomorrow for sure."

"What'll we do?"

"We take him down to the crick and let the gators eat him."

"He can be gumbo soup for alls I care, Cat."

"But we gotta hurry. Where's Tiddy?" As soon as he asked, he noticed her clinging to a far shelf. She was in shock but, near as Nate could tell, was unharmed physically. Midnight had made sure of that. Nate ran over and gave her a tight hug.

"You all right, Tiddy?" he asked.

She nodded. That was all she could do. Nate took her by the hand and led her out, making a wide circle around the fallen overseer.

As they moved toward the door Nate felt someone watching and, sure enough, he turned to the window where he himself had watched Midnight being whipped.

"What is it?" Midnight whispered.

"I don't know. Wait here." Nate went back to the flour rack and in a quick second saw the small musket laying near the pile of flour. He picked it up and walked across the room.

"Wait here, alright?" He opened the door and left the shack, leaving Midnight and Tiddy alone with Mallock. The two of them stayed clear of their tormentor and listened to the muffled voices on the porch.

"Whatcha doin' in there, Mr. Cat?" asked Joseph, a boy of ten or eleven.

"Mr. Mallock had a little accident."

"What kind of accident?"

"He tripped and hit his head."

"Should I fetch Massah LeBeaux?"

"No, he's busy at his social. He wouldn't take kindly to being interrupted. And, besides, I think Mr. Mallock is beyond hope."

Joseph peered through the window again. He saw Mallock spread-eagle on the floor and two fellow slaves huddled a foot or so away.

"I should go an' fetch the Massah."

Nate grabbed his arm.

"No. He's dead and it was no one's fault."

"But the Massah should know."

"Do you want him to hang Midnight? Master LeBeaux will find him in the morning. Let him enjoy his party."

The door opened letting out the soft light from Mr. Mallock's lantern.

"Cat, he's wakin' up." There was nervousness and anxiety mixed in Midnight's voice.

"You said he was dead."

"No, Joseph. I said he was beyond hope. There's a big difference."

"We have to help him," said Joseph

"To the crick." added Nate.

"No, Mr. Cat. To the doctor."

"Like he did for Mr. Rubideaux?"

"He's the overseer. We have to."

"He's a vicious man, Joseph."

"But he's the overseer." replied Joseph.

"He's the scum of St. Charles Parish, that's what he is. That's all he is."

"You let 'im die, Massah LeBeaux will tie a few boys from the neares' tree. Not jus' Midnight. Maybe poor Joseph here."

"Joseph, I don't have the patience for this. And Midnight doesn't have the time." Nate raised the blunderbuss at his side enough to get Joseph's attention. The boy had never seen a gun quite so close before. It had a subduing effect on him.

The three boys heard moaning boots scraping against the wood floor inside.

Midnight looked back into the shack. Tiddy was starting to shake at the prospect of Mallock waking up.

"He's startin' to stir, Catfish. He's gonna come to and when he does, I'm gonna be the sorriest slave boy that ever was born. Forget about my freedom in ten years time."

"Joseph, you better get back to your bed. If Mr. Mallock wakes up and sees you, you'll be part of it, for sure."

Nate didn't have to say anything more. Joseph nodded twice and disappeared into the dark.

Nate then turned to his friend and put both hands on his shoulders.

"Listen to me, Midnight. Listen careful. We gotta leave. The Plantation. All three of us." He let the words sink in. "Somehow, we'll get ourselves North, to Canada even, where you and Tiddy will be free forever. But, you know, it ain't gonna be easy."

"How can we do it, Cat? It's too far. And we never been there. We'll get lost for sure."

"We don't have a choice. If we stay, you're dead. We have to try."

"I've gotta say good-bye to Mama."

"No, there ain't time. And it's best they know nothing."

"Mr. Mallock will beat Mama. I know it. He'll be hard."

"Don't worry about him. You and Tiddy, go down to the crick. I'll be right behind you. We'll follow it to the River."

Midnight walked to the porch with Tiddy, and Nate watched the two of them cross the alley and head towards the Wood. He went back into the shack and closed the door.

Midnight and Tiddy walked quickly—and carefully—in a northwest direction past the Cimetière toward the Indian Wood.

Its shadowy darkness would offer them their best chance for reaching the Mississippi unnoticed. They crouched down in a field of wild grasses and waited for Nate to join them. To both of them it seemed like a very long wait.

Once they were reunited, the three of them moved quickly toward the Wood. Nate re-traced the route he used when he was looking for Rubideaux's book and kept them moving. While they ran, they kept looking over their shoulders for Mallock's men. At one point all three looked back at the same time and tripped over each others' legs in the process. The result was a clumsy somersault. The three lay just lay in the field catching their breath.

"You alright, Tiddy?" Nate asked.

"I'm alright, Cat."

"We bes' git up and head into the Wood. We'll be hearin' dogs soon enough." There was worry in Midnight's voice. Though they were all scared for different reasons, it was Midnight who actually struck Mallock. He had the most to lose.

"Can't we just rest? I'm tired." pleaded Tiddy.

Nate sat up and looked in the distance. He could see the dark outline of the Wood.

"It ain't far now, Tiddy," he answered. "Midnight's right; we gotta hide in there before anyone sees us." Nate stood up, and helped his two friends rise to their feet. He looked around his feet for the blunderbuss.

Tiddy reached out to Nate's forehead. "Cat, you're bleedin'!"

Nate touched his head and felt the warm blood. "I must have hit the gun barrel when we fell." He felt a bump on his head. "I'll be alright. C'mon, we gotta go." He reached down and grabbed the gun.

They started slowly at first and built up to a run. As they neared the Wood, they could hear the rustling of its billion leaves. The wind was a welcome relief on the hot night.

Now in the cover of the Wood, the boys and Tiddy ran as fast as they could blazing a freedom trail as they went. Midnight was close on the heels of Nate while Tiddy was a distant third.

"Hold on, Cat. Gotta rest," said Midnight.

Nate ignored his friend and kept on running. Midnight pushed a little harder and grabbed hold of Nate's shoulder, and pulled back like a brakeman.

"I said, *'Hold on,' Cat.*" Both boys slowly came to a stop and doubled-over in deep breathing. The words came out in a sput and a sputter.

"Cat, we'll be dead 'fore they ever reach us. Gotta slow down. Tiddy can't go so fast, and she's plumb tired."

"We gotta get as much distance as we can. Before the sun gets up."

"Or Mr. Mallock."

"Don't need to fret about him."

"What'dya do to him, Cat?"

"I finished him, for good." Even though he knew Mallock was completely evil, Nate felt guilty inside.

Midnight looked down at the gun Nate was still carrying.

"Don't worry about it," said Nate. "It's done."

"Ah, Cat. Why'da do that?" He looked up at the canopy of trees and the stars beyond. "You know, Cat, they could hang ya from the oak allée. And leave you there 'til ya rot."

"You tryin' to lift my spirit?" Nate was still breathing hard from the run.

"I want ya to go back, Cat. Tiddy and I—we'll go to the River and head North. We'll make it all the way to Canada."

Nate put his hand on Midnight's arm. "You can't go alone. You know why most slaves never make it? Do ya?"

Midnight shook his head.

"'Cause you need a white face to get you there."

Midnight pushed Nate's arm away.

"Minuit, we'll go out the front door, like we belong. Not through the swamps and back alleys. The dogs can stay in the woods. We'll be on the road."

"I don't know, Cat. I look pretty dark in the daylight."

"Yeah, well I have a plan. You and Tiddy, just follow me, and I'll get you both to freedom."

Nate put on his most confident face to assure his scared friend, but inside he wasn't so sure himself. He knew his plan was short on details. Reach the River, head North into town. He was painfully aware that leaving Vieux Saules would mean never being able to go home or see his mom again. He missed not seeing her this week.

The boys and Tiddy walked cautiously out of the dark Wood into an open clearing that separated them from the riverbank.

They would need to be careful along the River. Every square inch of the water's edge was owned by a planter. Unlike the rest of the South, the plantations in this part of Louisiana were thin wedges stacked along the river in a way to ensure each plantation had access to the Old Man River. What they really needed was a long stretch of virgin swamp all the way to Illinois.

"It's awfully quiet, Cat?" whispered Tiddy. It was the first she had spoken since entering the Wood.

"Yeah." Nate looked around on all sides. "I don't see any sign of anyone. Don't hear any dogs, either."

As they got closer to the River's edge, the only sound they heard was the peaceful lapping of water against the bank and the few trees that had fallen into the River.

Midnight walked into the River and stared across its darkness.

"I can't even see the other side, Cat."

"The ol' state of Mississipp' sure enough is out there somewhere, but we're goin' north." He cupped his hands and brought a part of the River to his thirsty lips. He spit it out in disgust. "Come on, y'all." He led them North along the River toward Blue Mounds, the plantation bordering Vieux Saules.

"What time ya think it is, Cat? How much more dark do we have?" asked Midnight.

Nate looked into the sky and guessed it was nearly midnight. Since he was a kid, Nate had always had a strong internal clock. To Nate's embarrassment, Diana told everyone she knew it was a sign of intelligence.

"We got maybe six hours to make some distance between us and this here plantation. Less time if they go lookin' for Mallock."

"How we gonna make it? We have no food."

Nate pointed to the wide River. "We have plenty of water, and I still got the twenty dollar gold piece." He put his hand in his pocket and double-checked it was still there. "That'll take us far."

"What about food?"

"I'm hungry too, Cat."

Nate rubbed his hand across his chin while he thought. He could hear his own stomach growling.

"I got it! Come on!" A Cat of an idea had seized him. He led them excitedly back toward the Indian Wood.

"Cat, where we goin'? We're goin' north, remember?"

He waved them along and in twenty minutes they were back in the sacred haunts of Rubideaux the First. Nate grabbed a stick and knelt down. He motioned Midnight and Tiddy to do the same.

"Look. Remember I said we need to take the road?"

The other two nodded.

"Well, we are goin to take the road. The watery one!"

Midnight and Tiddy gave him funny looks.

"Richard still has the canoe, and I know where it's hidden. His daddy won't let him use it for a month of Sundays, so no one will notice it missing.

"And we ain't goin' north either."

"Cat, are you crazy?" Midnight asked.

"It would take ten men to row a canoe all the way to Illinois against the current. We'll just take it out to the Gulf."

"And then what?" Midnight was skeptical.

"We hope—no, we pray—we find a British ship before an American one." Last year's history class was kicking in. "The British are against slavery. They wouldn't give two children back."

"What if someone else finds us first?"

"That's where the next part comes in. I gotta go back to the Main House."

"No, Cat. You can't do that. Someone'll see ya for sure. You'll never make it back," Tiddy pleaded as she tugged on his arm.

"Look, everyone's asleep by now. Not even a dog barking."

"Why do you have to go back, Cat?" asked Tiddy.

"First, we need food. Even going downstream, we'll never make it on empty stomachs. Second, we need passes—case we do get stopped. Listen, I've been in Master LeBeaux's study. I know where he keeps his papers. I can make up passes for you, and sign his name like he does. While everyone is looking for us to the north, we'll be miles past New Orleans. Free and clear."

"It's a fool's plan, Cat. And I don't like you goin' back to the House. If they catch you, they'll hang you. White or not, they will hang you."

"Midnight, it's the only way. We gotta eat, and we gotta have the papers. I'll leave the gun, and I'll be back in an hour. That'll still give us a good four hours of darkness to get miles down River."

Midnight and Tiddy were quiet.

Nate held each of their hands to reassure them. "It's the only way out for us."

"What if you get caught? What'll we do then? Live in the Wood the rest of our lives?

"No. I'll leave a note with my Mama and Brett. They'll come for you if I can't."

"If something happens to you, they won't be thinkin' of any-one else."

"You're wrong, Midnight. They'll come."

"Why?" asked Tiddy. "Why would they come for us?"

"Do you really have to ask, Tiddy? After all my Mama has done for you, for both of you."

"I don't mean it that way, Cat, but you're flesh and blood. If they lose you, they'll be heart-sick."

Nate faced Tiddy and looked straight into her marble eyes. "So are you, Tiddy. You are flesh-and-blood," he said softly.

"What?"

"You're—you're my sister—sort of. Brett—Brett is really your father." He stopped and let the news sink in. "I only found out myself."

"Your father is my father?" she asked skeptically. After all these years she was learning the biggest secret kept from her.

"I overheard my parents talking about it. That's why he came here. Then he met my mom and they fell in love. It's why we can't leave. He would never leave without you." Nate held both her hands. "And, Tiddy, you can't know how all of this is hurting him. He feels so helpless—ashamed really—that he can't free his own daughter. He's all torn up inside."

"I can't believe it. I have a father?" Her eyes were being filled with joy.

"Yeah. And a pretty good one. And some day the five of us will be free and together up north. And not so many years from now, Midnight, your Mama will join us."

"You seem so sure of yourself."

"On this one, I am. But I've gotta go so we can get out of here."

The three of them hugged and then the two watched Nate disappear into the dark foliage. There was nothing to do now but wait alongside the blunderbuss.

TIMOTHY PHILLIPS

Sunday

August 30, 1857

TIMOTHY PHILLIPS

22   CAPTIVE SOUL

Under a full moon the broad-leaf trees around the Main House and outbuildings cast large shadows across the lawn. Silhouette creatures that moved as Nate moved. He moved from shadow to shadow like a field mouse evading a hawk. Until at last he reached the Main House.

Nate peered through the window. It was well past midnight and all was dark inside. He stood on his tiptoes to get a better look. The nervous boy took a deep breath to try to force the collywobbles down to his bare toes. But he was having no luck in that regard.

He had to go in. It was now or never. As he reached up to open the window, Nate felt something sharp in his side.

"Well, well. The great cat returns."

'It can't be,' Nate thought.

"You shoulda finished me off when you had the chance, boy."

Nate turned to face his devil, who pressed the pitchfork further into his belly.

"I thought I had."

"Not nearly, boy. You ain't got the stomach for it." He gave a short jerk on the fork to make his point.

"Ow!" Nate moved his hand toward the tines of the fork; he had already sucked in his gut as much as he could. He was sure it was drawing blood by now.

"Not so fast, boy. Put your hands up where I can see 'em good.—Up, I said."

"Ow! You don't have to kill me."

"Oh, not yet. Not 'til I get my pretty Tiddy back and the darky Midnight. Now turn and face the House. Slowly!"

Cat obeyed. He had no other choice at the moment.

"Now put your hands behind your back." That's a good little cat."

Nate heard the distinct sound of chains closing around his wrists.

"That's a good little cat."

Mallock grabbed Nate's arm and pulled him away from the House.

"Where we going?" Nate demanded to know.

"Someplace sweet. Now, let's go." Mallock prodded Nate's back with the pitchfork. "Down the lane."

"It'd be easier if you went first."

"But not as much fun!" Mallock jabbed the fork again and laughed.

"You keep pokin' me, I'm gonna spring a leak."

"Don't tempt me, boy. You helped two runaways and nearly killed me. So I don't much care if your blood floods the lane. Until I'm ready, that is."

The angered overseer kept prodding Nate along the lane away from the Main House and further into isolation. Somewhere on the other side of the field was his own house where his parents were most likely sleeping soundly.

Nate had perhaps made a fatal mistake in telling his parents that he was spending the night at Midnight's. No one could know he was in grave danger, except perhaps Tiddy and Midnight, who were anxiously waiting for his return and their escape down the River.

Mallock gave Nate a swift boot in the backside, sending the poor boy face-first into the lane of dried mud. He laughed loudly at Nate's pain and hopeless situation. With the pitchfork he nailed Nate's shirt to the road.

"Get up, white boy! It's late, and I'm gettin' tired."

Nate turned on his side, ripping the shirt from the fork, brought his knees up to his chest, and put his weight on his knees to lift himself off the ground and back on his feet.

Mallock laughed. "Almost there."

Up ahead Nate could see the tall sugar mill with its partway coat of indigo paint. Nate wondered what Mallock had in mind. *'Why the sugar mill?'*

Nate's mouth was getting dry, and he could feel the bones in his legs giving way to jelly. He worried whether he had the strength to get out of this alive. Suddenly, the idea of being stuck in the car between Ryan and Patty through Texas didn't seem all that bad right now.

Mallock unlocked a small shed that was attached to the mill and threw the handcuffed boy headfirst into the dark room. It was a hard landing. The overseer put his boot in the middle of Nate's back and, pressing down hard, bent down and unlocked the chains.

"Get up!" Mallock lit a lantern and put it on a peg. It was a small room with little inside but scattered hay and cloth bags.

For the first time since the Cimetière, Nate could see Mallock's bloodied face and the huge lump on his head where Midnight had clobbered him with the board. Nate had never seen so much hatred in one pair of eyes.

Nate turned his attention to the only window and in that split second, Mallock swung his hand hard against Nate's face, cutting his lip and leaving a bright red mark on his cheek. The force of the hit knocked Nate off balance, nearly sending him back to the hard floor.

"Where are they?"

"I don't know."

"Liar!" He struck Nate again in the face. "You know and you're gonna to tell me. If it's the last words outta your mouth, you're gonna tell me."

Nate backed up against the wall. It was all the defense he could muster.

"You oughta be scared, boy. No one knows you're here. No one to help you out." Mallock pulled a riding crop out of his back pocket.

"I can always tell when someone's lyin'. It's in their voice. And I have no time for it." He ran his fingers along the small whip. "I've worked with slaves all my life, and I have never— never—let one run away. That is my one pride in life. Now, you've given me two black marks. You're gonna make it right, y'hear?"

"I don't know where they are."

"Liar!" He started to strike the whip across Nate's face but stopped.

"You lie like a slave so I'll treat ya like one. Now turn around!"

Nate stood there unable to move.

"Turn around, I said."

Nate shifted his feet. "I don't know where they are. They went north hours ago."

"Do it!" Mallock raised the whip as if to strike Nate across the chest, but Nate just hardened his look. "Do it, I say!"

Nate ground his teeth, gathering the spit in his mouth, while Mallock tightened his grip on the whip. The man and his captive glared at each other, waiting for the other to give. Nate made the first move, shooting his spit to the ground, just missing Mallock's dirty boots. He continued to stare and dare Mallock to blink first.

"Why, you son of a—" Before Mallock finished his own thought, he grabbed Nate by the shoulder and twirled him around. The force caught Nate by surprise and strained his right knee as he was flipped around. Mallock, facing open defiance for the first time, shoved Nate hard against the wall and pinned him at the neck with the whip.

"For a boy who plays with Nigras, you sure as hell don't act like one. Now you drop your britches right here or I'll break your neck." He dug the whip further against Nate's neck, making it more difficult for Nate to even breathe.

Truly scared, Nate fumbled for the front buttons and slid the suspenders off his shoulders. He closed his eyes, took a deep breath, and waited.

Mallock smiled as he watched Nate comply. The crazed man was discovering a new source of power—domination over another white soul. He took his time winding back and then—

—*Whack!* Nate's entire body flinched in reaction. He could feel the heat rising off his skin where the whip had struck.

The overseer wound his arm back and struck again. And again. The pain on Nate's bare backside was now intense. How he would endure this and live to see another day, he had no idea.

By the fourth strike Nate was forcing back his tears, but he couldn't stop his chest from heaving. He knew he had been caught by the Devil himself and he was paying the price. He knew now what Midnight had endured earlier and, perhaps for the first time in his life, understood a little what it was like for Midnight and Tiddy every day. Being in constant fear of crossing an invisible line.

"Ready to talk now, boy?" He looked down at the welts and new-formed bruises. "Had enough?"

He put his hand on Nate's face and pulled his body straight. The young face was literally a mixture of blood, sweat, and tears. And smudges of Louisiana mud thrown in. His left eyelid was beginning to swell shut.

"Your problem, boy, is you forgot that they ain't people; they're property. A notch above a horse, if that. If you're givin' up your life for property, you're a bigger fool than I thought."

Nate was silent as he pulled up his britches, and Mallock put the chains back on his wrists and tied his feet with rope.

"This is your last chance, boy. Last chance to tell me whatch ya know. When I come back, you'll be gator bait. Now where are they?"

"I don't know."

Mallock gagged Nate's mouth with a rag and threw him onto a pile of hay.

"Don't try beggin' for mercy tomorrow!" He blew out the lantern and closed the door. Nate heard the steel lock click tight.

The shed was musty and cold and with his mouth gagged, there was no way to breathe but through his nose. There was no way to avoid the strong smells.

As much as Nate wanted to escape, and knew he had to if he was going to live another day, he also knew there was no hope.

His hands were chained behind his back, and the door was pad-locked on the outside. There was the small window, but without a free hand to open it, and free feet to climb up to it, it was of little use to him.

He was tired as well. The beatings and adrenalin rush of being caught by Mallock—and the shock that he was still alive—had taken its toll on the boy. Nate fought to stay awake and alert. He didn't know when Mallock would be back. Could be in five minutes or five hours. There was no way to know.

His only hope was to survive into the morning and pray Brett and Jenna had discovered he hadn't stayed at Midnight's after all. He was sure that the news of Midnight's and Tiddy's escape would spread quickly through Vieux Saules.

But would anyone look for him in the shed beside the mill? Or, would they guess what should have happened—that he had escaped with them? Like everyone else, his parents would be looking for him outside the plantation, not in the middle of it. And that was exactly what Mallock was counting on.

Nate and Cat had never been in such a deadly situation. Neither had a ready solution. If only his hands were free, then he would have a chance.

He leaned against the wall and tipped his head back. From there through the window he could see a handful of stars. It was a cloudless night. He craned his neck to see more of the sky. *'Are you up there, God? Are you?'*

He wondered. Wondered a lot.

Before this week he had honestly never even given God any thought. He thought a lot about his father, the father he never knew, and always wondered why he had left. *'Why didn't he want to stay and watch me grow up?'* Yeah, he wondered about that. But about God, he never thought about Him.

'Things weren't that bad back home,' he told himself. *'Ryan and Patty are alright. Leave me alone mostly. And now mom doesn't have to worry about money.'* He remembered then all those times in bed late at night when he wished he lived in a different house, that he had had a different life in a different town.

Nate shifted his weight and stood up, a bit shaky at first, and shuffled over to the window. It was taller than his eyes, though, so he pushed a block of wood over with his heels. He maneuvered onto the block and took another view of the stars.

'Are you up there, God?' he whispered into the rag in his mouth. He tried to bring his hands up to pray, remembering how Jenna prayed, but his hands were secured behind his back by the chains. *'God, if you're there, I need your help.'* He could feel his emotions rushing to the surface. Nate struggled to keep back the tears, but he was too tired.

'I'm scared, God. Really scared.' He bit down on the gag and hoped that God was able to read minds. He looked over at the door, his only avenue for escape, and the only way in for Mallock. Nate didn't know when Mallock would be coming back, but he wasn't looking forward to it. Nate knew he could be only minutes or hours from death—a painful death he was sure.

The front of Nate's face was wet from crying, and the runny nose that followed made it hard for him to breathe. With his hands bound behind his back, he tried wiping it on his shoulder but finally had to settle on the rough windowsill. He felt like a real mess.

'Father—God, I can't die here. Not here, not this way. Midnight and Tiddy need me. They're stuck in the Wood, your Wood. I have to help them get away. And—and my mom, she doesn't even know where I am. She thinks I'm still in another room.'

Though totally spent, Nate slowly got down to his knees.

'I don't understand any of this, God. This week has been a mystery. You brought me back here for something. I didn't even know you existed, but you brought me here anyway. You led me down those stairs—I know you did. But I don't know why—but it can't be to die here, like this. It just can't be.'

Nate gazed into the stars. They seemed so close to each other but he knew from science class that they were actually millions, or billions, of miles apart. Right then, that's how he felt about God. Jenna said God was everywhere all the time. *'If that were true, then God must be here in the shack with me.'*

Nate looked all around the shack. *'If you're here with me God, why do I feel all alone? If you are here with me, you wouldn't leave me like this.'* Nate held his breath and pushed hard against the chains trying to break them, but they were solid, well built.

Worse than the thought of dying, he couldn't face another encounter with Mallock. He was a devil of a man, full of evil and hate. He knew there was nothing the evil Mallock wouldn't do. The weaker his target, the worse it came.

'God, hear me, I can't do this alone. I need you. Save me from this. For Jesus' sake, save me. Please.'

Nate walked on his knees to the pile of hay and fell down on to it, crying like a baby and saying the same prayer in his mind over and over again until at last he felt a peace and a presence surrounding him. Finally, he understood what made Cat different from him.

Sometime around four in the morning, totally exhausted, Nate finally fell to peaceful sleep. He was spent from hours of crying.

Meanwhile, in the Indian Wood Midnight and Tiddy huddled together for warmth and security. It had been at least eight hours past when Cat should have come back. It would be light in another hour or so, and there would be a mighty short trail for the dogs to find them.

"Where do ya think he is, Midnight?"

"I don't know, Tiddy. Cat's fast. Somethin' must be wrong."

"But he said he killed Mr. Mallock. No one else knew we was gone."

"Maybe Massah LeBeaux found him in his kitchen."

"Then why ain't the Massah in here now?" she asked.

"Don't know. Maybe the Massah don't know we ain't where we're supposed to be so he didn't ask him. Maybe he's just holdin' Cat 'cause he caught him stealin'."

"So wha'da we do in the morning when they find out we're gone? Can't outrun the dogs, not in the light of day."

"Well, we could stay in the darkest part of the Wood 'til tomorrow night, an' then look for the canoe like Cat say. Go south ourselves." He paused. "It'll be a lot harder without Cat. Two slave children in a boat'll look mighty funny. But it might be the only choice we have."

He tightened his arm around Tiddy. "It'll be all right, Tiddy. You'll see. God, He's on our side. An' on Cat's too. It'll be all right."

23   Blue Peter

Nate woke up with the roosters. His arms and legs were stiff, and he was anxious to have them free. He was also anxious to use the outhouse.

It was quiet outside. Not a single soul, slave or free, in sight. The mill was intentionally placed far from the main buildings so there was little use in screaming for help. Not that Nate felt like screaming. Unlike yesterday, he was calm, almost content. He felt God was with him now so he was no longer in this alone.

Nate pulled on the chains from time to time but they were solid. Mallock had also tied the rope around his ankles pretty tight. So much so that his feet kept falling asleep even as the rest of his body was on edge. Somehow, though, he knew God would find a way out for him.

Nate shuffled back to the window and hobbled up to the wood block. In the beginning light he could see a field of tall grass. He stared into the grass and saw a cat emerge with a small something in its mouth. Nate watched the cat intently and in a watery

blink it grew into a large cat—a lion in fact. He thought immediately of Midnight and his dreams about the African jungle. He
wondered how Midnight and Tiddy were doing. Nate felt guilty
for planning their escape so poorly. He should have had a con-
tingency plan in case he didn't return. He hoped that God was
with them now giving them the same sense of peace. Jenna had
said that God could be everywhere at the same time. He prayed
that that was true.

Nate also thought about the story he had read in the Bible
earlier in the week, the one about Daniel and the Lion's Den.
Looking around the shack and at the chains, he couldn't help but
wonder whether he was facing his own set of lions. *'Lord, am I
like Daniel waiting for the lions? Will you save me as well?'* He
wondered if was worthy of being saved.

Cat would not have had to ask, but Nate wasn't so sure. He
seemed to bounce from Trusting to Doubting and back again.
Round and round. For him, this week was the most time he had
spent hearing about God than in his first fourteen years combined. The modern boy wished he had the same faith as Cat,
but their moms were not the same and he hadn't had a dad to
bring him up in the Lord.

'So what happens next?' he wondered. It was now around
noon, and there was no sign of Mallock. Worse, the shed had
become like an oven. He was extremely thirsty, and he still
needed the outhouse. Nate was sure he would pee in his pants
the moment he heard the padlock opened. In the meantime he
hopped up and down to take his mind off that little problem and
to put blood back in his hands and feet.

He worried, too, about Midnight and Tiddy. The regretful
boy could only hope that they would try to wait it out in the
safety of the Wood until tonight. Maybe God would give him a
break and he could join them after all.

By two in the afternoon, Nate was ready to eat through the gag and munch on some of the hay. His stomach was growling every other minute. He no longer had to go to the bathroom, though the wet pants now stung his legs. While he tried sitting to give his legs a rest, the position was much too painful on his bruised backside. He was also wilting without water in the confines of the hot shed and assumed he would pass out at any moment.

Nate was finding out just how cruel—and how clever—a man that Mallock was. He could have swatted him like a fly hours ago, but instead he was letting the boy suffer the discomforts of captivity. For how long, that was the real question.

The scared boy kept looking out the window from time to time but even by mid-afternoon, there was still no one around. It was the slaves' only real day to relax and do as they pleased so none of them wanted to venture a foot near anything that reminded them of their work. And most of the white men, he ventured, were off looking for Midnight and Tiddy.

About an hour later, as Nate leaned in the corner trying to imagine where God might be in the shack, he heard the rustling of keys and the sound of the padlock opening. Despite Mallock's foul odor, the opening of the shed door seemed to bring in a wave of fresh air. Nate's pale face got back a bit of its color.

Mallock noticed the wood block right away. "Catchin' a glimpse of freedom, eh boy?" he laughed. "Well, look away all you want. Won't do ya no good now."

He removed the gag, and Nate immediately opened his mouth wide and took in a deep breathe. And then another and another.

"Like a rotten fish out of water." He laughed and then scowled. "What'dya do boy, wet your pants? I could smell you when I opened the door. You act more and more like a slave."

He untied the ropes and then the chains. Nate rubbed his wrists and shook his hands to bring back the circulation. He moved his feet around as well.

"Don't get too comfy. Not til I get what I want. And you know what that is, boy. Don't cha?" He slapped him across the face as he did the night before. The force of his hand turned Nate's face sharply to the right.

"Now, I'm gonna ask you one time, and one time only. Where'dya hide those slaves? You tell me and I may talk Massah into just giving ya a good lashin'. I may even forget you tried to kill me. Think hard before you speak, boy, or you may find yourself hanging from the nearest tree."

He thumped his finger on Nate's chest. "So what'll it be? Where are those darkies?"

Nate looked past Mallock and could see a sliver of light between the door and the wall. In Mallock's haste to confront Nate, he failed to notice it hadn't shut. Nate took a step back from Mallock while moving slightly to the left so he could see more of the light.

For the first time since yesterday, Nate felt there was some hope. He could see a way out. "Thank you, God," he whispered.

Mallock leaned in. "Wha'dya say, boy?"

"N—Nothing." Nate stuttered. He took another side step to the left, closer toward the door. Mallock did the same and was not in a position to see the same light.

"Where are they, boy? I'm losin' time with you."

Another small step, and Nate could smell the fresh air. "I'm not sure—I don't know where they're at now." He braved another small step to bring the door directly to his left. Mallock focused his eyes on Nate's face, wondering if he was telling him the truth. He prided himself on his ability to know whether a slave was lyin'.

"Well, where'dya leave them then?"

"You're scarin' me. I can't think right when I'm scared."

Mallock took half a step back and at the same time put a hand on the whip hanging by his belt. He felt an itch in his hand. He was looking forward to using it again on the scared white boy. "All right?" he demanded. "Where are they? It's gettin' late so there ain't much time."

At that moment a blue bunting flew onto the window ledge. Nate and the bird locked eyes and he wasn't altogether sure it wasn't the bird he had saved. The bunting broke into a song, and, for a moment, Mallock took his eyes away from Nate.

This was Nate's chance to escape, his only chance. Hoping the door was directly behind him, Nate took a leap of faith, turned and ran out of the shed. Slamming the door shut, he frantically swung the hasp and slid the padlock through the eye.

"If you wanna find Midnight and Tiddy, they're in the middle of Misery, you son of a bitch!" He slammed his fist on the door to further his point and then tore off toward the sugar mill.

Locked or not, the wooden door was no match for a grown man in boots, especially one as hot and angry as Mister Mallock. The door flew off its hinges on the third kick. He saw Nate run into the mill and followed him in.

Nate was nearly up the ladder to the loft when he realized that Mallock was close behind. He hurried up and ran over to the loft door and pushed it open.

'*Drat.*' The rope was gone from the pulley. Brett must have taken it down after he painted the last time. He looked around quickly. The only other way out was a catwalk across the middle of the mill. It was a thin walkway with short wooden railings on either side. It wasn't much, but he had no other choice. And, it was certainly better than being back in the shed.

He was halfway across when Mallock joined him on the walk. In his rush to get away—and because his feet were still cramped—Nate tripped and nearly fell over. By the time he stood up again Mallock was only a couple feet away.

The overseer whacked his riding crop across Nate's hand, cutting it open.

"Aw! Hell!" Nate screamed loudly in pain.

Mallock smiled. "Maybe you'll like this even better." He threw the crop over the side, and reached behind his back.

Seeing his last opportunity, Nate put all his weight on his hands and holding onto the railings, lifted his feet and pushed them hard against Mallock's gut. Mallock fell backward hard and because his hand was behind his back he couldn't quite catch his fall.

This time Nate heard Mallock scream in pain, and he had to admit it felt good to be on the other side of it. Instead of running, he waited to see what Mallock would do. He watched the man get up and pull out a large knife. It was long with jagged edges.

"I'll carve your guts out, boy, and with pleasure too."

The man lunged at Nate but Cat's instincts were working and the boy ducked low and charged Mallock's lower legs. He managed to push the force of Mallock's weight against the side railing. Fortunately for Nate, Mallock was standing at the spot where the railing was its weakest. The wood gave way in a snap and a crunch, and the wicked overseer found himself in a forty-foot free-fall headfirst to the rock solid ground. He was truly dead in that instant.

Nate stood on the catwalk staring at the contorted man down below. He had now seen two men die, both in one week. One good man and one bad.

He couldn't believe that what seemed hopeless just twenty minutes before had all suddenly changed. The cruelest man he had ever known could no longer hurt him or Tiddy or Midnight.

"Tiddy. Midnight!" Suddenly, Nate was reminded that he had a plan to fix. He ran along the catwalk back to the loft and quickly maneuvered the ladder. He took a final look at the newly deceased and then ran out of the sugar mill and down the lane toward the Main House. He was in no mood to bump into Mallock's rising ghost.

It was by now nearly five in the evening. He knew that the Family would be off at church so he ran quickly to the kitchen where Miss Nancy and Miss Alma were still working.

"Landsakes, Master Peter! You look like somethin' the cat drug in."

"Look at you boy! And your one eye is nearly shut. You get in a fight?"

"Yes, ma'am."

"What does your mama tell you about fightin'" lectured Miss Alma.

"Nothing good ever come of it," added Miss Nancy.

"Yessum. This one couldn't be helped."

"And what'chyou doin' here anyway," she lowered her voice. "Folks say you run off with Tiddy and Midnight."

"I can't rightly say. But I do need help. I need to see Benjamin."

"What you want with him? He won't help you."

"No, sir, he won't help you. He's blind as a white man."

Nate knew better. God had told him what to do. "He's the only one that can help."

"What if he won't? You could be in a heap of trouble."

"Tiddy and Midnight already are. I don't have much time."

Miss Nancy nodded to Miss Alma, who quickly left the kitchen and disappeared down the hall. In a few minutes she came back with the properly dressed butler.

He took one look at Cat and his mouth was frozen open.

Cat took a couple steps closer.

"Mr. Benjamin, I truly need your help. God has told me to come here. Told me you will help me."

"I'll take you there" He led Cat down the hallway to Master LeBeaux's study, leaving the two women in utter shock at what they had just witnessed.

Nate watched Benjamin hit a certain spot on the wall, and a door opened, leading them into the treasured study.

"How did you know what I needed?" asked Nate.

"I knows what people thinks about me. I knows what you think. But no one knows what I think. And last night, the Lord came to my room an' He told me you'd come, an' He told me what you'd need."

"What time did He come?" The boy was curious.

"Near to four, it was." It was the time when Nate finally felt at peace. "The ledger's over there." Benjamin pointed to a credenza by the Master's roll top desk.

"Ledgers? No, I need his paper. I need to write passes so we can get to freedom."

"There's blue paper on the desk. Massah always use the blue paper for importan' things. But the Lord say you needs the ledger."

Nate walked over to the credenza and looked at the ledgers lined up.

"But which one?"

"The one marked with the blue paper."

Nate picked up the ledger and opened it to where there were two sheets of paper.

"I don't understand, Benjamin. It's a birth register."

"Look at the names, Mastuh Peter. It'll be clear."

Nate ran his finger down the left margin until he saw Tiddy-Beaux's name. It listed her time of birth and her mother as *Martha, Slave*. For father, LeBeaux had written *Brett Hennessee, Irish painter*. Nate looked up at Benjamin and gave a quizzed look. Then he looked back down at the ledger and froze in disbelief.

On the following line, LeBeaux had written: *Midnight, Twin of Tiddy*.

Nate stood there staring at the word *Twin*. Brett had a son, a flesh-and-blood son. For some cruel reason, LeBeaux had chosen to conceal that from Brett and from everyone else. He wanted to ask him why and how anyone could do that to someone. To deny a child his father, and a father his son. But he knew time was already running short.

He grabbed a pen and ink and wrote a quick note to his parents giving them this news and asking them not to worry. To remind them that God could take care of them all.

He turned to the second sheet to write a pass, but it had already been filled out and signed.

"It looks so official. It has our names on it. I don't understand. Who did this?"

"You needn't know everything. But you must go. Massah LeBeaux will be back soon." Benjamin took the ledger from Nate and put it back in its place.

Nate folded the pass and put it in his pocket, and he and Benjamin walked back into the kitchen. Nate handed the note for his parents to Miss Nancy.

"Give this to my parents. Tell them not to worry." Nancy opened the folded note but it was in French. She quickly tucked it in her apron and nodded yes.

"Can you put some food in a sack for us? I'm going upstairs to get some of Richard's clothes. I'll be back in a few minutes." The women nodded and began getting food ready to go.

Nate tiptoed over to the back stairs and stared up at the long, narrow, dark stairway. The stakes were high. But he was confident. He would sneak up the stairs, change into Richard's fine clothes, and be back downstairs and outside in just a few minutes. But he had to hurry. The LeBeauxs could be back any moment.

"Hurry, Cat." pleaded Miss Alma.

"You hasn't much time," reminded Benjamin.

Nate took the first steps up the squeaky stairs. And then the next and the next. In short order he was at the top of the flight with his hand touching the knob. He wondered what he would find on the other side of the door. Which year? He knew that leaving Vieux Saules with Midnight and Tiddy would mean never going back home. It was a hard thing for him to think about, but his new friends needed him. Without him, they were doomed to slavery.

He opened the door to the hall and as he took a step in, he felt something inside pulling back. All of his muscles were being tugged backwards, more and more, and then, seconds later, they snapped back into place like a giant rubber band flicking his entire body. It numbed his skin, and he knew right then that for the first time in a week, he was truly on his own. The boy he had shared a body with was gone. He had stayed on the threshold.

Nate felt the void from Cat's departure. He walked into Richard's bedroom and stood there straining to see, to sense the presence of Cat. He knew his double would be there in the room; he knew what Cat was doing that very moment. He knew it as sure as—he reached into his pocket and pulled out the coin—he knew that the coin in his hand was gold. Gold from 1857.

He looked down at his feet that were once again in chalk white sneakers. His pants were fresh, and his shirt untorn. Headphones hung around his neck.

Nate was back in the present. He walked over to the mirror above Richard's dresser. The cuts and bruises were gone as were the aches throughout his body.

He stood in front of the picture of Richard and saw the planter boy differently now that he had had the chance to meet him, talk to him, see his world, and—yes—save his life. He looked out the window at the River in the distance and remembered their wild, rolling adventure chasing paddle wheelers.

He spread out his arms and waved them all around, thinking—hoping—that somehow he would catch the spirit of Cat. Nothing. Nothing was all he found.

An incredible sense of loneliness struck him as he thought about Cat and Richard. Tiddy and Midnight. And Brett and Jenna. He walked back across the hall and opened the door to the backstairs. He stared down into the darkness and listened for Miss Nancy and Miss Alma, but it was quiet. It was nearly closing time for the museum.

Before joining his family in the other room, he prayed for the first time as modern Nate. He closed his eyes and thought of his mother Jenna and how she talked to God. He could feel the water building around his eyes.

"Father God—I pray, um, with all my heart that the Irish Butterbyes will never take this week away from me. Thank you for saving me." He leaned against the doorjamb. "As my Maman Jenna says, 'Lead me, Father. Lead me to the light'. Don't ever leave me. And, if it's possible, let me see them all again. In Jesus' name, I pray."

24 THE HIDING PLACE

Nate could hear the docent talking in the parlor in the next room. He looked at his watch, which had reappeared on his wrist. It was 4:55pm. Despite all his adventures in the previous week, only a few minutes had actually passed.

Reluctantly, he left Richard's bedroom. It was, symbolically perhaps, taking him one more step away from the people of Vieux Saules whom he just gotten to know. He followed the high-pitched voice of the young woman who seemed to know all there was to know about this once vibrant plantation.

"Glad you could join us, young man," said the prim lady who was not that much older herself.

Diana rushed over to her errant son. "Oh, honestly, Nathaniel. Can you please keep up with the rest of us?"

"Yeah, Nate. Keep up," chimed Patty.

Nate looked around, but the grand room had lost all its life and color. Its glory days were gone.

"We are fortunate to have in this room not only some of the fine furniture from its heyday, but also these fine curtains that came all the way from Paris. They were quite expensive at the time."

Nate looked over to the windows and remembered the sad fate of Samuel and Ruth. The docent was right about the cost.

All eyes in the room followed him as he walked to the far window and looked through the bubbled glass. But last week's world was gone for Nate. The only things on the horizon were the dark clouds of another storm.

He turned to face the docent. "Are the ledgers still here?" he asked.

"I beg your pardon?" she replied.

"Master LeBeaux's ledgers. The Slave books. Are they still in the House?"

She ignored his question altogether and tried to refocus her thoughts on some of the colorful decorations on the west wall. All the while, though, she kept half an eye on the strange tourist boy.

Nate had had enough waiting on others. Seemed like that's all he'd done all his life. If he learned anything this past week, it was to take charge. Do something.

He walked deliberately across the room. Deliberate but respectful. So quietly that only his family, the black gentleman from New York, and the prim docent noticed him. When he reached the doorway, he tore off down the hall. That, everyone noticed, and the rest of the group followed him, as best they could.

Nate turned left and then opened a small door to his right. It was a part of the House the tour had not yet seen. Everyone was curious to know, especially the docent, if Nate knew in fact where he was going or was just a young troubled kid running amok in a treasured museum. Diana gave John her worried look that said *'Help!'*

The tour group and anxious docent followed Nate through the door and down another curved staircase leading directly into Master LeBeaux's private office. *The Rabbit Hole.*

The office looked just like as it did last Wednesday when LeBeaux had summoned Nate to thank him for saving Richard's life. The credenza behind the desk was now empty, so he frantically opened the larger drawers to the Master's roll-top desk.

The docent pushed her way through the crowd. "Take your hands off that desk, young man." Her voice was tense. "This is priceless furniture. Where are your parents?" She looked nervously around for any adult face that would give itself away as the owner of such an unpredictable child. She spotted Diana's face easily.

Nate stopped pulling out the drawers. "Where are they? Where are the ledgers?" with a mix of excitement and frustration in his voice.

"You need to calm down." The docent turned to Diana for support. "I'm going to have to ask you to control your son."

Nate stepped forward. "Where—are—the—ledgers?" he demanded.

"Nathan, honey." His mom reverted to a tactic that worked in second grade. "Let's go outside and get some fresh air."

The docent looked at her watch for the twenty-eighth time this tour. It was now a minute before five o'clock. "Yes," she said, "The Main House is closing. We should really move on to the gift shop."

"No!" Nate was firm. "Not until I see the ledgers. Please."

The young docent looked into Nate's green eyes.

"Please." he said softly. "Le maître voudrait que je les voie." *The Master would want me to see.*

Diana was shocked at the musical sound of French coming from her confident son. The docent seemed to understand something as well. She hesitated a second and then led him to the far side of the room where a cloth draped a small table. She removed the drape to reveal one of the Master's slave books.

"This was—the last book Mr. LeBeaux kept. The final entry was just a week before the Confederacy surrendered."

Nate's heart quickened as he approached the table. The rest of the tour was excited as well by this revelation. There was a sense that the tour had veered off its scripted page, and they were being given a rare treat. Something no other tour had ever seen before, and most likely none in the future ever would. Their disdain for the troubled blonde boy started evaporating. They were a fickle crowd.

The book was opened but secured beneath a glass case.

"The book is old and fragile. It is turned to the final inventory of slaves that was taken in March of 1865."

Nate stood in front of the glass case and leaned over to read the names. He was breathing so hard that fog kept forming on the glass and blocking his view. He rubbed it away with his sleeve and held his breath as he read the names that were in alphabetical order.

"It stops at 'G,' he said.

"Yes, and I'm afraid I don't have the key. I'm sorry." She turned to the rest of the group. "Well, ladies and gentlemen, I want to thank you for your kind attention throughout the tour, and for your patience in this past little bit of excitement. If you will turn and exit straight ahead. Thank you."

Nate was clearly disappointed. *'Maybe none of it happened,'* he thought. *'Maybe I was just daydreaming, like I do in class.*

Maybe my imagination created the whole thing.' His old lack of confidence was trying to push through even as his hand dug into his pocket and touched the gold memory. He smiled as his fingers connected with his recent distant past.

It had happened, just as his mind remembered. *But how, how, could he find out if Midnight and Tiddy had made it to freedom?* That was his only concern right then.

Nate had another idea. He pushed his way forward, parting the crowd like a little Moses as they pressed forward to get a glimpse of the just revealed treasure.

"Excuse me. Sorry, ma'am. Excuse me. Oh, sorry." Apologies peppered his escape. John, Diana, Ryan, and Patty followed closely behind.

When Nate exited the Main House, he turned left around the back gardens and took the path that had led him to the Cimetière so many times this past week.

A storm was arriving, sending the temperature south, thank goodness, and unloading drops of heavy rain. The family, still following, watched in astonishment as Nate maneuvered his way through the grounds. He seemed to anticipate what was around each corner.

Out of the corner of his eye, Nate saw the indigo sugar mill in the distance. He laughed inside at the color and remembered Brett fondly. He wished he could have seen his joy in reading his note and finding he had yet another son. He hoped that Cat and his parents and Tiddy and Midnight all made it to the north and lived together as a real family.

The sight of the sugar mill, though, brought back the nightmare of the day and previous night as he did battle with the Devil. But, then, he remembered how God had rescued him, and how he had visited Benjamin in the night to make sure all would go well.

At one point, as Nate approached the muddy ditch, he leapt across it as he had witnessed Richard's horse do. But the ditch had been dry the whole summer and was just now starting to collect the rainwater.

Nate was getting wet and sweaty at the same time. His heart raced between his lungs and his mind was already in the Cimetière. He didn't know what he would find there, but he had to try.

He came to where the old wooden bridge once stood leading into the Cimetière. It was now a monument of concrete form perfection. Up ahead he saw the rows of familiar slave cabins. Despite the years they were in remarkably good shape. The oak trees lining the dirt lanes were much taller and more mysteriously shaped than he had seen them the previous week.

Diana and the rest of the family watched Nate stop at a particular cabin and go inside.

"John, what do you think this is all about? Something isn't right."

"How did he know about those books?" asked Ryan.

"Why did he go into that cabin? Why *that* cabin?" added Patty.

"Why any cabin?" asked John.

Perplexed, the four of them walked closer to Midnight's cabin while, inside, Nate walked across the room to the old fireplace. He counted the bricks from the bottom on the left side as he remembered Midnight doing. He could almost hear Midnight whispering over his shoulder. *'Don't let the others see ya, Cat. This is my special hiding place, remember?'*

He found the magical brick and pushed on it until one side protruded. He could feel his beating heart all the way to his lower jaw. The rain in his hair ran into his eyes and onto the wooden floor. He began coughing from running so hard in the rain.

It was just like the night before when he ran from the Indian Wood to the Main House. He had been all out of breath when Mallock pressed the pitchfork into his side. He put his hand on his side, but felt nothing painful. The bruises, the welts, the cuts on his hand and face were gone. All had vanished at the top of the stairs.

With wet hands he pried the brick free. Midnight's hiding place. He put his hand inside, not knowing what he might find, if anything. It was his only hope of knowing. He closed his eyes and thought of his friend and of his prayer to God the night before.

His nervous fingers felt inside the darkness. He heard the soft clinking of glass and smiled. In his hand he pulled out a small leather bag. Midnight's prized marbles. The only possession he owned. The marbles were further proof he hadn't gone crazy.

He reached back into the hiding place and felt around. His hand touched a small book, and he remembered it was Rubideaux's. He had given it to Midnight to keep safe. Holding the book in his hand, it naturally fell open to the last page read by Rubideaux before he died. Nate re-read the first part of the poem.

> *She sits there in the blue of night*
> *beneath the dome of starry light.*
> *Day's end has shown a dazzling sight*
> *divinely placed in Heaven's height.*

The book and marbles were sure signs that Midnight had never returned to the cabin. That still didn't tell him, though, whether Midnight had made it to freedom. Nate put his hand back in the hiding place for a third time, but there was nothing else in the little vault.

He stood up and looked around the cabin. It had been rustic then, with rough wood and little furniture. It had since fallen into disrepair, and all of the furniture was gone.

He walked back onto the porch. The rain was coming down steady, and he could see his family across the alley huddled to stay dry under one of the oaks just like he had done with Midnight and Tiddy as they played marbles. They were staring at Midnight's cabin—at him—wondering what was happening to their son and stepbrother.

Nate didn't know himself. He knew that the craziest of crazy stories was true. He had the proof in his pockets, and there were no marbles lost. But he couldn't explain, to himself or anyone, how it all happened or why. He also didn't know what happened to Cat and his family. That question weighed on him more than the other two questions combined.

It had been an intense week, and he had bonded with them more than anyone else in all of his fourteen years of life on this earth. *What if he hadn't gone up to Richard's bedroom? Would he have found Midnight and Tiddy waiting for him in the Indian Wood? Would they have made it safely to the Gulf and ultimately to the north? Would he have lived the rest of his days in the past? Is that what he had been doing all his life anyway? Holding back, waiting for his father to return?*

He wished he knew the answers. But in one step across a threshold he had skipped ahead a hundred and fifty years.

As he stood on the porch, he remembered the fathers in his life. The first one who left him and his mom when he was only two. He never knew him, other than bits and pieces he gathered from his mom, especially when she was having a hard day. In school he imagined him to be a man of great importance, though deep down, he knew he was only a French chef. And perhaps not even a good one at that.

Then he thought of his borrowed Irish step-dad who struggled to be close to his daughter all the years Cat was growing up. The angst of watching her in slavery was always with him. Yet, until this week, Cat hadn't a clue. His father had enough love to share with him and with Tiddy. He treated Cat as if he were his flesh and blood. He was the father Nate had always wanted for himself.

Finally, there was Nate's own step-dad, a successful lawyer who was probably a decent guy. But Nate always found it hard to get his attention; Ryan and Patty were always there. *What does a man with two hands do with three children?* He would often ask himself at night when he was alone in bed and couldn't sleep. He never had the confidence to find out.

As Nate stood frozen on the porch, his step-dad ventured into the rain to cross the alley.

"Nate, what is it? What are you looking for?" his step-dad asked. At first, Nate couldn't hear him because of the rain, but his step-dad kept walking toward Nate and repeating the question.

"I don't know." Nate answered. Nate seemed at an emotional fork. John climbed the steps until he was eye to eye with his stepson.

"Why did you come here?"

"'Cause mom wanted to see the South."

His step-dad chuckled. "No, I mean why did you come here? Why did you run into the study back there?"

"I—I don't know. I'm just crazy, I guess."

"Nate, you're not crazy. But you are good at shutting people out."

Nate looked away toward the shack where the nightmare of yesterday first began. John turned Nate's head to face him again.

"You can't always turn away. Sometimes you have to face things."

"I face things. All the time." He looked at his step-dad. "You think I'm nuts. I know it, and I can see it. In all of you! I don't blame you—really. I'd probably think I was crazy too, except how is it that I know things about this place that Miss Primdocent doesn't? How did I know these—" Nate pulled Midnight's bag of marbles from his pocket and dangled it in front of his step-dad—"would be inside the chimney?

"Or, how is it that I know why that sugar mill is really bright blue? Or know the names of—" his voice now breaking "—some of the slaves and the whites who lived here?

"I have never been here before today but I know that on the other side of this Cimetière is a real cemetery." By now Nate was beginning to shake either from the rain or the emotions of the day. "And I know that in the northeast section by the River there should be a sacred forest, not oil pumps.

John gave Nate a blank look.

"Don't look at me like I'm crazy, 'cause I'm not."

"I don't think you're crazy, Nate."

Nate wiped the rain off his face. "I know a lot." He looked at John with almost pleading eyes. "But there's a lot I don't know. Things I just can't figure on my own."

"Nate, you may think I'm distant, but I'm not. I keep a close eye on you. I grew up without a father so I understand. It is not that I favor Ryan and Patty; it's that I know I can't just walk into your life and assume to be your dad. Fatherhood may be instant, but being a dad takes time and trust. *Mutual* trust."

Looking Nate straight in the eye, he spoke "I can't answer all the questions you've asked. Somehow back in that house something happened. And now you know things you didn't know before. Things that are hard to explain away." He laughed. "Like marbles in a chimney."

Looking at his mom and step-siblings, Nate said, "They won't believe any of this."

"Maybe not, but then so what? It's not for us to question. But the real question from me is what do you do now? Do you keep shutting us all out, including your mother? Or do you take a chance? How will you let your life be different?"

"If you've watched me so closely, tell me what I'm doing wrong with your twins?"

"That's your problem right there. They aren't my twins. They're your brother and sister. The three of you have a lot in common actually. You have all had to grow up with only one parent. You lost your father when you were two, and that was a terrible thing. But you never knew him. Ryan and Patty lost their mother three years ago. They know what they are missing, and it's very painful."

There was a long silence between them, with only the steady force of rain to keep the tempo.

"Do you believe in God?" Nate finally asked.

"Sure. Of course." John answered.

"Why?"

"It's how I was raised, I guess."

"But is it—" Nate stopped. He closed his mouth and breathed out deeply. His eyes darted up to the rafters of the porch for some hidden message. He was fumbling for the right question. "Is it what carries you through life?"

"I never think about it, really." He answered matter-of-factly. "I know God is there. I know He is powerful. I know He cares about me. Why do you ask? I mean, what exactly did happen back there? I know something did. I'm a smart enough lawyer to see that."

"I don't think you'd understand."

John put his hand on Nate's arm. "Like I said, you're very good at freezing people out. Maybe for good reason. But at some point you have to take a chance and let someone in. Let me in. Let me help you."

Nate laughed softly. "That's not it. I'm not freezing you out. There's a reason I don't think you'd understand, and it has nothing to do with you and me."

"Then what is it?"

"You want to know what happened back there, but the only way you could possibly understand is if you believe. Not in me— I'm just a confused kid, right—but you'd have to believe in God. Not because He is distant but powerful, but because He is the One and Only. He created everything. But—Dad,"—he used the word that would catch John's attention—"I'm not sure you be- lieve in God. Not really. And if you don't believe in God, trust me, you would never believe what I would tell you about where I've been."

"Trust me."

"It's not that simple." He pointed at the other crude houses. "You see these cabins?"

John looked around at the various cabins and nodded.

"This wasn't some slave quarters. This was like a testing ground for people who really believed in God. They stood up the best they could." He leaned in toward his new dad. "And I know it, because I saw it. I was there. Only for a week, but I was there."

John looked into his step-son's green eyes and, whether it was God working on his heart or not, something inside told him that the truth was living in Nate's words.

"So you were here?" he said.

"I was." He pulled the gold coin out of his pocket and handed it to John. John inspected it closely and turned it over to reveal the 1857 date. He knew it was in mint condition and also knew his son didn't collect coins. "Did you find this in the house?"

"No." Nate's tone was unmistakably bordering on the teen-age.

"You want me to believe that you went back in time?"

"No. I want you to believe that with God all things are possible. He created everything, including time."

"It doesn't happen that way, Nate. God doesn't just transport people across time."

"How do you know? How do you know how much you even believe? How much do you really know about God?" Nate started down the old wooden steps, Midnight's porch, for the last time.

"I know that God is logical." John replied.

"God is not a lawyer—He's a father. He does what He thinks is best. Maman told me that."

"Diana?" he looked over to his wife huddled in a sweater beneath an umbrella of oak and consternation.

"No, someone different" Nate said sadly. "Someone very different." He walked into the drizzling rain with John following closely behind. In truth, he was more puzzled than ever by his new son. Ryan had told him he was an odd one, and John wasn't so sure his son was too far off the mark. Still, there was the gold coin and the marbles. Tangible evidence for the lawyer's mind.

Nate walked past the rest of his family and back toward the footbridge leading out of the Cimetière, the place that had been his second home the past week. But instead of crossing the bridge, he walked along the creek now filling to the brim of its banks.

When he came to the spot where Tiddy has been baptized that very night, he stopped and looked up into the rain. From a distance, his family watched Nate talking up to no one, but John knew his stepson was talking with God.

"John, what's happening? I wish we had never stopped here. We should have kept going into New Orleans like you wanted."

John put his arm around his wife. "I can't explain any of this, Diana, but—"

"—But, what?"

"I don't know. Something tells me not to worry. Another part of me wishes I had stayed with him back there when he disappeared.

"Disappeared?" She looked at him in a funny way.

He waved aside the question and put his arm around her. "I think he's in good hands." he whispered. With Ryan and Patty at their side, the four of them huddled in the shelter of the oak as Nate walked in the rain.

The four watched Nate stop and then wade waist-deep into the muddy creek.

Diana put her hands up to her mouth. "Oh, my God, John!" She started to break free of her husband and run after her son, but John held her back.

"He's alright," he whispered. "Trust him. Just this once."

Ryan and Patty both turned to the adults. "I told ya he's crazy, dad," said Ryan.

"He's such a joke." Patty said to Ryan under her breath.

Nate raised his arms, and spoke in out loud. Through the muffling rain, Ryan and Patty thought they heard their step-brother claim he was a winner. But they were never always sure what the Geek was saying.

Then the soaked boy simply knelt in the shallow water, where his sister Tiddy had been saved, and bowed.

Diana watched but understood nothing. She started to approach him, and John was wise to let her go alone.

Halfway there, Nate turned around and looked at her and for the first time in a very long time he was smiling and happy to be alive. Actually, it was more than happiness; his expression was one of joy, belonging, and peace. Diana immediately found herself strangely happy as well, filled with some mysterious sense of hope for her son and for them all. It was an odd feeling for the anxiety-stitched woman.

EPILOGUE: THE CHATTERY

Two months later. Hoover High School, Whittier California.

School had ended for the week, and Nate was thankful. The year was starting out well enough for the ninth grader. The long ride home from Louisiana had given Nate a chance to talk to his stepbrother and explain a bit. It was a relief to finally look Ryan in the eye and say, "I'm sorry, Ryan." Tiddy had taught Nate to keep things simple.

Those three words were enough to break the ice between them, and each seemed more willing to accept the other. French and Irish warts alike. And, since the other kids—Patty included—took their cues from Ryan, relief came quickly for Nate. He was no longer the last boy standing on the sidelines.

Since his return from Louisiana, Nate had been caught in the limbo of not knowing what had happened to his family at Vieux Saules. It weighed on his mind constantly, especially in class. More than one teacher had to bring him back to the present. He was starting to get stern looks from most of the teachers, as well as the Principal. It was only a matter of time before his parents were called down to the office and told of his lack of focus.

But today was Friday, and Nate was upbeat. He closed his locker and swung his book bag over his shoulder. The hallway, as usual, was packed with self-absorbed high schoolers. Nate was once again low boy on the totem pole. This time, though, he wasn't on his own. Like the others, he tried to blend in and be unseen. Much the way Midnight and his friends tried to avoid the evil Mallock.

Though no match for the bigger upper classmen, his week with Cat had given him confidence and taught him to check his fears at the door.

"Nate."

"Yeah." He turned around to face Ryan.

"Robert and me are goin' to the Quad. Wanna come?"

The name invoked memories of Pouty Robert and Luke and George, and soon his mind was back with Midnight and Tiddy.

"Nate?" Ryan tapped his brother on the shoulder. "You comin'?"

"Naw, thanks. Miss Schmierer—she, uh—gave us all a bunch of homework to do in the library over the weekend."

"Again? C'mon, man. It's Friday. You can visit the dead poets tomorrow." He put his arm around Nate. "You're a new guy this year, remember? C'mon, leave the books and have a little fun."

Nate looked at Ryan. He had over the last four weeks some-how lost his knack for being a jerk. Nate was starting to wonder whether Ryan had taken his own stairway to someplace—and maybe even taken Patty with him. It was no longer the same house he dreaded to enter. Still, Ryan and Patty could never replace Midnight and Tiddy. And Nate desperately wanted to know what had really happened to them back in the Indian Wood.

"It'll take me twenty minutes, tops," Nate fudged. "I'll meet you at Central Park in twenty."

"All right, but don't be late." He gave Nate a soft jab on the shoulder and seconds later was absorbed in the crowd.

With his book bag on one shoulder Nate walked down Friends toward Central Park. It was an old-fashioned park complete with gazebo, fishpond, and a statue of John Greenleaf Whittier. Across the street was the large Methodist church with its tall steeple reaching toward God. Antique Victorian houses surrounded the other three sides of the park, each with a distinct name like the O'Shaunessey's own *Dreyer's Patch*.

As Nate neared the park, the bells from the Methodist Church chimed. He was a half-hour late. He looked around but Ryan and Robert were nowhere in sight.

He walked up Friends Avenue, reading the signs in front of each house: *Henny's Sway*, then *The Arbor*, and *Alley's Coop*, followed by *Jackson Bee* and *Bloomers*. Nate checked for traffic and cut diagonally across the intersection of Friends and Bailey.

Approaching the curb, he was blinded by the sun hitting a brass sign at the corner house. It was as bright as high beams on a narrow road. He squinted and turned his head, nearly tripping over the high curb in the process.

"You ok there, boy?"

Nate looked over at the front yard but saw no one.

Then he saw a bit of brown move, and an elderly gentleman, a gardener, stood up.

"You ok, son?" he asked again.

"Yeah," Nate laughed a little self-consciously. "Your sign blinded me." He looked over at the brass sign, one he had never noticed before, and stared in disbelief at the two incredible words:

The Chattery

"Where—where did you get that name? It's—it's unusual."

"It's a made-up name. My grandpa built this house and gave it the name."

Nate approached the sign and read the name again. *'How incredible,'* he thought. *'the same name as Cat's house. And this house is just around the corner from mine.'*

"Are you sure you're ok, son? You look a little pale."

"No, I'm fine." Nate bit down on his lip thinking. *'Could there be a connection?'* he wondered. *'How could there? What would be the odds?'*

Nate looked up at the two-story house with the fine wrap-around porch.

"Care to look inside? It's a fine house, one of the oldest in Whittier," the elderly man offered.

"Uh, thanks, but I should get home. I live at Dreyer's Patch around the corner."

The man's face burst into excitement. "You're Ryan's new brother?" he asked.

"Yeah."

He walked over to the wrought-iron fence. "I've known John O'Shaunessey since he was just a boy your age. He's a good man."

"Yes, sir." Nate adjusted his book bag and started toward home. He stopped and took another look at the house, wondering if there was a connection with the name.

"C'mon, let me show you something I think you'll enjoy. You can call your father and tell him you're here."

Nate hesitated and then followed the white-haired man up the brick steps onto the shady porch and into the oak entryway. Though not as simplistically furnished as *The Chattery* in Louisiana, everything inside seemed to be just as old. The place was a treasure trove of antique Americana. Nate rubbed his eyes wondering if he had gone back in time again.

"Wow," Nate said simply.

The man laughed. "I get that reaction a lot."

The boy walked into the front parlor and looked around. The late afternoon sun highlighted the dust swimming in the air. Nate crossed the room and stood in the center, in the spotlight. He was very much at home in this room; it felt like the old Chattery.

Nate noticed an old violin in a built-in bookcase.

"Do you play?" Nate asked.

"No. Haven't got much talent for music, I'm afraid. My Grampa, though, was quite a player."

Nate walked over to the violin, and the owner, sensing Nate's question, said, "Go ahead."

The awe-struck boy put his hand carefully around its neck and placed the body in the other hand. He remembered playing the fiddle with Brett in *The Chattery*. He could picture Jenna sitting in a chair nearby, both hands clapping to the music.

"Do *you* play?" the man asked Nate.

"I did, a long time ago." Nate raised the fiddle and bow, and, tentatively at first, began to play "*Galway in the Morning.*" He remembered it was Brett's favorite.

Nate closed his eyes as he played and saw Brett and Jenna sitting together on the couch watching him, beaming with pride as he played.

When he finished, he stood without moving, his eyes still closed. After a moment, he opened them, and where Brett had sat, he now saw the elderly man wiping his eyes.

"That was beautiful, son" he said softly.

Nate cradled the fiddle in his arms before returning it to the shelf. As he backed away, he saw a daguerreotype picture on a shelf below.

The man stood up and walked over to Nate. "That was my grandpa; he was a little older than you are now. Had an interesting life, he did; grew up on a plantation down in the South. What did they call that place?" He snapped his fingers softly, attempting to bring his old mind to attention. "Old Something."

Nate stared at the boy in the picture. He had recognized him at once, and now it was Nate whose eyes were welling.

"—Vieux Saules." Nate looked into the man's eyes for a sign of Cat. "Vieux Saules." he repeated.

"Yes," the man nodded and gave him an off look. "How did you know?"

"Old Willows, I believe," the boy added.

The gentleman looked at Nate's face closely, and then down at the picture, and up again, while a queer expression came over his face.

"They say a cat has nine lives," he said. "Maybe it's true."

"He has at least two," responded Nate. "At least two, I think."

The relative calm of the past eight weeks was broken. It was clear to Nate that his adventure was not yet over.

Map of Vieux Saules
August 1857

TIMOTHY PHILLIPS

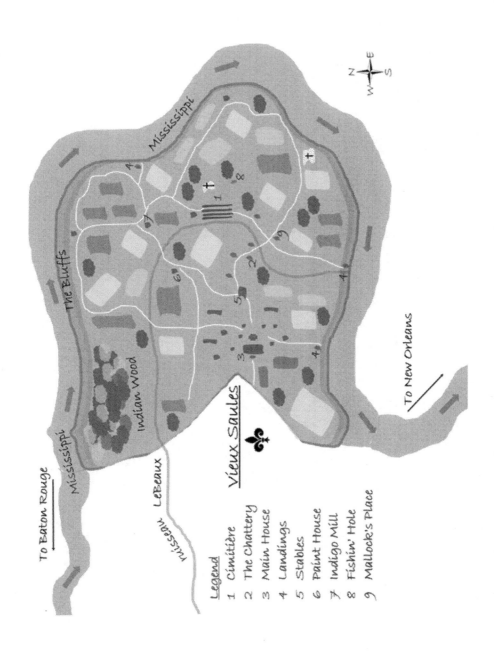

Legend

1 Cimitière
2 The Chattery
3 Main House
4 Landings
5 Stables
6 Paint House
7 Indigo Mill
8 Fishin' Hole
9 Mallock's Place

Vieux Saules

TIMOTHY PHILLIPS

About the Author: Timothy R. Phillips

Timothy Ray Phillips grew up in the Amish country of Lancaster County, Pennsylvania. There, he found his poetic heart and began writing poetry at the age of thirteen. The small Moravian town of Lititz was a perfect backdrop for Timothy's earliest poems. Much of his work reflects his experience and affinity for small town America.

At seventeen Timothy moved South and began college at Virginia Tech in Blacksburg, Virginia. He graduated cum laude with a Bachelor's degree in Accounting. In addition, he holds a Masters in Business Administration from Azusa Pacific University in California. He is both a Certified Public Accountant (CPA) and a Certified Internal Auditor (CIA). Currently, he is the Chief Financial Officer for a manufacturing company in West Virginia. He jokes that he balances numbers by day and words by night. Timothy is an admitted night owl and it is in the small hours that his most creative work surfaces.

In addition to writing poetry, Timothy has penned a handful of novels that provide a nice counter-balance to the old television set in the basement. *Midnight Matters*, a labor of love for nearly twenty years, is his first published novel.

TIMOTHY PHILLIPS

Timothy and his wife Debbie live in the beautiful Ellett Valley just east of Blacksburg. Their empty nest includes two lemon-white beagles, a Maltese, a parakeet named Leo, and, at last count, twenty-three wild deer, a college of cardinals, and boundless native creatures of the Blue Ridge Mountains.

More from Timothy Phillips

Visit *twaaneviepublishinghouse.com* for more information.

In Loving Colour explores life using the unique colours of a crayon box as a reference. Written from a father's perspective, *Colour* provides the straightforward common sense wisdom he would want to pass on to his children to better equip them for a well-lived adulthood.

The Ark of Lumijnfroost is a collection of 58 poems—a menagerie of verse, in form and theme. Within the *Ark* you will find politics, nostalgia, life, death, money, spells, a block of ice, a parliament of owls, and even a goggle box or two. Come meet the Lady of Marlborough, Mirabel, Oliver and other characters of life.

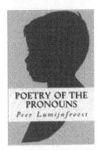

Poetry of the Pronouns is a book of 100 poems arranged in a planetary scheme according to the stages we all go through, from birth to death and in between and then, ultimately, heaven. Fortunately, the poet has not yet arrived on Jupiter and remains aware of both his faculties and his humanity.

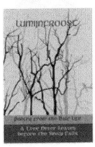

A companion to the novel *Life in the Half-Life*, the poetry book was written by the character Lumijnfroost over a span of 500-plus years. Arranged in eleven themes named in the poet's adopted Irish, the work covers the major aspects of modern civilisation—both the highs and lows—as observed firsthand by a well-traveled soul.

TIMOTHY PHILLIPS

73477717R00211

Made in the USA
Columbia, SC
16 July 2017